It was like
being six again

Kristina was getting more than a little crazy, letting this rush of emotion overtake her just for a couple of lighted Christmas windows. "You've been out in the cold too long," she muttered.

But it did look nice, didn't it? She imagined Tucker Bennett behind those windows, doing whatever people who owned toy companies did when the night grew long.

"I want to see," Kristina admitted for the first time. "I want to go up there." Gathering the wisps of her courage together, she put her head down into the wind and angled around to the back of the house. As promised, the back door was open, and she slid right in....

Toyland magically greeted her with all its treasures. And Tucker Bennett, with his beautiful body and the power to make her dreams come true, was waiting.

ABOUT THE AUTHOR

Julie Kistler believes that it takes a curious mix of discipline and creativity to think up new, fresh characters and plots, to actually finish what you've started and then send it off into the world. Julie has always loved the fantasy world of movies and books, and she feels that writing is a perfect outlet for her creative talents.

Books by Julie Kistler

HARLEQUIN AMERICAN ROMANCE

Don't miss any of our special offers. Write to us at the following address for information on our newest releases.

Harlequin Reader Service
P.O. Box 1397, Buffalo, NY 14240
Canadian address: P.O. Box 603,
Fort Erie, Ont. L2A 5X3

JULIE KISTLER

CHRISTMAS IN TOYLAND

Harlequin Books

TORONTO • NEW YORK • LONDON
AMSTERDAM • PARIS • SYDNEY • HAMBURG
STOCKHOLM • ATHENS • TOKYO • MILAN

To Corinne, who thought of the idea, thought of me
and finally managed to get the book out of me.
You're wonderful!

Published December 1991

ISBN 0-373-16418-1

CHRISTMAS IN TOYLAND

Chapter One

*"Silent night, holy night,
All is calm, all is bright..."*

"Don't you just love Christmas?" chirped a fur-coated blonde clutching too many parcels.

Since Kristina was the only other occupant of the elevator, and since she worked for Austin's Department Store, she knew she had to muster some sort of cheery response. Good customer relations were, after all, Austin's hallmark.

She stifled a sigh. A headache had been lurking around the corners of her mind for hours, and it showed no signs of letting up. Idly, she wondered if she could spare the time to get to her office to find some aspirin. No such luck. Too busy.

She managed a smile for the blond shopper, hoping it didn't look too phony or strained. It wasn't this particular Christmas lover's fault if Kristina had had another rotten day. But having to listen to sappy Christmas songs every time she rode up or down in the elevator during her current twelve- to fourteen-hour workdays was quickly pushing her over the edge.

Faced with a perky customer happily humming along with the yuletide soundtrack, Kristina felt like Scrooge. It wasn't like she hated Christmas or anything. Okay, so maybe she wasn't all that fond of it. But it wasn't even Thanksgiving yet, and Austin's had already been bombarding its upscale patrons with holiday cheer for weeks.

It didn't help matters that Kristina was personally responsible for providing all that Christmas spirit—the elaborate window displays, the lush in-store decorations, the overflowing gourmet shop, even the half-buried gift wrap department. And they were all going to hell in a handbasket at the moment.

Special Areas—that catchall name for the catchall department she managed—was full to the brim with headaches.

"One more and we'll explode," she muttered.

"What did you say?" her elevator companion inquired cheerfully.

"Oh, nothing." She smiled weakly, trying to sound convincing.

Thankfully, the elevator doors slid open, and a sweet electronic voice interrupted the music to announce, "Second floor. Children's Clothing, Toys and Furnishings, and the Little Miss Posh Boutique. Please step out now."

As the door closed behind her, swallowing up the blonde and Bing, Kristina took a deep breath to fortify herself for her next crisis. She rounded the corner and there she was, in the toy department, as ordered.

At the main entrance to Toys, dolls and teddy bears exquisitely decked out in velvet and lace were gently galloping along on their perpetually rocking horses, welcoming kiddies to Austin's version of an opulent Christmas fantasy.

Here, the soundtrack featured childish voices caroling sweetly about the Little Drummer Boy, while tiny mechanized mouths on the dolls and bears opened and closed in time to the music. It was like a Victorian flock of Teddy Ruxpins.

Well, the displays looked perfect from Kristina's vantage point. So what was the reason for the urgent summons to the second floor?

"Santa," the floor supervisor explained grimly. "Or rather, no Santa."

Ah, yes. Now that she looked more closely, Kristina saw that Santa's elegant velvet wing chair was conspicuously empty. Nearby, an antique wicker easel held a sign that proclaimed, in flowing script, *Santa Is Away For A Moment. Please Come Back!*

"He *is* coming back, I hope," she said with a sense of dread. It had taken three weeks of interviews to find a Santa with a résumé good enough for Austin's, and she wasn't prepared to lose him easily.

A low, cultured voice interrupted her from the direction of Santa's wing chair. "That man is certainly not coming back. Not while I have anything to say about it."

Mrs. Mirabel Austin, the grande dame of the store, swept into view, leaving one immaculate hand carefully draped on the velvet wing of the chair. Since Mrs. Austin was very tiny, Kristina hadn't noticed she was there behind the wing chair. But Mirabel never went unnoticed for long. Even though she was at least seventy years old, and couldn't have weighed more than eighty pounds, the total package exuded power and presence.

Where Austin's was concerned, Mirabel's beady little eyes missed absolutely nothing. If there were a string on the arm of a Balenciaga evening gown, Mirabel would be sure to spot it. If a scratch marred the buckle of a Hermès bag, Mirabel's radar would catch it from the other side of the store.

And if Santa Claus weren't up to snuff, Mirabel would have him banished back to the North Pole without a second thought.

Kristina hurried to make amends before the grande dame decided to banish *her*. "Hello, Mrs. Austin. So nice to see you. Is there a problem with Santa?"

A wan smile crossed Mirabel's small, patrician features. "There was a problem. There isn't anymore. I fired him."

Exactly what she'd been afraid of.

"He wasn't suitable in the least," Mirabel continued grandly. "Not for Austin's."

"I see." What she saw was a whole new headache looming on the horizon. "Was there something in particular you didn't like, just so we don't repeat the problem?"

"He simply wouldn't do," the older woman insisted.

"No problem," Kristina managed, wishing she meant it. "Mrs. Austin, it would be helpful if you could tell me what was wrong with that Santa. So that I won't make the same mistake with the next one."

"Just find a better one," Mirabel replied. "Someone with distinction, elegance. It shouldn't be difficult."

No, not difficult. Merely impossible.

Kristina glanced at her watch. It was now almost 4:00 p.m. on Tuesday, two days before Thanksgiving. By Friday at 7:00 a.m., when Austin's doors opened to the biggest shopping day of the year, every rich kid in Chicago plus innumerable sets of rich parents were going to be clamoring to see Santa.

In other words, if she didn't find a new—and improved—Santa by Friday morning, she might as well kiss her job goodbye. But when was she supposed to find the time to go back through the files, get in touch with po-

ential choices, interview them and push the paperwork
through if she *did* find someone presentable?

Meanwhile, Mrs. Austin had sauntered away to create
havoc somewhere else, leaving this little gem of a prob-
em behind.

Kristina was left to punch the button for the elevator.
Damn Mirabel anyway. There hadn't been one thing
wrong with that Santa.

The elevator doors slid open noiselessly, and sweet
music came rolling out.

"Here we come a-wassailing among the leaves so
green;
Here we come a-wand'ring so fair to be seen
Love and joy to you,
And to you your wassail too..."

"HELLO OUT THERE," Tucker Bennett called, bending
forward to speak carefully and loudly into the intercom.
"Can we get rid of the Christmas music? It's not time for
that yet, is it?"

His sister came bursting through his office door with
bright spots of color staining her pale cheeks. Wearing a
too-large gray flannel dress that didn't suit her coloring,
Tegan looked like a waif out of Charles Dickens.

Her words belied that image.

"Tucker, you idiot, you don't need to shout into the
damned speaker! I can hear you just fine."

"Sorry." Annoyed with himself for yet again irritating
his sister, Tucker tossed the full weight of his long body
into the back of the huge leather chair. If he could only get
comfortable in this thing.

"You're going to tip it over if you're not careful," Tegan warned. "How many times do I have to tell you not to play with the furniture?"

"Okay, okay." Gingerly pulling himself out of the ornery chair, Tucker angled his body onto the edge of his father's polished cherry desk instead. He could see objections forming on his sister's face, and he raised a hand to forestall her. "Don't tell me—Dad didn't sit on the desk, either. Too bad. Dad's not here. I am. I sit on desks."

"Right," she said stiffly. "So what was it you yelled into the intercom?"

"Oh—the music. I can't work with that stuff piped in here." Tucker picked absently at a thread near the button on his suit jacket. "I think people work better to Eric Clapton, don't you?"

His sister sighed loudly, clearly doing it for the effect.

Tucker frowned. "I suppose old Mrs. Partridge left instructions that say the Christmas music gets turned on— what is this?—the Tuesday before Thanksgiving, and you don't feel brave enough to buck tradition, even though Mrs. Partridge retired six months ago."

"Well, she did leave instructions. Only the Christmas music was supposed to start yesterday. But I forgot."

Unable to ignore how silly that sounded, Tucker grinned, while Tegan looked like she was trying to maintain a severe expression. "I'm just trying to do a good job!" she protested.

"I know. It's not your fault." Tucker shook his tawny head. "But it's like we're playing office, like it's not real." He got up and stuffed his hands in his pockets, purposely ruining the line of his expensive suit. "The old man's been gone six months, and I still feel like Toyland is his company."

"It *is* his company," Tegan pointed out. "He still owns sixty percent, even if he's not doing anything with it at the moment."

"He's retired, Tegan. And you know his health as well as I do. No matter how much of a mess I make of things, he can't come back." Pulling his hands from his pockets, Tucker straightened his tie. "I'm the president. And I'm supposed to be acting like one."

"Come on, Tucker. Don't be so hard on yourself. So you don't have the hang of the intercom, or the chair." She tucked back a lock of her hair, exactly the same shade of brown as his, and regarded him with blue eyes that mirrored his own. "Are chairs and intercoms important?"

"No." Tucker paced back and forth in front of the long, dark desk. "Chairs and intercoms can take a flying leap. But the Christmas season is about as important as it gets."

In the toy business, the Christmas season wasn't merely important. It was everything. World peace could come and go, as long as Christmas sales were coming in strong.

"Any preliminary figures from the major toy companies?" he asked.

"It's too early, Tucker. You know that."

"Yeah, I know. I'm just..."

They both knew he was just anxious because this was his first Christmas in charge, because this season's numbers would determine whether Toyland saw feast or famine for the next two years or more.

Impatient, he sat back down in the chair and did a quick spin or two.

"Tucker..." she began.

"Damn it, Tegan, this is the toy biz." He looked up at her with missionary zeal. "Toys, Tegan. Fun, excitement, Christmas morning in a kid's eyes. Not toilet paper or pencils or canned pineapple—*toys!* We're supposed to be enjoying ourselves. But how can running Toyland be any fun if I can't spin in my damned chair when I want to?''

"Don't give me that wistful, gooey stuff. We're trying to run a business here." She relented enough to sit on the side of his chair and drape an arm around him. "And besides, you're in no position to complain. This was all your idea, if you remember."

"I remember." As the oldest son, he'd known his duty the moment Dad began to feel chest pains. It was unwritten law in the Bennett family that someday Tucker would take over. He might not want to be the big cheese, but he didn't have a choice.

"My goal in life is certainly not to be your administrative assistant," Tegan continued. "But you said I had to be here to help you out. And if I have to be here, then you *sure* do."

"Yeah. I know."

Life had seemed so much easier when he was running the design department. It wasn't his problem if a toy was wildly impractical; his dad would say no, but Tucker would've had the fun of playing with the thing anyway. If sales were down, if Toyland's market share was slipping, the buck stopped with the senior Mr. Bennett.

But then Harley Bennett, for forty years the guiding force behind Toyland, Inc., had suffered a heart attack. And suddenly it fell to his oldest son to step in, to try to be as wise, as practical, as patient, as his dad had been for so long.

So Mom and Dad took off on a round-the-world cruise, designed purposely to keep the old war-horse out of commission for a good, long time. And Tucker took over the big office, with his sister Tegan pitching in as his assistant and his hotshot little brother Trey picking up the slack in Design.

Gone were the work shirts and blue jeans of the design department. Now Tucker was stuck inside Brooks Brothers suits and ties, perfect for hobnobbing with other execs about town. Trey had picked out the clothes, and Tucker hated them with a passion he couldn't even express.

He pulled at his collar. "Hey, Teeg, you don't want to be president, do you?"

"I don't even want to be administrative assistant."

Taking his sister's hand, Tucker squeezed it gently. "I guess we have to do what we have to do."

"I know. But I don't have to like it."

Tucker said softly, "I do. I can't do it if I don't like it."

"Okay, good. Learn to like it." Smoothing imaginary wrinkles form the lap of her plain flannel dress, Tegan fortified herself for the world outside Tucker's office. "Settle into your chair, stop shouting at the intercom and get ready for the Zappers and Spinners presentation. Trey will be up in a few minutes to show you what he wants to do with next year's cars."

"Zappers and Spinners," he muttered.

He'd loved the high-speed cars when he got to pick which ones had fins and which ones had firebolts. Now they were just one set of numbers among piles and piles of similar sets. He wasn't even sure he could remember which were Zappers and which were Spinners anymore.

And his tie was chafing his neck something fierce.

"Tegan," he called out, catching her before the door shut. "Don't forget—Eric Clapton."

In a few moments, the glorious sound of "Layla" filled the room. Unbuttoning his top button, Tucker loosened his tie and carelessly tossed his five-hundred-dollar jacket at a coat tree on the other side of the office.

Smiling broadly, he propped his hands behind his head, balanced long legs on the corner of the desk, and leaned back as far as he could on his father's chair.

There were, after all, ways to make this job bearable.

"POLLY," Kristina called out to her secretary, "do you have that other file of Santa applicants? The guys in this batch look like they belong on *Hee Haw*."

There was no answer except the ticktock of her wall clock.

Almost eight. Good grief. Was it that late already?

Her secretary had undoubtedly left hours ago, with all the rest of the office staff. If Kristina didn't get out of there, she'd end up spending the night.

"Santa, Santa—my kingdom for a Santa," she muttered, cramming a few files into her briefcase. "So, Mr. Claus, why are you causing me all these problems?"

The silence of the empty office hung around her like an accusation.

"Okay, so I was never crazy about Christmas. Is that a crime?"

There was still no answer, of course, because there was no such thing as Santa Claus. At least not at Austin's this year.

Undaunted, Kristina continued her little soliloquy. "If I promise to get a tree and start hanging lights, will you take pity on me and bring me a decent Santa for Christmas? And can I have him for Thanksgiving while you're at it?"

One good thing about being in the office later than anybody else—there was no one to hear the audible evidence that she was losing her mind. All she needed was for Mirabel Austin to round the corner and find her asking invisible Santas for favors.

Stifling a laugh, she held her hair out of the way long enough to button her coat. When she could face this kind of catastrophe with a smile, she *knew* she was losing it. Clearly, she was so tired she was getting hysterical.

Or maybe just escaping from the store after such a long day was the tonic she needed. Whatever the reason, leaving Austin's put a spring back in her step, and her mood had definitely improved by the time she got to her car.

And she realized she couldn't look as haggard as she felt when the parking-lot attendant—who was all of sixteen—winked at her and asked if she was busy Friday night. As he waved her through the gate, she saw the tattoo on his arm that announced *Born To Raise Hell.*

"Sorry," she told him, rolling up her window and getting out of there with all due haste. But it gave her a much needed laugh, even if she didn't date sixteen-year-olds.

It had been an unusually warm November thus far, but the air felt chilly enough tonight. Shivering inside her trim wool coat, Kristina turned up the heat in her Toyota as she headed north on the Edens Expressway.

"If that guy could come up with a Santa, I might actually go out with him," she mused. "Now *that's* desperate."

Finally, home was in sight. It wasn't grand or exciting, despite its fashionable Winnetka address. When Kristina was a child, the other school kids had teased her that she lived in the smallest house in all of Chicago's wealthy northern suburbs. As a teenager, she would've given anything to be as cool as the kids who lived on palatial estates, and she'd told herself she hated the little white Cape Cod.

But now that it was all hers, she'd developed a real fondness for the place, with its pretty shutters and peaceful, tree-shaded corner lot. Yes, it was all hers, and that was what really mattered.

She had already pulled into the driveway and gotten out of her car to open the garage door when she noticed the strange man standing on the sidewalk near the corner. There wasn't anything in particular about him that was strange, but merely the fact of his existence. Men loitering on street corners were not normal occurrences in Winnetka.

Although he seemed grave and composed, there was a hopeful light in his eyes, and a funny little half smile hovering around his lips. Clearly, he'd been expecting her. But who in the world was he?

As she gathered her things together, Kristina regarded him dubiously. After all, he could be a weirdo, stalking her for some ugly reason. On the other hand, he could also be an emissary from Ed McMahon, here to tell her she'd won a million dollars.

To be honest, however, he didn't look like he fit the profile of either a maniac or a sweepstakes messenger. Elderly, probably at least in his sixties, he carried himself beautifully, even though he was wearing a green zipped jacket and a matching cap—clothes that didn't speak of wealth or status. Under the cap, he had kind eyes, a rather vague smile and a neatly trimmed white beard. From this distance, she couldn't read the inscription on the hat, but the letters were red-and-white striped, like candy canes.

He must be freezing standing out on the street without a better coat. But who was he? She couldn't recall knowing any older men with beards.

The reality of the beard hit her all at once. *Heavens to Betsy,* she thought, *it's Santa Claus.* After all, she *had* asked for him for Christmas.

But this man was too tall and elegant looking—in a scruffy sort of way—to be Santa Claus. Where was the tummy like a bowl full of jelly? Or the plump cheeks and snub nose?

He's tall, she thought suddenly, and it began to add up. Tall and in his sixties. With a beard partially obscuring features she might otherwise have recognized. And waiting for her.

"Oh, my God. It can't be," she whispered.

She'd been praying for—and dreading—this moment since she was ten years old. Abandoning her briefcase on the passenger seat, she strode over to where he stood at the front of the lawn.

Without pausing, she demanded, "You're my father, aren't you?"

Chapter Two

The man stared at her, surprise written in his mild blue eyes.

"I've been expecting you," she whispered, staring right back. "I knew you'd come back someday."

"Pardon me," he said quickly. "But I think there's been some sort of mistake. I'm not who you think."

Kristina froze, noting the faint British accent that colored his words. Even if he hadn't told her, that voice would've revealed he wasn't her father. Disappointment mixed with relief seeped through her. "So you're not my father."

"Oh, dear me. I certainly didn't intend you to think *that*. No, my dear, I'm afraid I'm not your father. I'm just the postman."

This was all too confusing. She hadn't got past the "I'm not your father" part. "I beg your pardon?"

"The postman." He tapped the front of his cap to point out the Holiday Courier inscription, written in candy-cane letters. "Or rather, the delivery man. That is to say, I don't work for the regular post office, the United States Postal Service, that is. I work for a more specialized delivery service."

It would be something like that, something mundane and real. After all, except for his height, he didn't look a thing like her father should look. She remembered that much.

So this man, with his kind gray-blue eyes, was clearly not her father. And suddenly she felt very, very silly.

"I'm really sorry," she managed.

"Oh, no, please don't apologize. It's rather flattering being taken for the father of such a lovely young lady."

It wasn't in her nature to dither, but dithering seemed to be the only thing to do at the moment. Good Lord, she'd accused a perfect stranger of being her father!

"I really apol—"

"Please, don't think about it another moment. Simple mistake," he insisted.

"It's just the timing," she told him, trying to muddle through. "The Christmas season never fails to get to me. My father left—years ago—on Christmas Eve, and I always thought he'd come back at...well, this time of year. Oh, dear."

She was normally so reserved with strangers. What was wrong with her? Quickly, she tried to shift the conversation onto less personal ground. "Did you say you had a package for me?"

"Don't worry, Miss Castleberry," he offered kindly, ignoring her question as he patted her arm. "I don't think any less of you for making the mistake. Why, in your shoes, I'd probably think I was my father, too."

She didn't even try to figure that one out. "Don't you have something to give me?" she asked again.

"Oh, ah, yes." He took the large, scarred leather pouch that hung at his side, pulled it around to the front, unzipped the flap and then sifted through its contents for some moments. "A very special delivery, as it happens."

"Yes?"

Still he poked through the bulky pouch, picking out and putting back several packages and envelopes. Finally, when Kristina was just about to call it quits, he settled on one ragged-looking envelope. "Yes, yes, here it is." Beaming with success, he waved it in her direction. "Your special delivery."

"It's just a letter."

"Yes. *Your* letter, as a matter of fact."

"Right," she agreed, craning her neck to try to see more of it. "Do you suppose I could have it now?"

"Certainly, certainly." With a half bow from the waist that bespoke a more courtly era, he presented the letter. "It's rather old, as you'll see."

The envelope looked decrepit and rumpled, as if it had gone around the world and back by banana boat, and the return address was completely obliterated by an ugly brown stain. Kristina noted that it was indeed addressed to her but to "Krissie" Castleberry, rather than Kristina.

"No one's called me Krissie in years," she mused.

"Perhaps eleven years?"

"Well, yes, that's about right." She narrowed her gaze. "How did you know?"

"Because that's when the letter went astray." He pointed to the faded postmark, which read 1980 if you looked very closely. "I'm afraid the regular post office— that would be the official, United States Postal Service— misplaced this, back in 1980. It has only recently been re-discovered in the bottom of an old bin, and I've been asked to hand-deliver it right to you, to make sure there's no mistake this time."

"I—I see." Surely if a letter resurfaced after so many years, it had to be significant; it smacked of fate or karma when something so long lost popped up again.

Oh, nonsense, she told herself firmly. It was probably an ad for encyclopedias, or a plea for money from the Save the Plankton Foundation. Nonetheless, Kristina's hands trembled as she tried to pry it open. She told herself it was just the cold making her fingers so stiff and clumsy.

"Is there something wrong?" her friendly messenger asked.

"Oh, no, of course not." She called upon inner reserves to compose herself. She was, after all, her mother's daughter, and her mother was the soul of reason and calm common sense.

"Look," she said suddenly, sliding the mysterious letter into her pocket with determination. "We're both freezing. Why don't you come inside and have some hot chocolate with me?"

It was unlike her to make friends with a virtual stranger on the spur of the moment, but after all, she'd already blurted out her life's secrets to this man. What harm could a cup of cocoa do?

"Why, thank you, Miss Castleberry." His eye twinkled as he hefted his pouch on his shoulder and accompanied her up the walk to her cozy Cape Cod. "And perhaps I can be of some help to you as to what to do about your letter."

"What to do...?" But that sounded like he knew what was in it. Kristina shook her head. Probably every employee at Holiday Courier, whatever that was, had steamed open her letter and read it.

But, no. Somehow, she just couldn't believe that of this nice man. He was so sweet, taking her arm to help her up the walk, telling her how much he liked her house, even carrying her briefcase for her when they retrieved it from the car.

"Yes, indeed. This is a lovely home, Miss Castleberry," he repeated, as she led him in the front door. She led the way back toward the kitchen, but he stopped and looked around the living room. "A lovely home."

She had no illusions; there was nothing spectacular about her house. But the plain beige carpet and pale yellow walls in the living room were soothing, if not spectacular, and the lemon-striped love seats flanking the small plaster fireplace looked very inviting at the moment.

"Thank you," she said, tossing her coat over the back of an armchair. "You're very kind."

Kind and sweet and sympathetic.... In fact, if her long-lost father *had* walked back into her life after all these years, she'd have wanted him to be just like this man.

In a flash, before she'd had a chance to say yes or no, he'd found the firewood bin and started a rosy little blaze going in her fireplace, something she hadn't done since last winter. With the flames crackling and dancing, the small room became even cozier.

"And that," he told her, pointing to a corner space next to the stairs, "is where your Christmas tree should be. When will you be putting it up?"

"Oh, I don't usually get one. I'm not really home enough to enjoy it. And all those needles on the floor— you know," she finished lamely.

His blue eyes were solemn. "Everyone should have a Christmas tree, Kristina."

"Yes, but..." She broke off suddenly. "How funny. Just today, I said I'd put up a tree if I could only find..."

He stood there expectantly, rolling his hat with its candy-cane letters between his hand. "Yes? If you could only find what?"

"Santa Claus." Kristina considered her mysterious visitor. "You know, Mr... What is your name, anyway?"

"Um, it's, well it's Nick."

"Nick...?" She paused, waiting for a last name. "Nick what?"

"Well..."

With anyone else, she would've been suspicious when he couldn't seem to recall his own name. But Nick was so darned nice, she found herself overlooking the odd behavior. He was getting on in years, after all. Maybe he just forgot for a moment.

"Your last name?" she asked helpfully.

Gazing down at the cap in his hands, he offered suddenly, "Nick Holiday. That's it. Nick Holiday."

"Holiday. Oh, of course." She nodded, remembering the letters on his hat. "You must own the delivery service."

"Yes, that's right," he said brightly.

"Well, anyway, as I was about to say, Mr. Holiday—"

"Nick, please."

It felt a little funny to call such a distinguished older man by his first name, but if he insisted, she'd try.

"Nick, then. As I was saying, I had this sudden idea. You're not the usual Santa Claus type, you know—round and jolly. But maybe that was Mirabel's problem—that the Santa I found was just like everybody else's." She shook her head. "I should've known that the Burl Ives type was a little too down-home and comfy for Mirabel."

"What precisely are we discussing?" Nick asked politely.

"You, Nick, *you!* You have the beard, and Mirabel said she wanted someone with class." The more Kristina thought about it, the better this idea seemed. "That accent... Well, it oozes with class, Nick. Really. And you're such a good listener. I never talk this much, but around you, I seem to be spilling all sorts of things."

"Why, thank you, my dear."

"You're welcome, but Nick, I can hardly be the first one to notice. I mean, you're tall, you're slim, you're very elegant in—oh, I don't know..." She searched for the right image. "Like a butler in an old movie."

"I beg your pardon?"

Maybe that hadn't been the best way to put it. "Obi-wan Kenobi?"

"Obi what?"

"Alec Guinness? You know, in *Star Wars?* The movie?"

He shook his head. "I'm sorry. I don't see many movies."

"Well, it really doesn't matter. But what do you think?"

"About?"

"Being Santa for me at Austin's." Kristina allowed herself to hope. "We'd put you in a deep, rich color—like maroon instead of red. And forget the goofy hat with the fur ball on the end. Instead, we'd do a little wreath of holly and ivy, like the old Victorian Santas." Circling Nick, she nodded. "Yeah, that's it—I can see it now. We'll get you a long, darker robe, in a really nice velvet or brocade."

"I'm afraid I haven't the vaguest idea what you're talking about, my dear."

"Santa Claus!" she told him. "Only this isn't just any Santa Claus. Austin's needs a more upscale version, like Saint Nicholas instead." Pausing, she focused on Nick's genial face. "That's odd, isn't it? Saint Nicholas, and your name is Nick."

"Quite a coincidence," he said gravely.

"More like fate." Kristina shook her head. "I don't know. I don't believe in that stuff—fate or destiny or whatever you want to call it. But first that letter arrives out of the blue and now you pop up when I need Saint Nicholas." Turning away, she asked slowly, "Do you believe in fate, Nick?"

"I'm not sure. But I do believe you should open your letter."

Kristina felt her face flush with warmth. She was only too aware that she'd been studiously avoiding actually looking at the thing.

"Don't you think you'd better?" He inclined his head toward her coat, where the letter peeked out of one pocket.

"It's just..." Once again, she found herself wanting to share all her secrets with Nick. He was so easy to talk to, so nonjudgmental.

"I don't want to open it," she admitted. "With something like this—a bolt out of the blue—it has so much promise, and I hate to ruin it."

Nick looked confused, and she elaborated. "It's like it ought to be important because it's old, but I'm afraid it will be something really dumb and ordinary, and I'll be disappointed. While it's still unopened, all the promise is still there."

"I understand, Kristina, but you're going to have to open it." His smile was gentle. "What if it's something wonderful? Shouldn't you open it up and get at it?"

"Yes," she said finally. "I suppose I should."

She strode to her coat, and pulled the thing out of the pocket with determination. But once again, her hands trembled, betraying her anxiety. Maybe if she were alone...

"Look, Nick, do you mind? Maybe you could get the hot chocolate while I look at it."

"Certainly. Should I...?" He tipped his head toward the kitchen.

"Right," she responded absently, concentrating on the letter. Nick disappeared into the kitchen, and she called in after him, "Cocoa packets are in the smallest canister and mugs are in the cabinet next to the sink. Just go ahead and microwave it."

"Cocoa packets? Microwave?" From the kitchen, Nick's voice sounded baffled.

"Right. Just put water in the mugs and stick them in the microwave for about a minute and a half each."

Taking a deep breath, Kristina sat on the edge of the love seat. "Okay," she murmured, "this is it."

With one quick and careless rip, the envelope was open and the letter lay unfolded before her. Its brightly colored masthead, with tiny building blocks forming the letters of the company's name, caught her eye immediately.

"Oh, my God," she whispered. "It's from Toyland. I haven't thought about them in years."

With growing disbelief, she scanned the lines of her letter.

Christmas, 1980

Dear   KRISSIE CASTLEBERRY:

Congratulations! Your design for SANTA'S MAGIC WORKSHOP   is one of the five finalists in the "Toyland Christmas Toy Supersearch Contest"! You have been chosen from among a record number of entries in our tenth annual search for the best in new and innovative toy designs. We hope you're as excited as we are by this once-in-a-lifetime chance to help create Christmas joy for boys and girls across America!

Please submit a prototype of your toy by February 15, 1981, for judging consideration. Our panel of ten toy experts will examine, scrutinize and *play with* all five finalists. These experts include Harley Bennett, president and CEO of Toyland, Inc.; Mrs. Mary Tate, 1980 Elementary School Teacher of the Year; and Bethany Rogers, 1980 Poster Child for the Disabled Children's Foundation. They will ultimately choose the one toy that best meets the following criteria, based on Toyland, Inc.'s founding philosophy:

* Is it fun?
* Will it inspire a child's imagination?
* Is it realistically marketable to America's children?

If your SANTA'S MAGIC WORKSHOP is chosen as the best of the best, it will be mass-produced by Toyland, Inc. for sale as our *premier* Christmas toy for the 1981 season. If you have any questions, please consult the complete rules of the contest attached to your original entry blank, or contact us at Toyland. We'll be happy to help.

Again, we offer out heartiest congratulations. Here's hoping *your* toy becomes the biggest success story since the teddy bear!

Merry Christmas from your friends at Toyland!!!!

Yours,

Tucker Bennett

Toyland Inc. Marketing Department

"A finalist..." she murmured. "All those years ago, and I never knew. I can't believe it."

"Who is it from?" Nick asked, hovering in the doorway to the kitchen.

She had the funniest feeling he knew before she told him, but she pushed the thought away. "Toyland, the toy company. They make Blox, the construction set. And GoBlox and GloBlox and SpaceBlox and all the rest."

"Yes, I know those sets. Good, sturdy toys. You know, Toyland has been around for some time. Even back in my day, they made the Master Building Blocks set."

"Nick, you amaze me. Why on earth do you know so much about Toyland?"

"Well," he said helpfully, "you might say that toys, in general, were once part of my business. And of course I knew the various companies as well as I knew my own name."

Since he hadn't been all that sure about his name only a few minutes ago, Kristina didn't press the point. "Okay. Well, Toyland sponsored a contest every year when I was a kid."

"A contest?"

"To design a Christmas toy." Smiling wanly, she recalled her youthful foolishness. "I fancied myself a toy designer, you see, so I entered their contest." She bit her lip. "I thought I'd die if I didn't win. I was so *sure.* Anyway, I watched my mailbox every day for a letter. But no letter came. I—I finally admitted that I didn't win. And there went the toy design dreams."

"I'm sure the postal service regrets the error."

"What? Oh, sure."

Glancing again at the lines of the letter, she couldn't help but remember the girl she'd been, daring to dream. She'd been positive she'd win that toy-design contest, even though her mother thought she was being ridiculous. And Mother had been right, as far as Kristina knew then. No letter, no victory, no dream career as a toy designer.

No, she'd been good and practical, just like Mother wanted. She'd gotten her MBA and gone to work as a middle-level grunt for a computer giant with cogs instead of employees. And just last year, she'd moved up and into the plum job she now held at Austin's.

All because she'd lost the Toyland Christmas Toy Supersearch contest all those years ago.

"It's very odd to be so sure you're doing the right thing, and then have something like this happen." She shook her head. "I still can't believe it."

"What was your toy, Kristina?"

Confused, she looked up to meet his gaze. "Excuse me?"

"What did you send in to the contest?"

"Oh." She smiled, remembering. "Santa's Magic Workshop. It was this gorgeous thing, all in miniature—like a gingerbread house, only the roof came off so you could play with the stuff inside."

It was all so vivid in her mind, it might have been yesterday, not over ten years ago, that she'd created Santa's Workshop. "There was a fireplace with tiny logs, and a comfy chair for Santa, and a workbench and a whole bunch of little toys to paint and put together."

"It sounds lovely."

"It was."

"Kristina, my dear, I hate to interrupt," Nick said tentatively, "but the cocoa in the—what was that thing?"

"Microwave?"

"I don't think it's getting any hotter," he said dubiously.

"Did you turn it on?"

Nick's eyes held mild rebuke. "You didn't say anything about turning it on."

She tried not to laugh as she put the letter aside and joined him in the kitchen. "You've never used a microwave before, have you, Nick?" she asked, as she set the timer and clicked it on.

"Certainly not," he replied with dignity. "I have a very nice wood-burning stove."

"A wood-burning stove?" She tried not to look as incredulous as she felt. "Where do you live, Nick? The woods?"

"Well, I don't live in the city if that's what you mean. I prefer the outdoors, and I like it cold. So I live..." He stopped suddenly.

Busy stirring cocoa mix into the hot water, Kristina missed his hesitation. "Up north?" she asked.

"Yes," he said. "Way up north."

"Hmm." She handed him a mug. "Where would that be?"

"Far up north."

"Far? As in Canada? Minnesota?"

"Minnesota. That's it. Minnesota."

"I hear it's beautiful there."

Nick's eyes seemed far way. "It is. Deep, deep snow, and the air so cold and clean...." Catching himself, he took a quick sip of hot chocolate. "Yes, well, I like it there."

Funny, but it hadn't occurred to her that Nick and Holiday Courier might be based out-of-state. This development could pose a definite problem. "I suppose it's too much to hope that you'd be willing to take a job here? Even for a little while?"

"This Santa business?"

Nodding, she set her cocoa down on the counter. "The store is Austin's, downtown on North Michigan Avenue. Have you seen it?"

He shook his head.

"Oh, Nick, it's fabulous. And at Christmas, it's nothing short of spectacular." She leaned forward, hoping she sounded persuasive. "Do you like children, Nick?"

"Well, yes, I do."

"You like kids, you already said you know a lot about toys—what could be easier?" Delicately, she laid a hand on the thin fabric of his jacket. "And it pays well."

His smile was serene and amused, as if he knew exactly what she was thinking, and dismissed the idea out of hand. "I don't worry much about money, my child. I find that life provides."

Maybe if you worried a little more about money, you wouldn't have to stand outside freezing in a thin jacket. But she bit her tongue.

"More cocoa?" she asked instead.

"Oh, no, my dear, I'm afraid I must be getting on my way now that I've successfully made my delivery. But Kristina," he ventured. "Before I go, I do feel I need to ask..."

"Yes?"

"What are you planning to do about Toyland?"

She shrugged. "What can I do? That was years ago. It's nice to know I might've won after all, but there's nothing I can do about it now."

"No?"

"You think there's something I should do?"

"Oh, no, I wouldn't presume. That's *your* decision." His mild blue eyes held her for a long pause. "But I might consider very carefully, if I were you. I might mull it over, and make sure I really knew what it was I wanted to do."

"And you think about the Santa job, okay?" His expression was too ambiguous to read, but she pressed on. "As a favor to me, if nothing else."

"I shall think on it with all due consideration."

"Good. And since you don't live in town, if you need a place to stay for the duration of the job..."

Even she didn't believe the words coming out of her mouth. Kristina Castleberry was turning into Lady Bountiful all of a sudden. But she couldn't bear to think of this sweet old man wandering the streets without a warm coat.

"I shall consider it," he said again, and she knew that that would have to do.

She walked him back to the living room, helped him with his heavy mail pouch and then held the door open for him.

As he turned to leave, she suddenly realized she had no way to find him again. "Nick, wait! Is there somewhere I can reach you? To find out what you've decided?"

"Why don't I contact you?" he suggested. "Tomorrow, one way or the other, at your Austin's."

And then he ambled down her front walk and disappeared down the street.

"This has been," she said to her empty living room, "the screwiest day of my entire life."

But as she turned out the lights in the living room, and made ready to go upstairs and go to bed, she found herself humming "Santa Claus Is Comin' to Town."

She had to laugh. "I wonder how long it's been since I sang Christmas carols."

She didn't need an answer. She knew.

It had been a long, long time.

Chapter Three

The letter from Toyland just sat there, looking at her, no matter how hard she tried to ignore it.

"I'm not going to dredge up something that died ten years ago," she told herself firmly, and pulled a heavy folder over on top of the letter.

Okay, back to the latest crisis in Special Areas. This time, a whole shipment of Christmas decorated gourmet chocolates had gotten frozen en route to Austin's, and she had to track down who'd screwed up where and get the shipment replaced.

But her mind wasn't on chocolates.

Dangling a pen over the pink copy of the shipping order, Kristina stared into space, envisioning the perfect, miniature Santa's Workshop of her imagination. She tried to pull herself back to the plight of the frozen candy, but all she could think of were reindeer and elves and tiny toys....

"It could have been so great."

"What's that?" her secretary asked, edging her way through the door with a new pile of folders.

"Hmm?"

"What could be so great?"

"Oh, uh, chocolates," Kristina improvised, jabbing her pen at the pink sheet in the middle of her desk.

Polly, a plump young woman with lousy clerical skills but a very good disposition, shrugged. "If you ask me, chocolates are always pretty darned good." With a carefree smile, she dumped her armload of files onto the high pile already stacked on Kristina's desk.

"Wait, Polly, before you go—have I gotten any calls today?"

"Sure, lots." She pointed to the mountain of yellow message slips, impaled every which way on a spindle dangerously close to pitching over the edge of Kristina's desk. "Any one in particular you want to know about?"

"Nick, my Santa Claus. He still hasn't called?"

"Kristina!" Polly protested. "You've already asked about him a million times."

"I know." Kristina thumbed through the pile of messages, in case Polly had missed something. "But this is an emergency."

"Yeah, I hear you. At least five of those messages are from the floor supervisor on Children's, wanting to know when the new Santa would be here." She rolled her eyes. "Whew. You should be glad I took the calls."

Kristina frowned, noting the increasing urgency of her messages. "I see what you mean."

"You better get somebody quick."

"Thanks, Polly. I know that." As her secretary once more turned to leave, Kristina added, "And if Nick calls, please let me know right away."

"I will, I will," Polly promised. "Geesh, Kristina, chill out, wouldja?"

Kristina let that one pass and tried to get back to the chocolate problem. Not to mention the design supervisor's impending maternity leave and the little difficulty of the special Christmas wrapping paper stuck somewhere in far-off Peru. . . .

She managed to stay hard at work for at least five minutes before Polly interrupted.

"Excuse me, Kristina, but you did say to let you know right away if that Nick guy—"

"Nick? He called? Is he still on the line?"

"Oh, no, he's not on the phone."

"Did he at least leave a number where I can reach him?"

"No, because he didn't call." Looking utterly confused, Polly paused. "He's here—well, out there. By my desk."

"Here? Great!" This was the best news she'd had in a long time. "This must mean he's willing to do it. Bring him in, will you?"

Polly nodded and scrambled out the door. "Go right in," she called out, and then there he was, standing in the doorway, hat in hand.

"What are you going to do about Toyland?" he asked gently.

Kristina rose from her desk, a look of surprise on her face. But she recovered quickly. "What's to do? Toyland is yesterday's news." Leaning across the edge of her desk and sliding aside a stack of computer printouts, she motioned for him to sit on the chair. "Let's talk about today's news, okay? I'm so glad you've decided to be Saint Nicholas for me. This will be great for both of us."

"I haven't actually decided as of yet."

"No?" Disappointed, Kristina sat back down. "Why not?"

"I realize you're in a bit of a bind, and I'd like to help you, really I would."

"Yes?" she prompted.

"It's just that I'm rather busy myself at this time of year."

Kristina nodded. "Deliveries, of course. It's the Christmas season."

"I do have very good helpers back at home, but I don't feel quite right, leaving them to manage alone."

This was not what she needed to hear. "Nick, I need you. What can I do to get you to accept?"

"Well, there is one thing...."

"Yes?" she asked eagerly. "Name it, and I'll do it."

"I want you to answer your letter from Toyland." His words hung in the air for a long pause.

When she didn't respond, he added, "It's important that you revive your workshop, Kristina. Why not go to Toyland and see what can be done?"

"I—I don't understand, Nick." Kristina fidgeted with her letter opener. "What possible difference can it make to you if I answer that letter?"

"It's difficult to explain, but...well, being in the delivery business, I feel rather responsible that your letter went astray." Looking very sincere, he came in closer to her desk. "It's my way of making it up to you, for not giving you what you wanted...that is to say, on behalf of the post office, for failing you all those years ago."

It made no sense whatsoever. But impulsively, she moved aside the folder, revealing the Toyland letter. "I have been thinking about it."

"Yes, I knew it." His smile was encouraging. "It's never too late to pursue a dream."

"But I can't...." She broke off. "It's impossible, Nick. That's a dead end. My future is in being a manager. That's what I'm good at. Toys were a dream, but that's all. I have to be practical."

"You don't always have to be practical," Nick put in. "Besides, you're being half practical at least, since it will get you the Santa Claus you so desperately need."

"Well, that's true enough," she said dubiously. "Tell you what—I'll think about it. Is that good enough?"

As he leaned in closer, his blue eyes lost their mildness. "You mustn't just think about it, my dear," he urged. "One week from today, I want you to have made an appointment with the head man at Toyland."

"Nick, I don't know if—" she began, but he shook his head.

"Once you've thought this over properly, you'll know what your decision must be, Kristina."

"I'm glad one of us is so sure."

"I'm merely righting a wrong, my dear. I can afford to be sure."

"One week, huh?"

"One week." Laying his hat on her desk, Nick bowed ceremoniously. "And in the meantime, you have acquired a new Santa, Miss Castleberry. My humble person is at your service."

"Nick, you're a lifesaver." Dragging him along in her wake, Kristina made for the door. "I'll have Polly take you down to Personnel to do the paperwork, and then we'll get somebody up here from Design to take fittings for your costume. Remember, you can stay with me if you want to—if you need a place, I mean. You don't mind wearing the regular red outfit until we get the new costume, do you? Oh, and Nick, if you see a very small woman with a fierce look on her face, act classy."

"TUCKER, what are you doing?"

He glanced up uneasily, for the moment ignoring the

untied laces on his Nike basketball shoes. "Nothing. Why?"

His younger brother frowned, giving a gloomy cast to a face so much like Tucker's they could've been twins. "Why are you dressed like that? You know we have a press conference." He gestured toward Tucker's faded blue Bears jersey and cutoff sweatpants. "That isn't exactly the right outfit for this kind of thing."

"I know." Studiously, Tucker finished tying the laces on his high-tops before standing up and facing his brother with an easy grin. "Look, Trey, I need a break. I'm going out to shoot some hoop."

"Tucker, you can't—" his brother began, but they both knew Tucker was ignoring him. Fishing a black-and-red basketball out from under his desk, he started to whistle "Sweet Georgia Brown."

"Tucker, what do you think you're doing?" Tegan hissed from the doorway. After slipping in, she eased the door shut behind her. "You've got a room full of appointments out there and I don't think they're waiting to see you play Michael Jordan."

"Cancel my appointments."

"I'm not your secretary!" Tegan protested. "Who do you think you are?"

"So tell my secretary to cancel my appointments. I need some air," he said carelessly.

"You can't cancel appointments that are already here," Trey put in.

"Then you talk to them. You know more about this stuff than I do anyway."

A dangerous light glinted in Trey's blue eyes. "You want me to take over? I can do a damn sight better job than you're doing."

Tucker unfolded to his full height, using his extra inches to face off against his brother. "Look, little brother, don't get any ideas. I'm in charge and I'm staying in charge. This is the way Dad wanted it, and that's the way it is. Losing a few appointments isn't going to kill anybody. And I need the space, okay?"

"Yeah, sure," Trey grumbled.

"Besides, I happen to believe that frequent breaks stimulate creativity." He grinned. "I had the whole design department out playing field hockey, and it worked great. Really cleared the air, geared everybody up for mega-work."

Without further comment, Tucker slid open the window on the far wall, and then fit his long body through the opening. Both his siblings watched in disbelief.

Tegan trailed after him as far as the window. With her head through the opening, she shouted after him, "That's the garage roof, Tucker. You could fall and kill yourself. You can't go climbing around on roofs!"

As he jumped off the short garage roof and landed neatly on the ground, he called back, "Toss me the ball, will you?"

"Better he sneaks out on the roof than going out the regular way, walking past his appointments wearing those ratty clothes," Trey noted with disdain.

Down below, Tucker cupped his mouth with his hands. "The ball, Tegan! Throw me the ball!"

Shaking her head, she retrieved the ball and pitched it out the window after him. Within moments, there he was, on the basketball court outside the Toyland building, happily perfecting his hook shot. "I don't believe this."

"Face it, Teeg, he's a disaster as a manager." Trey shot her a hopeful look. "He'd take it better if you told him to step down."

"He's not stepping down, so you might as well forget it. It would kill him to think he disappointed Dad, so he won't even think about it." Turning back from the window, Tegan sighed. "What am I going to do with all of his appointments? One woman has been waiting all afternoon."

Trey grinned, and for a moment, he looked as carefree and reckless as his older brother. "Is she good-looking?"

"Actually, she is. In an uptight, prissy kind of way. You know—hair pulled back, tiny gold earrings, knockout suit." Noting the look in his eye, she added, "And much too old for you."

"Sounds perfect," he told her. "Just my type. Why should Tucker have all the fun?"

Tegan smiled. "She's all yours, Trey."

KRISTINA COULDN'T BELIEVE what she was hearing. "What do you mean, he's not available? Why couldn't somebody tell me that hours ago?"

The young man shrugged. "Sorry. A business emergency came up. But I'd be happy to help if I can."

There was no way this youngster could help her, even if he was pretty cute, with his clear blue eyes and impish smile. The tailored suit and impeccable haircut put him squarely into the category she thought of as her type. If only he weren't so young.

She could hardly offend him by asking his age, but she felt like it. "Well," she began, as she pulled her letter out of her briefcase, "Tucker Bennett is the one who signed my letter, so I really think I should speak to him." She announced pointedly, "I had an appointment. I made it a week ago. Surely that means something to Mr. Bennett."

"Sorry," her young man repeated. "Are you sure I can't help?"

If her assessment was correct, this guy was only twenty or so, hardly old enough to remember the days when Toyland ran a contest. "How about Harley Bennett?" she tried, picking his name out from the middle of the letter. "President and CEO?"

"Sorry," he said again. "He retired six months ago. Tucker is the president now."

"Then I guess it's him or no one."

She had to admit to feeling distinctly peeved. When she'd finally given in to Nick's prodding and called Toyland, she'd been told that Tucker Bennett's schedule was full through Christmas and after New Year's.

But she'd refused to take no for an answer. Even though she hadn't been all that sure to begin with, and she had no idea what she was going to say once she got her foot in the door, being thwarted seemed to harden her resolve. So, after much persistence, she'd been given a one o'clock appointment.

Except she'd been waiting for three hours and still no Tucker Bennett. And now she was being told her appointment was canceled. It was enough to make her grit her teeth and dig in her heels.

"Well, Mr. Tucker Bennett who cancels his appointments, you don't know Kristina Castleberry," she said under her breath.

The youngster grinned amiably. "*I'd* like to. Kristina, was it?"

Surprised, she lifted her gaze in time to catch the sly look on his face. He certainly seemed eager to please. "Is it possible you could get me in to see him for a few minutes?"

But he shook his head. "I wish I could, but there's just no way. He's tied up...for a while, and then he has a press conference. If you could wait till after that," he said, clearly trying to be charming, "I might be able to corner him for a few minutes."

She looked doubtfully at her watch, only too aware of how long she'd been away from her own office. After all, she had lied about having a doctor's appointment.

Nick would be disappointed if she left—he seemed to find this whole Toyland thing simply fascinating—but she'd been practical and sensible too long to ignore her duty to Austin's now.

Finally, regretfully, she concluded, "I can't wait that long. I really have to get back to the city."

He reached past her to open the door into the hall. "This way. I'd be happy to walk you out."

"That's not really necessary."

"Oh, no, my pleasure." He grinned again. "I'm Trey Bennett, by the way. And I'm very happy to meet you."

There was something to be said for youthful charm. Kristina smiled back. "Nice to meet you, Trey."

Toyland's main offices were not in an office building, and not in the city. Instead, Toyland was inside an old Victorian house way out in St. Charles. It was a pretty little suburban town, built around the Fox River some forty miles west of Chicago, and it boasted several ornate old homes like the one housing Toyland.

As Kristina had driven into town, she'd noted that one big house was now a decorating business, and another a bookstore. This one, a four-story beauty dripping in gingerbread, was the unique, charming headquarters for Toyland, Inc.

Because the layout was relatively simple, she didn't need help finding her way out of Mr. Bennett's office, in what must have originally been some kind of second-floor parlor. It was a straight shot from there out into the main hall, down the curving front stairs, past a receptionist and out the front door.

But her young admirer insisted on accompanying her, and he led her back behind the receptionist, into a rabbit warren of cubicles and desks, bulletin boards and drafting tables.

"Marketing," he told her. "And on the other side is Personnel."

If she hadn't guessed before, she knew now that Toyland was a small concern. They couldn't have had more than twenty or twenty-five employees. So how in the world had they sponsored that contest, and tackled product lines that rivaled the major companies?

"Is this all there is?" she ventured. "To the company, I mean?"

"Well, Design is upstairs. I head up Design," he announced with a touch of arrogance.

Sure you do, she thought. No company in her experience had kids right out of college who managed their own departments.

"But if you mean manufacturing," he went on, "that's done wherever we hire it out."

Her heart sank. There was no way this place could do her Santa's Magic Workshop, even if they'd wanted to. Not that she'd planned on pitching it, of course. It was, after all, a ten-year-old idea, and she was only here on a wild-goose chase in the first place.

But a small part of her had held on to the hope that just maybe...

Oh, well, it didn't bear thinking of now. She hadn't gotten in to see Tucker Bennett, her ten-year-old workshop hadn't wowed him so much he'd immediately seized it and hailed her as the next wizard of the toy industry and her childish dreams were not going to come true.

She argued with herself to give up once and for all as Trey led her through the marketing department and into what was still a kitchen.

"By the way," he said, with an odd, conspiratorial sort of look on his face, "if you should change your mind and decide to come back later, this back door is always open. After business hours, I'm sure I could get you as much time with Tucker as you want."

"No, I don't think so—" she began, still heavily into her struggle to give up on toys.

But Trey held up a hand and continued speaking. "Go do whatever it is you need to do and come back tonight. I'll be waiting for you. Just come up to the third floor and look for the playroom. I can introduce you to Tucker, and you can talk to him about whatever it is that's so important."

"I never said anything was so important."

"Then why were you upset with Tucker for canceling your appointment?"

"It's the principle of the thing," she maintained stubbornly.

"Well, whatever—I still think you should try again. If you decide to come back tonight, look for me on the third floor." And he opened the back door for her, ushering her out onto the sidewalk. "See you later, Kristina."

"I'm not coming back," she told him, but he only grinned at her again.

"He probably thinks I'll come back to see *him* again," she said with a laugh as the door closed behind her. "I should've asked him his age. I mean, he can't be more than nineteen. Then I could've pointed out the fact that I'm ten years older than he is, and this flirting thing is hardly appropriate." She paused. "But he *was* cute. Okay, so maybe he's twenty, even twenty-one...."

She was still mumbling under her breath as she made her way down Toyland's sidewalk, next to a flower bed, forlorn except for a few hardy mums this time of year. The persistent sound of a hard ball pounding against cement invaded her consciousness, until she finally looked up.

Directly ahead of her, across from the Toyland house's small garage, she found her target. It was a full-size basketball court, carved out of the next-door lot. She'd heard of taking extra lots and making them into gardens, but basketball courts? This one had the regulation two hoops, lines painted on the cement and even lights for night games.

"Toyland must really be into employee physical fitness," she decided.

Especially if the lone player was any indication. He was tall and slim, with the kind of easy grace she drooled over in secret when she saw the likes of Michael Jordan sailing down the lane for a lay-up, or Joe Montana hiking back to throw the long bomb. As she watched, the man drove out from the basket, spun and then sent a fifteen-foot jump shot swishing through the net.

In her real life, meaning the part of her life she admitted to, she had no fondness for jocks. In her experience, they were cocky and macho, and very immature. But in her fantasy life, in that small segment of her time when she turned to the all-sports network at three in the morning to watch team handball or college baseball, she had an undeniable *thing* for long, fit bodies that jumped and ran and flew through the air.

And this guy had one of the best.

Inside a Chicago Bears jersey that had seen better days, the man's shoulders were broad and strong. When he went up to shoot, his jersey rode up just enough to see a hard, flat stomach and a narrow waist. And his lean, well-muscled legs went on forever in those ghastly shorts of his.

Kristina held her breath. Whew. She'd definitely been working too hard if a stranger's body hit her like this.

"Get a grip," she told herself. Clutching her briefcase, she forced herself to stop gawking and start walking. But when she tried to ignore his body, she saw his face.

It was the mirror image of the youngster who'd escorted her outside, with the same sparkling blue eyes under straight brows, the same clean jawline and the same aristocratic, impudent nose.

But this one's light brown hair was a tad shaggier, and his face was stronger, more clearly defined, with character lines etched around his eyes. This one was older.

And suddenly it all became clear. Two men who looked alike but were about ten years apart in age—they must be brothers.

And Toyland was a small, family-run company, where a kid might actually manage a major department, *if* he were a family member. So what did that make this set of brothers?

Bennetts, that's what, as in the Bennetts who owned and ran Toyland. She remembered now that Trey had introduced himself as Trey Bennett, and it hadn't even registered that he might be related to the man who wrote her letter.

So this dazzling basketball player was a Bennett, just like her young pal Trey.

Chewing her lip thoughtfully, she narrowed her gaze at Mr. Wonderful. *He* was Tucker Bennett. And he'd skipped out on her appointment to play basketball.

She swept down the sidewalk and past the basketball court without giving Tucker Bennett another glance. Stand her up for basketball, would he?

"I'll be back, Mr. Bennett," she promised him, even though he was well out of hearing range. "You haven't seen the last of Kristina Castleberry."

Chapter Four

It was dark and cold by the time she returned to Toyland. Kristina stood for a moment, back on the sidewalk next to the tall Victorian house, shivering as she stuck her hands farther into the depths of her coat pockets.

The house was chock-full of charm. She had to admit that, even as she frowned, gazing up at it. A thin layer of snow had frosted the windows and painted delicate edges on the wooden shakes, giving it the look of a gingerbread house.

But charm and gingerbread didn't add up to real life. Real life was her overflowing desk at Austin's, and back home in Winnetka, an answering machine full of calls from her mother.

She decided then and there—she didn't care if she was a chicken, or if Nick never forgave her—she wanted to go home. But when she turned to walk back to her car, she couldn't resist one last look up at Toyland.

It was then she saw the glowing windows from the other side of the third floor. There were lights on—inviting, seductive lights, spilling out into the darkness and promising warmth and laughter and...

And she didn't know what.

It was like being six years old again, nose pressed up against the window of the toy store, wishing for Patty Kay, the beautiful baby doll who came with her own velvet dress and shiny black shoes.

She was getting more than a little crazy, letting this rush of emotion overtake her just from a couple of lighted windows.

"You've been out in the cold too long," she muttered.

But it did look nice, didn't it? She imagined Tucker Bennett behind those windows, doing whatever people who owned toy companies did when the night grew long. Was he winding up speedy little cars and racing them again and again? Or maybe building new galaxies out of the latest models of erector sets?

Or perhaps Tucker Bennett was at this moment ranting and raving, fighting with his designers over whether the newest Toyland toy should be blue or green or violently purple.

"I want to see," she admitted for the first time. "I want to go up there."

Gathering the wisps of her courage together, she put her head down into the wind and angled around to the back of the house. As promised, the back door was open, and she slid right in.

And Tucker Bennett, with that beautiful body and the power to make her dreams come true, was waiting upstairs.

Toyland was completely silent and eerily dark as she made her way through the first floor and up the stairs. Finally, when she reached the third-floor landing, she thought she heard muffled voices.

She crept down the corridor toward the voices, feeling like a cat burglar, until there it was, right in front of her—

a rather beaten-up door with the word Playroom sten-
ciled on it.

As she raised her hand to knock and announce herself,
the door creaked and swung open a few inches on its own.
It was unnerving. With her heart pounding, she snatched
back her hand and stepped away from the door.

"Tucker!" she heard Trey's voice boom out into the
stillness. "You can't be serious! That's the stupidest thing
you've said yet, and you've said some pretty dumb things
in your time."

"Can it, little brother. If I wanted your advice, I'd ask
for it."

That voice could only belong to Tucker Bennett. And
what a voice it was—deep and rich, with a hint of a growl
in it. It dipped inside her winter coat, bypassed her wool
suit jacket and cool linen blouse and purred right up her
spine.

"Give me some credit here, Trey." The voice dropped
a notch, not so angry now, but still a little rough around
the edges. "Trust me, little brother—faster and flashier,
not more expensive, is the answer."

The voice continued in an undertone, keeping time with
a series of footsteps that paced impatiently across the
hardwood floor inside, charting a path closer and closer
to the door.

Kristina took another step back. If they were arguing,
she couldn't very well interrupt, could she?

As she edged even farther away, a worn floorboard
creaked loudly under her foot. The footsteps inside the
room stopped abruptly.

"Who's there?" Tucker Bennett called out. "Come on
in and join the fun, especially if you're on my side."

Accepting her fate, Kristina slid in around the edge of
the door. And there he was, all six-foot-whatever of him

wearing worn jeans, a softly tattered flannel shirt unbuttoned over a white T-shirt and an openly curious light in his blue, blue eyes.

He gave her a slight, quirky smile and then stood there, looking at her, while she did her best to get her heart to start beating again.

Why did he affect her like this? She was a smart, capable person, who dressed well and looked good and knew all the right people. He, on the other hand, was a vaguely scruffy, decidedly eccentric toy designer whose hair was so carelessly shaggy that her fingers itched to reach out and fix it.

There, now she felt better. But she still couldn't take her eyes off him.

"Hello," she said finally, sticking out a hand and trying to sound businesslike. "I'm—"

"Kristina!" Trey interrupted. He bumped Tucker out of the way and took her outstretched hand between both of his. "Glad you could make it."

It was a surprise to realize again how much the brothers resembled each other. Trey might be wearing a crisp button-down shirt and neat khaki pants with a perfect crease, but his features were startlingly similar to his brother's. She offered him a smile. "Hello, again, Trey."

Tucker immediately retreated. "What a shame," he said with a sigh. "You're with him."

"Well, not really. That is, I'm not with anybody." Pulling her hand away from Trey, she followed Tucker with her eyes. "Actually, I came to see you."

Tossing his brother a superior grin, Tucker said, "Smart girl."

"Kristina was one of the appointments you canceled this afternoon," Trey shot back. "I told her to come in tonight when you'd be more likely to sit still and talk business." He turned to Kristina. "I was planning on introducing you to Tucker, but I guess you've already figured it out. Anyway, this is my brother, Tucker Bennett."

"Nice to meet—" she began, when Trey suddenly broke in.

"Did you hear that?"

Kristina was mystified; she hadn't heard a thing.

Tucker seemed equally confused. "Hear what?"

"The fax," his brother told him with excitement. "Didn't you hear the beep? This could be it!"

Nodding, Tucker threw an arm around his brother. "Let's hope so. And that the news is good."

Kristina looked back and forth between the anxious faces. "Excuse me?"

"We've been waiting for the first of the Christmas retail figures," Tucker explained. "The reports are late. But maybe this is finally it."

"Come on, Tucker," Trey put in. "Let's get it over with."

Quickly Tucker turned to Kristina. "Do you mind excusing us for a few minutes?"

"No, of course not."

"Make yourself at home. We'll be right back," he told her, flashing a grin as he backed out the door after his brother.

"Well, okay," she murmured, but the Bennett brothers were already gone.

She shrugged, wondering what she should do until they came back. How did one make oneself at home when this was nothing like one's home? Quietly she slid out of her coat and hung it on a hook near the door, but that was all she did to get comfortable.

Humming to herself to fill the silence, she turned around and let her eyes wander around the big space they called the playroom. Her humming faded.

While Tucker had been in the room, she hadn't noticed much else. But now ... Even the remarkable Tucker Bennett paled by comparison to this place, this magical toy kingdom right out of her childhood imagination.

She didn't quite know what to make of it.

It wasn't that it was fancy. Oh, no, just the opposite. Uncarpeted and unadorned, it was a big, practical room, overflowing with bits and pieces of toys and games from every possible surface. On three walls, top-to-bottom shelves offered a hodgepodge of dolls, bears, cars, soldiers and colorful building blocks. The debris spilled from the shelves and pooled on the floor, as though a whole kindergarten class had been in the process of playing with it only moments ago.

Above her, a host of kites hung from the high ceiling, their bright tails dipping down to touch the roof of an elaborate dollhouse in one corner, and an equally impressive castle, complete with turrets and drawbridge and flags flying, on the opposite side. She bent to peer inside the dollhouse, catching a glimpse of miniature Persian rugs and dark wood furniture. It was exquisite.

Reluctantly leaving the dollhouse, she wandered back to the middle of the room, where two huge tables took up most of the available space. The larger of the two held the most complicated train set she'd ever seen, with hills and valleys and several towns for the train cars to pass through. The other table was heaped high with glue and scissors and tape, pieces of scenery and track, and enough cords and batteries to keep the Pentagon running.

''Wow,'' she whispered.

Every child's fantasy, it was exactly what Kristina had imagined when she'd first conceived the idea of growing up to be a toy designer. When she was about twelve, she'd told her mother about her dream, and Betty Castleberry had pressed her lips together in a bitter frown.

Even now, so many years later, Kristina could still see that frown, and hear the angry words that followed.

"Why would you want to do that?" her mother had demanded. "You're pretty and smart, Kristina. Why work in some dingy, dark place with bugs and mice?"

Mrs. Castleberry had been referring to Mr. Castleberry's workroom in the basement, at that point abandoned for two years or so. When he was still around, he'd spent most of his time down in the basement, in his funny, crowded little room, where it always smelled like the burnt wire and scorched wood of failed inventions. Even after it became patently clear to everyone that his designs were not going to make ten cents, let alone the millions he'd pinned his hopes on, George Castleberry had stayed hidden in his basement workroom, puttering away on his faster-than-a-speeding-bullet tugboat—whose motor frequently caught fire—and Thor's Flying Hammer—which had an unfortunate tendency to rebound and hit its owner on the head.

She never told her mother that, unlike her father, her idea of being a toy designer didn't include basements *or* solitude.

Kristina envisioned a bright, cheerful place, full of sunlight and laughter, where other people worked right along beside her. At some level, if she were scrupulously honest, she supposed those mythical "other people" included her father. In the lavish toy workshop of her imagination, Mr. Castleberry and daughter toiled side by side in perfect harmony. In a place just like this one.

Running loving fingers over the edge of the train table, she knew exactly what she was feeling. A secret, intense, shameful longing.

She coveted this playroom.

It was like a physical ache, right there under her rib cage. If she weren't careful, she'd wrap her arms around the dollhouse and beg to be allowed to stay.

Get over it, she told herself firmly, forcing herself to pull her hand off the train table. *This isn't yours, and it never will be.*

But it made her want to share her workshop idea with the Bennett brothers, to make them understand how special it was. If she couldn't be a part of their fabulous playroom, maybe her Santa's Magic Workshop could.

Taking one last look around, she shook her head at the sheer size of the place. "What could this possibly have been?" she asked under her breath.

From behind her, Tucker cut in before she'd even realized he was back, and she spun around guiltily.

"It was originally a studio when the house was built in the 1890s," he said easily, strolling over in her direction with his hands tucked in the pockets of his disreputable jeans. "The lady of the house was a retired ballerina, and her husband built her a place to dance."

It was irritating that he'd interrupted her reverie, but downright maddening that he'd guessed what she'd only whispered. "How did you hear my question?"

"I didn't. It was written all over your face. You looked so completely amazed, like, 'What in the world could this have been in a normal house?'"

Quickly she tried to compose herself. She didn't want anything written on her face, especially not her feelings about this room. "And then?"

"What?"

"After the ballerina?"

"Oh." Tucker grinned. "My folks bought the house in the fifties and moved the company headquarters here. This seemed like the natural place to throw all the leftovers and actually play with our toys—to see if they worked, to see if they were fun."

"It's wonderful," she murmured, moving away from the train table and brushing the tail of a kite with her fingers. Encouraged by this enchanted playroom, she found Santa's Magic Workshop on the tip of her tongue. "You're in charge now, right?"

"Right."

Behind them, Trey snorted. "That's debatable."

Kristina turned, surprised. She had forgotten all about him. "Did you get the news you were hoping for?"

"Sort of," Trey allowed grumpily. "Although not as good as it could be."

"Trey, don't start this again, please? We have a visitor, and I'm sure she doesn't want to hear your complaints about how I'm running the company."

"Look, I'm sorry. I seem to have barged right into some sort of—" she searched for the most diplomatic word "—difference in philosophies. I didn't mean to intrude."

"Oh, don't worry. We're always fighting about something," Tucker said quickly. He hitched a thumb in the direction of the bigger table. "If not the company, then the train set. Trey has a lot of dopey ideas, so I have to keep pointing out the error of his views."

"My brother, Mr. Crash and Burn," Trey muttered.

Tucker only smiled. "Unlike my brother, I'm sure you understand what I mean—fast is where it's at."

"F-fast?" Her gaze seemed fixed on his. "I'm sorry?"

"Trains," Trey said with disgust. "He thinks speed is everything, whereas *I* say trains sell because—"

"Because of fancy cars and towns and corny little people," Tucker finished for him. Equally disgusted, he shook his head. "Forget all the accessories—they'll bankrupt you. Run at the highest possible speed, and make sure there are lots of good crashes."

This did not accord with her own personal philosophy, and it certainly didn't fit her Magic Workshop. "I don't know anything about trains," she began carefully, "but I do know retail. I work at a department store, so I see the people who buy these things, and I think Trey is right."

"No, no, you don't understand." Impatient, Tucker moved back to the train table. "Here, I'll show you what I mean. I'll prove it."

"Tucker, you don't need to do that," the others chorused, but it was too late.

On one side of the massive train set, he pulled a switch, jolting a long section of cars to life. Quickly he slid around to the other end of the table, where he set a similar length of train in motion. Finally, pulling a few random cars and an engine off the spare parts table, Tucker started a third train going, too.

Kristina's eyes widened. She hadn't even had a chance to check out those adorable trains, and he was sending them dancing around the track so fast their logos blurred.

Electricity buzzed through her, as tangibly as it propelled the trains around the curves. As she watched, fascinated and horrified all at the same time, the brave little trains chugged faster and faster, with Tucker flipping switches here and there to control their direction. Steadily, inexorably, Tucker's plan became clear as all three trains began to converge on a perfectly pretty little town built on a hill near the center of the long table.

Kristina couldn't take her eyes off the speeding trains. The tension in the room—the tension inside her—crackled higher with each passing second, as the trains rocketed along the track toward destruction.

"Trey," she tried, feeling faint-headed. "Stop this. He's going to wreck them!"

"Come on, Tucker," Trey interceded. "You're heading them toward Whoville, and I just made the post office. Tucker, I only finished the benches in the Whoville Station yesterday!"

Before she could move forward—to either throw herself onto the tracks or rip Tucker Bennett's hands off the controls—the first train came blazing up to Whoville, with the second train only inches away from meeting it there with a big bang.

But at the last possible instant, with a flick of a gear, number one careened into a hairpin turn while number two slipped right past. Directly behind this near miss, the third train spun into the tiny Whoville Station, out of the path of disaster, without a centimeter to spare.

She couldn't quite believe her eyes. How had he known that train number three would fit exactly in the station? How had he timed it so perfectly that each of the trains emerged unscathed? She shook her head and stared at the track, only now getting her heartbeat under control.

"Well?" Tucker prompted. "Didn't I tell you it would be exciting?"

She closed her mouth and forced her gaze away from the trains. Her voice was shaky when she mumbled, under her breath, "Heavens to Betsy."

"Tucker, you are a jerk," his brother said stiffly. "You almost ruined six months of work."

''I didn't ruin anything,'' Tucker protested. ''Not one brick of your precious town is touched. That was the whole idea.''

''But you tried, didn't you?''

''I wasn't trying to wreck your town. I was just trying to prove a point, that flash is more fun than details, that—''

Trey's eyes glittered with hostility. ''You were trying to get me all hysterical that you were going to wreck my town, and then *not* wreck it, just to make me look like an idiot.''

''Calm down here. Let's not blow this out of proportion.'' He held up a conciliatory hand. ''I know you're steamed because I won this round, but it has nothing to do with—''

''Don't tell me what it has to do with,'' Trey shot back. ''This involves a lot more than train sets.''

''Oh, yeah? Like what?''

''How about the way you're screwing up the company with your stupid emphasis on *fun?* Who cares about fun, when it comes to matters like prestige and profit?''

Tucker shook his head. ''Look, kid, I know you have some beefs about my management style—''

''That's a laugh.'' Trey interrupted him. ''You don't have a management style. Or do you call *neglect* a style?''

There was a long pause.

Finally Tucker spoke, in a low, slow voice that ruffled the hairs on the back of Kristina's neck. ''Maybe you'd better go somewhere and cool down, little brother. Before you say something you regret.''

''My only regret is that I didn't say this sooner, while there was still time to convince Dad to leave me in charge, instead of you.''

"Call him up," Tucker suggested softly. "I'm sure there are phones on cruise ships. Bother him in Tahiti, or wherever they've gotten to by now. Let's see if he changes his mind."

Anger colored Trey's handsome features, but he said nothing.

"In fact, why don't you call Dad right now? Use the phone in Design. It's the closest." Tucker turned his back on his brother and began to remove the now idle train pieces from the track.

"I know where the damned phone is." Wheeling, Trey stalked out the playroom door without a backward glance.

Kristina stayed where she was, trying to seem inconspicuous. She hated arguments; she could never witness one without somehow feeling that it was all her fault, and that she ought to thrust herself in between the combatants and make things all right. She felt the familiar panic that arguments engendered, and all she wanted to do was sink quietly into the floorboards before either Bennett brother remembered she was there.

Quietly she tried to escape toward the door before Tucker turned around. But she had gone less than two steps before he moved to put a section of track back on the worktable, and caught her in the corner of his eye.

"Oh." His blue eyes were wide and unconcerned, as if no battle royal had raged here only moments ago. "What was it you wanted to talk to me about?"

"I don't think this is a good idea," she managed to say. "I've kind of changed my mind about it."

"No, no, that's okay. You can tell me now." But her face must have shown her discomfort, because he relented. "Look, don't let that little scene with my brother throw you. I don't know if you and Trey are friends or something..."

"Well, no. I mean, I only met him today, when I was waiting for you." It was out before she could stop it. "You know, when you were playing basketball."

"Aw, hell." He winced. "I suppose Trey told you where I was?"

"Actually, I saw you," she admitted.

"And so you think Trey was right when he was shooting off his mouth about me neglecting Toyland?" He shook his head. "Sometimes I go crazy in the office, and I need a break so bad I can... Well, anyway, I'm sorry about the appointment. It's not a usual occurrence, if that helps."

"That's okay," she found herself saying. Clearly, happy-go-lucky Tucker Bennett wasn't so happy these days, even if he did get to play with toys for a living. She, of all people, understood job pressures. She understood wanting to play hooky, to feel free for a little while.

"I guess I'm not making much of an impression, am I?" he lamented.

If only he knew. She kept trying to be miffed—about the missed appointment, about the train set nonsense—but all she could think of was the warmth in his blue eyes and his touchy-feely voice. "I think your impression has been just fine," she said weakly.

A wan smile curved his mouth. "About the thing with Trey—we've been through this more times than I can remember. Brothers—you know."

She shrugged helplessly. "I'm an only child."

"It's just a—what did you call it?—difference in philosophy." He ran a hand through his hair. "I like the simple toys—fast, fun, no frills. Trey wants to turn this place into a yuppie playground, with electronics and gimmicks, and everything priced sky-high. I just can't see it."

Unfortunately, that "difference in philosophy" made it even more unlikely he'd approve of her exquisite, expensive idea for Santa's Magic Workshop.

"We'll patch it up," he added. "We always do."

"Maybe you should talk to him," she suggested softly. "See if there's not some compromise you can come to."

A brief smile flickered across his lips. "What, and let my little brother win one?"

A lock of hair had slipped down to ruffle his forehead, and she had an overwhelming urge to tuck it back where it belonged. A very dangerous urge, considering she was all alone here with the engaging Tucker Bennett so late at night. "I—I'd better be going," she told him.

"No, wait. You have to give me your name so I can watch out for you, when you make a new appointment." He pulled a small, crumpled piece of paper out of the back pocket of his jeans, and then searched his other pockets, apparently looking for a pen.

Without thinking, Kristina bent to offer him one from her purse. She was always well-supplied with that kind of thing.

He took it absently, balancing paper and pen against his knee. "Well?"

"What?"

"Your name?"

"Oh, right." She wasn't sure she wanted to reschedule her appointment, but it seemed easier just to go along for the time being. "Kristina Castleberry," she told him. "That's Kristina with a *K,* and Castleberry just like it sounds."

His pen stopped in midscrawl. "Castleberry? As in George Castleberry?"

"My father?" A chill seemed to settle over her. "What do you know about my father?"

Chapter Five

"Do you believe it, Nick?" She was so keyed up, she couldn't even think of sleep. All the way home from Toyland, she'd tried to make sense of this amazing development.

Thank goodness Nick was still up—he'd been staying with her for almost a week now—so she had someone to talk to when she got home.

"My father has been writing letters to Toyland, proposing toy ideas, steadily for the past fifteen or twenty years." She shook her head. "I still can't believe it."

"Very unexpected, yes," Nick murmured.

Brimming with nervous energy, she stooped and peered into the refrigerator. After rearranging the butter tub and the lone diet soft-drink can, she slammed the door shut and regarded her companion thoughtfully. "You know, Nick, you don't seem very surprised."

His gentle eyes rebuked her. "It's not my father who's suddenly reappeared."

"He hasn't exactly reappeared." As she tried hard to look on the positive side, the negatives kept getting coming back to haunt her. "He hasn't come back into my life, or tried to see me, or even written to me. He might be interested in keeping ties with Toyland, but not to me. That hasn't changed.''

Nick said nothing. It was as if he were waiting for her to make her own conclusions.

''But this is better than not knowing anything,'' she decided after a moment. ''At least I know he's alive. And that he's still trying to design toys. Tucker says he's been sending them new ideas practically every week for years and years.''

Nick smiled, and a twinkle reached his eyes. ''Tucker, is it?''

''Now, Nick. Don't get any ideas.'' She poked around in the kitchen cabinet for some crackers. ''I know you have this bee in your bonnet about me and Toyland, but trying to fix me up with Tucker Bennett isn't going to help things.''

Nick only smiled.

Dangling the whole packet of crackers, Kristina allowed a picture of the wayward toy inventor to sneak into her brain. ''I will admit that he's...interesting,'' she murmured. ''He has blue eyes—really blue, none of this wishy-washy stuff. And his voice, well, I've never heard a voice that like that before. Low, kind of rough, kind of...'' She searched for the right image. ''Intimate. Tucker Bennett is one of those guys who smiles and just takes your breath away before you even realize that...''

Catching herself, she stuck a cracker in her mouth before she had a chance to say anything worse.

''And how did Mr. Bennett react to Santa's Magic Workshop?''

Carefully she chewed and swallowed. ''I didn't tell him.''

''You didn't tell him? But, Kristina, wasn't that the purpose of the visit?''

"Well, yes." Twisting the tie on the package, she turned away long enough to stick the crackers back into the cupboard. "But first, Tucker and his brother got into an argument, and it didn't seem like a good time. And after he dropped the bomb about my father, well, it definitely wasn't a good time."

"And what happened next?"

"Well, I asked him what he knew, and he said not much, that my dad had been sending in crackpot ideas for years and years." She managed a rueful smile. "You might say that my dad is a legend around Toyland."

"Is that good or bad?"

"Terrible," she said softly. "And it looks like the Magic Workshop is on the shelf for good. I can hardly pitch an idea to a company where my father is a big joke."

"But the Magic Workshop is too important to abandon!" he insisted.

"You and I think so, Nick, but I'm sure my father thought that about all of his ideas, too. And they were stinkers, every one." She sighed. "So what does that make the Magic Workshop?"

"There, there, my dear. I'm sure your father's ideas, no matter how odd, don't reflect on you in the least."

"It doesn't make any difference, anyway," she said with resignation. "I didn't exactly leave Toyland with Tucker dying to hear my idea."

"What do you mean?"

"After he told me about all the letters from my father, Tucker said I could see the files sometime if I wanted...." Even now, the very idea made her stomach do flip-flops. "If I wanted an address. To try and reach him."

"Yes." Nick patted her hand kindly. "And what did you do?"

"I didn't do anything. When he said that about the address, I panicked even more and I bolted." Tilting herself back against the kitchen counter, she stared down at her carefully manicured nails, resisting the urge to chew on them. "I'm sure Tucker thought I was crazy, running out like that. I mean, I never did tell him what I was doing there in the first place."

"I'm sure he understands. It's not every day one gets news of one's long-lost father," Nick offered encouragingly.

"*I'm* sure he doesn't understand. He undoubtedly thinks I'm nuts, too, the crazy daughter of a lunatic toy inventor...."

"Kristina," Nick said firmly, "it's late and you're being much too hard on yourself. I'm sure the young gentleman does not think you are a lunatic."

Immersed in her thoughts, Kristina ignored Nick's kinder perspective. "When you stop to think about it, it's pretty weird. Tucker Bennett is a stranger, and he knows more about my father than I do."

"I'm quite sorry this didn't turn out as we'd planned," Nick said quietly.

"I didn't exactly come home the new queen of the toy world, did I?"

"No, but you are home now, and you have some very important issues to ponder," Nick reminded her. "So I suggest you try to get some sleep and do just that. It's very late, my dear."

"Ponder while I sleep?"

"Certainly."

"But how can I sleep? I've never felt so awake in my life!"

"Come along now," the older man directed, tucking her arm inside his and leading her toward the stairs. "One of the reasons I agreed to accept your hospitality during my Santa Claus tenure was that I perceived a very great need here.''

''Meaning?''

An affectionate smile curved his lips. ''Meaning that you have been neglecting yourself awfully, but now that I am staying with you, you must eat and rest properly. Or my name isn't. . .''

''Nick Holiday,'' she finished for him.

''Yes, that's right.'' His smile grew more mischievous. ''Nick Holiday.''

FROWNING, TUCKER HUNG UP the phone. Spinning around in the tall leather chair, he contemplated the blank wall of darkness visible out his window. He undid his tie with a quick yank, deciding it was okay to let loose a little if it was already dark outside. Unfortunately, there weren't any answers out there, either.

Why couldn't he get through to Kristina? If her secretary was passing on his messages, and he didn't see any reason why she wouldn't, then Kristina must know that he was trying to reach her. And since days had gone by, and she still hadn't answered any of his messages, he could only assume that she didn't want to be reached. But why?

Maybe he should try her at home again. Another message on her answering machine couldn't hurt any more than the ones he'd already left at her office.

He had his message all planned—something appropriately interesting without sounding threatening—when to his surprise, the phone was picked up on the other end.

''Yes, halloo,'' a respectable older man's voice announced. ''Miss Kristina Castleberry's residence.''

It sounded like the butler. Was she the type to have a butler?

"Is Kristina there, please?"

"No, I'm sorry. Miss Castleberry is not at home presently."

"Do you know when she'll be back?"

"I'm sorry, but I believe she plans to be away all evening," came the delicate reply. "Of course, I should be happy to relay a message. Might I tell her the reason for your call?"

That was the stumper. Tucker himself wasn't quite sure about the reason for the call.

"I, uh..." He persevered. "The last time I saw her, she was kind of upset. I just wanted to make sure she was okay."

"She's fine, I assure you." There was a judicious silence. "You wouldn't by any chance be Mr. Tucker Bennett, would you?"

He was mystified. Did that mean she'd mentioned him to this person, this butler? Was that good or bad? "Yes, I am," he answered. "I've been trying to reach her for several days."

"Of course you have," the man said cheerfully. "And I've been trying to get her to return your calls. She has the most wonderful idea she really ought to tell you about, but she's a bit hesitant. I can't say I understand why."

"Idea?"

"For a toy. It's simply lovely. She came to see you about it, you know, but then, due to an unfortunate bit of timing, she learned about her father, and I'm afraid it quite put the toy idea out of her head."

"So she does want to see me?"

"Oh, no, she doesn't," the other man answered, sounding perfectly logical. "But she should."

"I don't understand."

"I'm not a bit surprised." The cultured, vaguely British voice lowered. "Confidentially, I don't think Kristina does, either. Understand, that is."

"Okay." Mentally, Tucker tried to regroup, but he kept coming back to the same point. "And who exactly are you?"

"Call me Nick. Everyone does."

"Sure. Great. Nick. Are you Kristina's uncle? Grandfather? Something like that?"

"No, no. Not at all." He put in helpfully, "Simply a friend. Kristina has kindly extended her hospitality while I undertake a position at her store. Austin's. It's a lovely store. Have you been there, Tucker?"

"No, not recently." He asked casually, "And what do you do at the store?"

"Why, I'm Santa Claus. It seems Kristina was in a bit of a pickle regarding her previous Mr. Claus, so I've stepped into the breech, and am now the official Austin's Santa."

"I see. How nice for you."

"I'm quite enjoying myself, actually. A change of pace." Nick clucked his tongue softly. "But you haven't called to chat with me, have you, Mr. Bennett? As I said, I'll be happy to give Kristina your message. But I can't guarantee that she'll ring you back. She seems to have got it into her head that you wouldn't want to see her again."

"But I do," Tucker said quickly.

"Yes, I can hear that in your voice. Might I tell her why?"

"I'm not exactly sure."

Tucker tried to sort it out. It was partly because she was very pretty; he'd allow that. It wasn't every day beautiful young women with long, dark hair and prim, cherry-red suits slipped into Toyland and captured his imagination.

And he knew she was his "type"; just like his little brother, he had a thing for cool, professional women.

But if anything, that worked against her. After all, his ex-wife was the same type—hell, Vanessa even wore the same kind of suit—and he thought he'd sworn off smart, self-possessed women for good.

But Kristina was different. Maybe it was the way her eyes had gotten all round and soft when she'd taken a good look at the playroom, or how breathless she'd gone when he'd staged the near miss with the trains, or even the flush on her cheeks and the uncertainty in her eyes when he'd casually mentioned her father's name.

He liked to play his impulses out, to see where they led. Right now, Kristina Castleberry was more than an impulse. She was a question mark, a beautiful, scared question mark.

"I'd like to see if I could help," he answered finally. "She seemed like she could use my help."

Nick chuckled. "I don't think she'd like to hear you say that, my boy. Our Kristina doesn't think she needs anyone's help."

That fit the profile, but it didn't dissuade him. "Will you tell her I called, that I'd like to see her?"

"I think I can do better than that," his newfound friend declared. "I've just had the most delightful notion. Here's the thing—Kristina has gone off to a fancy dress party tonight, a benefit as they say, where I believe anyone is welcome who cares to make a rather substantial contribution...." There was a long pause. "Do you perhaps own a dinner jacket, Mr. Bennett?"

KRISTINA SIPPED CHAMPAGNE from a fine crystal flute, and wished the Austins kept their ballroom less chilly.

"I also wish I'd brought a date," she murmured under her breath.

"Don't talk to yourself, darling," her mother told her as she slid noiselessly into place next to her. "People will think you're odd."

Just what she needed at this moment. Kristina loved her mother, really she did. She just didn't need to see her or hear her *at this moment.* She made herself smile. "Hello, Mother. How are you? You look wonderful."

"Thank you, darling."

Bitsy Austin, formerly plain old Betty Castleberry, was a vision of pastels and creams, with her pale, perfect skin and cool blond hair.

Bitsy prided herself on knowing exactly what to wear to set off her petite figure and porcelain good looks; it had been her calling card throughout her days as manager of Posh, Austin's ultraexclusive designer boutique. Tonight, she wore a cream-colored sheath, hand-beaded, elegant and very, very expensive.

Examining her daughter, Bitsy said, "You look so tired, darling. And you could have done something more interesting with your hair." She fussed over a stray strand of Kristina's hair, left long and straight tonight, before stepping back to survey her handiwork. "The outfit is nice, though. Did I buy you that?"

The outfit in question was a plain black silk dinner suit, with a long, double-breasted jacket over wide trousers. "Nope, sorry." She smiled. "I got this one on my own."

Bitsy bit her lip, considering the suit. "Very nice. Anyway," she went on, "the point is that in this business appearance is everything."

Kristina took a long swallow of champagne. "I thought tonight was a social occasion."

"Darling, darling... When Mirabel is your boss, no occasion is purely social. Besides, they won't think you can handle the job if you look all worn-out and frazzled."

"But, Mother, I *am* worn-out and frazzled."

Bitsy clicked her tongue. "Oh, Kristina. Sometimes you worry me, you really do." It was the first volley in a familiar argument. "You know, darling, Windy only gave you the job as a favor to me."

"Yes, Mother, I know." It was hard to forget when Bitsy reminded her at least twice a week.

"And Windy is such a dear."

"Yes, Mother, he is."

At first, Kristina had been delighted her mother was marrying Windham "Windy" Austin. After all, the man was stinking rich, and he wasn't even a bad guy. He'd lived under the thumb of his own domineering mother, the indomitable Mirabel, for so long, Kristina knew he'd knuckle under to Bitsy without a whimper.

And he had. Betty, now called Bitsy to sound a bit more upscale, had resigned her position at Austin's to concentrate on being Windy's pampered wife, and then she'd managed to maneuver her daughter into the plum job in Special Areas.

"Windy really went out on a limb for you," Bitsy admonished, "so you have to do an absolutely fabulous job to show him—and that evil little mother of his—how deserving you are of his support and trust."

Kristina's lips curved into a semblance of a smile. "I'm trying, Mother."

"I know you are, darling." Dashing away an imaginary spot of dust on her daughter's lapel, Bitsy beamed encouragingly. "But you must try harder. Austin's is a demanding place to work, my dear, and it requires the best from its girls."

The word "girls" grated, but she knew her mother was speaking from a perspective some twenty-five years in the past, when Bitsy had begun her career as one of Austin's "girls."

"So, when I tell you—" Bitsy went on, but Kristina cut in, trying to get them onto other conversational turf.

"Are you enjoying yourself tonight, Mother? Mirabel really outdid herself with this one, didn't she?"

"This one" was Mirabel Austin's annual Christmas benefit for the symphony, called the "FaLaLa-GaLa" behind Mirabel's back. Anyone who was anyone was invited, and anyone who wanted to be anyone at Austin's had better attend, with a fat check for the symphony in hand.

"La-di-da," Bitsy tossed off, negligently waving a pretty little hand weighted down with a very large diamond. "They're all the same."

"And where is Windy tonight?"

"No doubt Mirabel has cornered him somewhere to rail at him about the store," Bitsy sniffed. "As if he doesn't deserve a night off to simply enjoy a party."

Kristina wondered what her mother would do if she was reminded of the maternal lecture *she'd* just been handing out. But, playing the dutiful daughter, Kristina chose to sip her champagne and keep her mouth shut.

"And what are you up to these days, darling?"

"Hmm. What have I been doing?" She knew better than to mention anything about Toyland, ten-year-old toy designs or the fact that she'd recently stumbled over evidence of her father's continued existence. If she wanted to keep the evening on an even keel, those subjects were right out. She'd learned at the age of ten; anything that might remind Mother of Daddy must be avoided at all costs. "Not much," she said finally. "Working hard. You know Christmas."

"Of course." Bitsy smiled wistfully. "I always loved Christmas at the store. The days just fly by when you work that hard."

Kristina came to the conclusion, not for the first time, that she and her mother were cut from different cloth. Mother was a workaholic, and Kristina yearned for something different from a nine-to-five routine, something creative and fun, something like designing toys. Not that she dared tell her mother that.

"We missed you at Thanksgiving, dear," Bitsy went on. "I was hoping you'd join us."

"I was so busy," she murmured. "I had to find a new Santa Claus on a moment's notice, and I . . ."

Taking a long drink of champagne, she let her voice trail off. Actually, she hadn't been able to bear the idea of spending Thanksgiving at the cold Austin mansion, trying to make chitchat with Mirabel and Windy and the rest of the frozen clan. Nonetheless, she finished with the truth. "I was at the store trying to catch up."

"That was so industrious of you, darling," Bitsy said approvingly. "I must remember to tell Windy."

Just what she didn't need. Kristina drained her glass, exchanging it for a full one from the nearest tray. Tuning out her mother's familiar diatribe on work ethics, she let her gaze absently follow the waiter as he swept her glass away through the throng of party-goers. Almost at the doorway into the cavernous entry hall, the waiter stopped and then turned, offering a glass to a newly arriving guest. From the back, the man's broad-shouldered, slim silhouette looked vaguely familiar.

No, she told herself, stifling a sigh as she refocused on her mother. Just wishful thinking. Tucker Bennett wouldn't be caught dead in evening clothes at a snobby, pretentious symphony benefit.

And wasn't that a shame.

ACROSS THE ROOM, Tucker almost caught her gaze, but it skittered away too quickly. Had she seen him? He didn't think so. Nonetheless, he backed off, leaning against a wall behind a potted palm that was taller than he was.

He wasn't quite ready for Kristina to see him yet. He needed a game plan first.

Fancy place, he thought, casting a casual glance around at the ballroom of the Austin family mansion. The floor beneath him was marble, and the ceiling above arched high with elaborate plaster moldings. The inside wall was mirrored—giving it that Versailles look—while the far side was all glass, with doors out to what he supposed must be a terrace.

They didn't make this kind of overblown museum anymore, even for museums. If the Austins really got off on recreating Versailles, maybe somebody ought to tell them what happened to the last folks who lived in that particular palace.

"Off with their heads," he offered cheerfully.

Waiters in tuxedos carried silver trays of champagne and extravagant little hors d'oeuvres around and around in a never-ending circle that he could've intercepted, if he'd wanted to. He didn't. He hated the stuff. Luckily, he'd thought to drive through McDonald's on the way there.

Calculating his next move, he ventured another glance at Kristina, who was tossing back champagne like there was no tomorrow as she chatted politely with a small, cool blonde. Her boss, he figured. But not a friend. Not if Kristina's attitude was any indication.

At least she wasn't with a guy. Nick—that character right out of a Charles Dickens story—had assured him that Kristina wasn't bringing a date to this evening's soiree, but there was always the chance she'd meet someone once she got there.

But not tonight. Except for the chilly little blond woman, Kristina was all alone. He smiled to himself, thinking how very nice it was to see her again.

The first time, she'd looked pretty, but a tad stuffy in her buttoned-up blouse and severely cut suit.

But this time, she was simply dazzling. Her long, deepest brown hair was straight and sleek, all pushed to one side to spill negligently over her shoulder. She looked good in black, he decided; it gave her a hint of drama.

And she looked *very* sexy in that long black suit—all tall and slim and feisty.

Her expression was, however, neither dramatic nor feisty. Instead, her face was eloquently blank, as if she were bored to tears or depressed beyond belief, but doing her best not to show it.

"Well, if she's bored, I can fix that," he said with an easy grin. "Tucker Bennett to the rescue."

He ambled out from behind his potted palm and started over in her direction.

It was time to make contact.

Chapter Six

As her mother continued on in the same vein—something about gratitude and trying extra hard for Windy's sake—Kristina delicately downed the last drops of her third glass of champagne.

Looking down at her empty glass, she decided she had found something good to say for the Austins; they served remarkably fine champagne. And she had developed a sizable thirst. As a result, this dull and depressing evening was beginning to look downright rosy around the edges.

She caught the shine of a silver tray in the periphery of her vision, and she cleared her throat. "Waiter!" she called out. As she held out her glass, hoping to see it quickly replaced by a full one, she noticed the way the light from the chandelier in the center of the ballroom shot color through the fluted crystal. "Hmm," she said, "isn't that pretty?"

"Beautiful," returned a deep, resonant voice almost at her elbow.

Once again, that voice undressed her, caressed her.

"Tucker," she whispered. It couldn't be true. But when she twisted around ever so slightly, there he was. Maybe her fairy godmother had waved a wand, and poof, Tucker appeared. "You really are here?"

"At your service," he said softly.

Neatly, before she'd even noticed, he removed the empty glass still dangling from her fingertips. Leaving her for a moment, he set it on a waiter's tray, and then sent the young man away.

She tried not to notice how *fine* he looked, with the black-and-white elegance of his evening clothes emphasizing his broad shoulders and long, lean torso, and the wings of his starched white shirt edging his cleanly shaved jaw. Swallowing, she could only hope the hunger she was feeling didn't show on her face.

But he looked wonderful, he really did, from the top of his tawny head to the tips of his shoes. Shoes. Her scrutiny stopped there.

The man was wearing black canvas high-tops with formal evening wear. Her eyes met his in disbelief.

"Well, they are black," he offered.

He presented her with a bright, breezy, incandescent smile, and she felt the corners of her own mouth curve up in response. Her world was a bit hazy at this point, but Tucker Bennett's high-voltage grin was coming through loud and clear.

"Oh, uh…champagne," she said suddenly, needing an escape. "I was planning on another glass. Can you get the waiter back?"

"Are you driving tonight?"

"Of course." Seeing Tucker, she felt like she was positively brimming over with saucy repartee. "Do you think I plan on walking from the wilds of Lake Forest all the way back to Winnetka?" she inquired, in her best version of a silky purr.

"If you're driving, maybe you'd better lay off."

That wasn't the effect she was searching for. "What do you mean—?" she began, taking a step toward him, but her mother cut in.

"Sensible young man," Bitsy offered, catching Kristina's elbow and pulling her back next to her. She hissed, "Drinking so much in public? Good Lord, Kristina, what's wrong with you? And who is he?"

"We haven't met," he said smoothly, stepping right up and into their conversation. "I'm Tucker Bennett."

"Bitsy Austin," she replied cautiously. She added, in a significant tone, "Kristina's mother."

"Oh, really?" His eyes lit on the tall brunette and small blonde in turn.

Kristina put a hand up. "Before you say it—we know we don't look alike."

"I wasn't going to say that."

She sighed. "Of course you were. Everybody does."

"Well, you do look too young to be anybody's mother," he said, giving Bitsy a charming grin.

Bitsy began to warm up. "What a lovely young man. And how do you know Kristina, Mr. Bennett? I'm usually acquainted with Kristina's escorts."

"That's because you usually arrange them," Kristina said under her breath. Her mother's expression didn't change, so she didn't think Bitsy had caught the ill-advised words, but the naughty smile playing about Tucker's narrow lips told her he definitely had.

She tried to contain her answering smile. "Mother, he's not my escort," she said solemnly, trying very hard to feel sober. "We hardly know each other."

"Well, you must have met him somewhere," Bitsy returned. "I simply asked where he knew you from. It's a reasonable question. Don't you think so, Mr. Bennett?"

"Of course. My mother would probably ask the same thing. As a matter of fact, I met Kristina when she came out to my company."

"Your company?" Bitsy asked. "What company would that be?"

Alarms flashed in her brain. *Whatever you do, don't say the word* Toyland. Before he could open his mouth, she jumped in.

"Tucker is the president of a company out in St. Charles. I was out there on business—for Austin's—and I happened to run into him."

"President, did you say? Well, isn't that nice?"

Even half-sloshed, Kristina could read her mother's thoughts like a book: *He's gorgeous, must be rich to shell out the big bucks for this benefit and owns a company.* Looks, money, power—what else could a girl ask for?

But once Bitsy knew what that company was, she wouldn't be so accepting.

"My father retired earlier this year, and I've taken over," Tucker added.

"How very enterprising," Bitsy cooed. "But I must say I'm surprised to see you pop up this evening."

"So am I," Kristina murmured, so that only he could hear.

His lips curved into a secret, intimate sort of smile, as Bitsy continued. "Kristina hasn't said anything about dating someone new. Darling, were you keeping Mr. Bennett a secret?"

"A secret?" she asked, immediately feeling guilty for all the secrets she *was* keeping. "Mother, I told you before—Tucker and I hardly know each other. Besides, I don't have time to date anyone."

Bitsy's eyes narrowed. "Time can be made, Kristina."

"I agree with your mother."

"Isn't he just a sweetheart?" Bitsy linked her arm through his. "Now tell me more about this company of yours."

"To—" he began, as Kristina took his other arm and yanked him around behind her.

"I really need to talk to you," she insisted through her clenched teeth.

"No problem," he murmured, adjusting himself to move in even closer.

When his hot breath ruffled her hair and his long arm casually pulled her up against him, she gasped. She forced a smile for her mother's benefit.

Bitsy's severely arched eyebrow spoke volumes as she gazed meaningfully at the relative positions of her daughter and this young man. Not even a quarter inch separated their bodies, and nobody was making a move to change things.

"Excuse us?" Kristina asked breathlessly. "It's important."

Bitsy murmured, "I'll just bet it is."

Tucker held onto her firmly as Kristina managed to pull them both out of her mother's vicinity.

"I didn't know you wanted to be alone with me so desperately," he whispered in her ear. "I'm not complaining, just surprised."

She took a deep breath and forced herself to think rationally. "Why did I drink so much champagne?" she lamented.

"I don't know," he answered reasonably. "Maybe you were having a rotten time and you wanted to get smashed."

"I don't do that kind of thing."

"You did tonight."

She shook her head, trying to clear the cobwebs. "I haven't been myself lately."

"So who are you?"

"Somebody else," she moaned. "Some total basket case."

She realized she'd spoken a little too loudly when the party-goers around them began to stare.

Taking his arm again, she marched him over to the far end of the ballroom, where the potted palms took over and the crowds thinned.

"I still can't believe you showed up," she said dazedly. "What are you doing here, anyway?"

"Talking to you. What does it look like I'm doing?"

"You're impossible," she muttered, dropping his arm. She shook her head, wishing she didn't feel so muddled. Damn the champagne, or Tucker's overwhelming presence, or whatever it was that had filled her head with fat, puffy clouds.

But there was no help for it. Determined to pull herself together, she risked looking full into his eyes. "You didn't crash this party, did you? I mean, people are not going to be dragging you away and throwing you out, right?"

His face was all innocence. "What do you take me for? I'm the president of a company—I get invited to these things all the time."

"You mean you paid to get in?" He nodded. "But, Tucker!" Raising a hand to her flushed cheek, she tried to lower her voice. "This thing cost a *thousand* dollars."

He shrugged. "I decided to kick in my fair share for the symphony. It's a good cause."

"You could've written a check—you know, a hundred bucks. Maybe two hundred if you really wanted to be generous."

"Okay, okay, I admit it." He leaned in closer, fanning her ear with his warm breath when he spoke. "I wanted to see you again."

"See me?" she whispered. "For a thousand dollars? You've got to be kidding."

He just looked at her for a long moment. Finally he asked, "Would you like to take a walk outside?"

"Outside?"

He nodded. "These doors open on the garden, don't they?"

"Well, there's a terrace, and then formal gardens." She regarded him with horror. "But, Tucker, it can't be more than thirty or forty degrees out. You can't seriously want to..."

"Do you have a coat?"

"You're crazy!"

"I've been told that." Clasping her hand, he tugged her along behind him, out the door and into the cold. Gazing into the sky, he stopped abruptly, and she bumped into him from behind. "Look, it's beautiful," he whispered in that gorgeous voice of his. His thumb caressed her palm. "A hunter's moon."

She felt a chill creep up her spine, but her shivers were not from the temperature. As a matter of fact, it wasn't all that cold. It was an odd night, slightly hazy but with no wind to speak of. There was only the moon and a few stars.

And Tucker.

"I'm afraid you're mistaken," she returned primly, yanking her hand back. "A hunter's moon is a full moon. This one is only a crescent." *You're babbling again,* she told herself, but she couldn't seem to stop. "And a hunter's moon is in October or something. There's no way you'd see a hunter's moon in December."

"Good grief. I'm out here on this spectacular night, with the most literal woman on the face of the earth." He sighed. "So why do you know so much about moons?"

"Astronomy class."

"I should've known. I keep telling myself, don't go after smart women, they're a pain in the a—"

"You're going after me?" Her hand on his sleeve, she forced him to turn and face her. One high heel wobbled slightly, so she had to concentrate on standing very still. *Damn that champagne.* "What do you mean, going after me?"

"Is it that hard to understand?"

"But you just met me, only a week ago. Why on earth would someone like you decide to—"

"I like you."

She shook her head. "You don't even know me."

"I saw you at Toyland. You feel the same way I do about it." His voice dropped into its softest, most persuasive register, as he lifted a finger to trace the curve of her cheek. "Why shouldn't I pursue a beautiful woman when I see one?"

She tilted away from his hand. "I'm hardly beautiful."

"Who told you that?"

"Tucker," she warned, "this isn't going to work. I don't know why you're being so nice to me, but I know what kind of impression I made at Toyland. And all that stuff about my father..." Angling away, she gazed out at what was definitely not a hunter's moon. "I'm sorry I behaved like a fool, running out of there like that."

He shuffled impatiently. "You didn't behave like a fool. You acted like a normal person who heard surprising news."

"Look, this is all very kind, but I don't want to talk about it, okay?" This was much too private a topic to be discussing with the likes of Tucker Bennett. Briskly she edged around him and took the first step off the terrace, down the wide stone staircase and into the formal gardens. "Since we're already out here freezing, you might as well see the grounds. They're a lot nicer in the spring and summer, of course, but there's still a medge haze—"

"A medge haze?"

"A maze. The hedges make a maze," she said slowly, carefully, cursing herself for sounding like some dippy, tipsy schoolgirl.

"The medge haze it is," he declared. After a glance at her expression, he said lightly, "You don't have to be perfect all the time, you know. Imperfection is endearing. I mean, look at my hair."

"I don't want to look at your hair." But she did. She also wanted to run her hands through it.

He strolled after her, much more mobile in sneakers than she was in high heels on the frozen ground. Trying to set a lively pace, she almost slipped several times, before he took her arm firmly and pulled her in close to guide her along.

"Damn that champagne," she muttered. If only his long, hard body didn't feel so warm and so right, pressed up against her this way.

"I don't mind giving you a hand." As they entered the maze, the lights from the terrace dimmed, and he tightened his hold against the cold and the darkness. "In fact, I kind of like it."

"Me, too," she whispered, hoping he didn't hear.

They negotiated their first bend in the maze with his arm still firmly encircling her, and, the funny thing was that she didn't feel cold at all.

"Kristina," he ventured, "now that we're in the maze..."

"Yes?"

"You do know how to get out, don't you?"

"Sort of."

"Young lovers found frozen in winter maze...."

She cleared her throat. "We're hardly lovers."

"That can be remedied."

"Well," she said breathlessly, breaking away and spinning to face him, "we're not all that young, either."

"Young enough."

"How young?"

"Me?" He considered. "Thirty-four."

"You don't act thirty-four."

"I know. But my twenty-two-year-old brother does. So I can act twenty-two in his place. Except when I'm being president of Toyland, of course, when I have to act about fifty-five."

A small giggle escaped her. "I see." It escalated into a full-blown laugh, and she covered her mouth with one hand. "Tucker, you're so...odd."

He brightened. "Thank you."

So he thought being called odd was a compliment. She couldn't recall ever knowing anyone like Tucker Bennett before. Slowing her steps, she watched him for several seconds. "You really came here tonight just to see me?"

"I told you I did."

A wall of hedge greeted them, and they were going to have to choose a direction. Kristina hesitated. "But how did you know where I was? To find me, I mean."

"Oh. Nick told me."

"Nick?" She hadn't expected that. "You know Nick?"

"Well, now I do." Reaching out to disentangle a strand of her hair that had caught on a brier, he wound the end around his finger. "He told me he was Santa Claus."

"He shouldn't have told you anything," she avowed softly. She couldn't look away from the hot light in his eyes.

"If he's Santa Claus, does that make you my Christmas present?"

"I—I don't think so." Regretfully, she tried to smooth her hair back into place, but a current of electricity remained as the strand slid slowly across his fingers. Her gaze fixed on the image of her own dark hair against his pale, moonlit skin.

Swallowing, she murmured, "I can't believe Nick did this." Purposely taking a step away from Tucker, so that her hair had no connection to anyone but her, she picked up her volume to change the mood. "For some reason, Nick can't leave well enough alone when it comes to my life." Suddenly suspicious, she inquired, "He didn't happen to mention anything else, did he?"

There was a pause before he said, "He told me that you have a wonderful toy idea that I'd be crazy not to pursue."

"I knew there was more." She jammed her hands in her jacket pockets. "That darn Nick...."

His eyes continued to hold her. "So far, you haven't said a word about an idea. Why not?"

The answer leaped into her brain before she could squash it. *Because I couldn't bear for you, of all people, to think Santa's Magic Workshop is stupid.*

Instead, she said, "It's not that good an idea."

He lifted his shoulders in an expressive shrug. "Sometimes the craziest ideas are the best ones. Where do you think the Slinky and Silly Putty came from?"

"Bad ideas?"

"Wild ones, anyway. And then there's Cabbage Patch Kids and Teenage Mutant Ninja Turtles. Come on," he coaxed, "you can at least try me."

"But my father—"

"Your father sent in a truckload of bad ideas, okay? Do you think he's the only one? And even if he were, so what?"

He swore quietly and glared at a spot on the ground. Then, shifting back to her, he braced her shoulders in his hands. She tried to concentrate on the moon over his head, to forget the firm pressure of his hands and the fire in his eyes, but it wasn't easy. Not when he was staring at her as if she were the only person on earth who mattered at all.

"If you ever wanted to know if your idea was any good," he said softly, urgently, "now's your chance. Don't you want to know, one way or the other?"

"Yes." She backed off, away from his hands. "Yes, I do."

"Then tell me."

She managed to say, "Santa's Magic Workshop." Under her lashes, she glanced up. He hadn't said it was stupid yet.

"That's a start. Go on."

She raised her hands in defeat. "It's just a workshop."

He nodded. "Right. Santa's Magic Workshop. You said that. But what is it?"

"It's not that easy to describe."

"But you came to my office, all ready to sell me on it. Right?"

"Well, yes."

"So you must have had some idea of what you wanted to say."

"Not really." She cast her mind back to that night. "I think I was going to start with the contest. The Super-search Contest."

"The one that we ran at Toyland? Okay, so you entered this Magic Workshop idea of yours in our contest?"

"Yes, that's right. In 1980."

"But you didn't win? Look, Kristina, don't let that bother you. I mean, you were only a kid, right?"

"I was eighteen. But that's the thing." She paused. "I did win—sort of. At least, I was a finalist. You signed the finalist letters, and that's why I came to see you."

"Ten years late? You waited ten years to come see me?"

"Actually, it's eleven." She noted the sardonic curve of his lips, and remembered him calling her the most literal woman in the world. "But who's counting? Anyway, I *was* a finalist, but I didn't get the letter. It got lost in the mail or something. When it was found, after all these years, Nick was hired to deliver it. And he got this idea in his head that I should resurrect Santa's Magic Workshop, and contact you. I don't know why exactly, but Nick is a pretty determined guy once he gets going."

"Wait a minute. Are you trying to tell me that Nick came to deliver a letter and never left?"

"Well, yes, as a matter of fact." She dug her heel into the hard dirt and almost fell over, but Tucker reached out to steady her.

"Don't you think that's kind of weird?"

"I needed a Santa Claus," she said logically. "I convinced him to stay. He agreed to be my Santa, if I would come and see you and tell you about the Magic Workshop."

He ran a hand through his tousled hair. "It's got to be one of the strangest reasons anybody ever came to me with a toy idea, but I'm game if you are. What *is* Santa's Magic Workshop?"

"It's, uh . . ." Fear was blocking her brain and making her inarticulate. "It's just a workshop."

"A miniature workshop, right?" he asked impatiently.

"Yes. Santa's workshop, you know."

"Anything like a dollhouse?"

"Well, smaller than the dollhouse you have at Toyland."

"How much smaller?"

"Not even half as big—only one floor."

"Okay," he said encouragingly. "What's inside it?"

"Oh, the best stuff." Suddenly, the mental image of her workshop overtook her fears. "The roof lifts off so you can play with all the things—a workbench, a fireplace with tiny little logs, a comfy chair for Santa to sit, a couple of elves, oh, and a bunch of toys that you can put together and paint—like a sled and a bicycle—and everything fits inside the house."

"It sounds nice." His eyes were warm on hers. "Very nice."

"Do you mean it? You really like the idea?"

"Of course I mean it. Now don't get carried away," he warned. "I like the idea, but that doesn't mean we can produce it tomorrow."

"No, I understand. That's fine. Really." But she could hardly contain her excitement.

"What we need to do next is schedule a meeting before the board at Toyland. We'll get preliminary approval, enough to get started with the workshop." She could see the gears turning. "And then ask for a final okay once we have something to show them—you know, like a model of the workshop."

"Okay, sure."

"Okay, then." He smiled and the darkness in the maze brightened considerably. "And Kristina?"

"Yes?"

"I have a very good feeling about this."

She nodded slightly. "Me, too."

Glancing around at their position in the maze, he raised a hand. "Which way to get out of here?"

Well, that was the problem. "I don't exactly know. Maybe the best idea would be to go back out the way we came in." She added, "If we can remember."

"No problem." He grinned. "I left a trail."

"A trail?"

His grin widened as he pulled a tiny green pellet out of his pocket. "A trail of Tic Tacs."

She laughed out loud, but she couldn't argue. It was a cinch following the trail of green pellets out of the maze, and a race up the terrace to the ballroom.

Inside the doors, Tucker suddenly stopped. "Look," he said mysteriously, pointing behind him, to a garland tied above the frame of the French doors. "It's mistletoe."

Her gaze followed to the supposed mistletoe, and she shook her head. "That's not mistletoe. It's just holly or something."

"Kristina?" Once again, his voice wound around her, enchanting her. "Tonight it's mistletoe."

And then he bent down, bringing his mouth softly against hers. It was a chaste, warm, sweet kiss, nothing too pushy or overbearing. But the pressure of his lips was steady and strong, and she sighed with pure pleasure, tightening her arms around his neck and kissing him back without even thinking.

"Uh-hem." The loud, throat-clearing noise came from behind Tucker. Kristina pulled herself far enough away to look around him. And right into her mother's disapproving frown.

"What can you be thinking of?" Bitsy mouthed at her daughter.

Kristina tried to signal Tucker, to head him off before he said anything damaging, but it was too late.

Clearly interpreting her odd gestures as a desire to end the kiss, he straightened, but still held her hand in his. He brushed a kiss against her fingers. "What's wrong?" he asked, gazing down at her panicked features. "Are you worrying about the Magic Workshop again?"

She considered kissing him again to stop the flow of words, but it was too late.

"What is there to worry about now that you've told me? I'll call a board meeting at Toyland as soon as I can manage it."

"Toyland? What is he talking about?"

As Bitsy stepped forward, snapping with hostility, Kristina began to feel dizzy.

"You had some crazy idea about winning their contest when you were in high school, didn't you?"

"Yes, Mother, I did, but—"

Beside her, Tucker draped his arm around her as a symbol of support. It was a nice gesture, but on the whole, she would've preferred that they both slip away right now, before the shouting started.

"I hope this doesn't have anything to do with that, Kristina. I told you then that there was no point in pinning your hopes on something as foolish as that contest, and I thought you'd learned your lesson."

"Mother, I—"

As Bitsy lost her temper, her sophisticated veneer slipped away, revealing plain old Betty Castleberry. "Your father was always sending things off to that place. He was so sure every single one of his asinine ideas was going to be the one that would bring in millions." Her mouth twisted with bitterness. "Couldn't get a real job. No, he had to play with toys."

Kristina said nothing. Misery didn't require words.

Bitsy pressed her lips together in a rigid line. "You can't have anything to do with Toyland, Kristina. I forbid it."

"I don't think that's your decision, Mrs. Austin," Tucker said quietly.

"Tucker, please—"

"It certainly isn't your decision, Mr. Bennett. Toyland?" Bitsy sniffed. "What kind of a place is that for a grown man to work?"

"My father ran Toyland, and his father before him." He stood firm. "There's nothing wrong with Toyland. I can understand if you have some problem with the toy business. I mean, I don't know your ex-husband, but—"

"How dare you?" Bitsy gasped. "I will not discuss my personal affairs with you. Please take your hand off my daughter, and leave here immediately."

"I'll be happy to leave." His eyes were a dark, troubled blue when his gaze swept down to meet Kristina's. "I'd like to drive you home, though. Is that all right with you?"

"No, it is not all right," Bitsy said angrily.

Regretfully, Kristina agreed with her mother. "There's no need to drive me. I have my car here."

"We'll take your car, and I can come back later for mine." Tucker's smile coaxed her. "All that champagne..."

The effects of the champagne had long since vanished, and they both knew it. But still Kristina hesitated.

Should she do what Tucker wanted, and agree to leave? Or should she do what her mother wanted, and tell Tucker to take a hike?

She knew what Kristina, the good girl, should do.

But she also knew, deep in her soul, what *she* wanted. She wanted to go with Tucker. At this moment, he represented more than just an attractive man. He was acceptance and approval and the possibility that dreams could come true.

"All right," she said. "Let's go, Tucker." She held her breath. "Good night, Mother."

"Kristina!" Bitsy choked out, but her daughter didn't listen.

Chapter Seven

"I'm sorry." His words hung softly in the silent car. "I would have avoided mentioning Toyland if I'd known."

"It's not your fault."

"I know." Nonetheless, he wished her expression wasn't quite so grim. All he'd wanted to do was help, not make things worse. "If it's anybody's fault, it's your mother's," he pointed out. "She's obviously being unreasonable, so I suppose this argument, or whatever you want to call it, had to happen sooner or later."

"Not if the Magic Workshop goes nowhere," she replied quietly. "She never would've known."

He couldn't believe what he was hearing. "And keeping it a secret, letting her think she gets to decide what you do and don't do—that would've been better? You've got to be kidding."

"Do I look like I'm kidding?"

"So you want her to keep thinking she can push you around for the rest of your life?" He was so annoyed he almost forgot to watch the road. "Don't you think it's better for her to know how you really feel, to get it out in the open once and for all? No matter what happens to Santa's Workshop, you're still going to want to design toys, right? I mean, you can't give up on something you've wanted ever since you were a kid, just because your mother doesn't approve."

"You make it sound like I have this big secret career I'm hiding, but there's only one dumb idea." She gave him a very direct glance. "Which will most likely amount to absolutely nothing. Right?"

Reaching over to squeeze her hand, he cajoled, "Come on, kiddo. Where's your confidence? I told you I liked the idea. What more of a recommendation do you need?"

She smiled wanly. "You're just being nice and we both know it."

"I'm crushed," he claimed. "Not trusting yourself is one thing, but not trusting me is quite another."

"I trust you," she murmured.

"Then what's the problem?"

"My mother," she said slowly, "is furious with me. And Mom is married to Windy Austin, my boss. So not only have I alienated the woman who raised me, sweated, saved and agonized over me, but I've also probably screwed up my job. And all over something as unreliable as Santa's Magic Workshop."

"Your mother will feel differently once she's had a chance to think about it." Speaking from his own frame of reference, with more understanding parents, he offered reassuring words. "She loves you. I'm sure she'll realize that this is the best thing—"

Kristina broke in with considerable heat. "Tucker, you don't know my mother! She hates my father with such venom *I* can't even believe it after all these years. She will never forgive me if I try to be a toy designer. It's like betraying her for him."

"Maybe it's time she got over it."

"She's not going to get over it."

Once more, he squeezed her hand. "Be glad that you're finally doing what you've wanted to do for so long. You've gotta go for it. Life's too short to leave loose ends."

"Okay, okay, you can stop the Pollyanna routine. You know, Tucker, with all this stuff about life being too short and going for your dreams, you're starting to sound like Nick."

"Well, that's good, isn't it?"

"I wouldn't say it's *good* exactly. Different, maybe."

"Santa Claus-meets-English-butler—it's not a type you run across every day," he remarked, happy to get them onto a more cheerful subject. "Especially one who can get himself a cozy place to stay just by delivering a letter. I wish I had his powers of persuasion." He grinned suddenly. "If I bring in your mail, can I stay over?"

"I told you," she said, with a touch of defensiveness. "I invited him to stay with me because I desperately needed a Santa Claus. He didn't have anywhere else to go."

"What a scam. I've got to meet this guy," he commented as he pulled the small Toyota into her driveway. "Why don't I come in and meet him right now?"

Her hand hesitated on the door handle. "It's late. I doubt he'll still be up."

"We can see, can't we?" Actually, he didn't care if Nick had been asleep for hours. The truth of the matter was that he wasn't ready to say goodbye to Kristina yet.

"I don't think so," she objected. "Maybe some other time."

"You have to let me in long enough to call a cab." He put on his most persuasive face as he leaned completely over her to unlatch her door. "This is your car, remember? Mine's still at that museum of the Austins'."

"Oh, right." Tucker followed close behind as she led the way up the walk to the house. He noted immediately that a light had been left on in the window of the small, neatly kept house. It made the place seem cozy and warm. Somehow the house wasn't what he'd expected.

"Nice place," he said softly.

"Thank you."

She switched on two more lamps the moment she got inside the door. Apparently she felt safer if the place was flooded with light.

"But no mistletoe," he said, trying for an easy, mocking tone. It came out a little huskier than he'd planned.

It sounded much too intimate, too hungry, that way. He told himself it was the nature of the place, or perhaps the lateness of the hour, making him feel so vulnerable.

He took a step closer to Kristina without even meaning to, wishing the few inches between them didn't feel so far *or* so near. As his eyes held her, he saw her swallow slowly, and then she, too, moved a little closer, as if invisible strings pulled her toward him.

One more inch, and he'd be out of control. Already, he was swamped with feelings. When his glance fell on her hair, it made him want to stroke the long, glossy strands between his fingers. When he looked into her eyes, he read a touch of apprehension, a hint of fear. *If only I could hold her and tell her everything will be okay.* But once he got started, that wouldn't be nearly enough.

So he looked away.

But then he caught the scent of her perfume, a sweet, delicate fragrance that was barely there at all. He could only imagine the source of that fragrance—beneath one ear, perhaps, where a soft, dark tendril curled, or along the curve of her breast, where the black silk of her jacket gapped to reveal soft, pale skin.

Oh, God. Imagining was worse than looking, and his gaze flickered back to her.

She reached out her hand to him, ever so slightly, and he felt his own fingers unbend and begin to stretch toward her. Her voice was breathless when she murmured, "Don't mention mistletoe too loud, or Nick will be stringing some up tomorrow."

"Good for Nick."

"Did I hear my name?"

The cheerful words came from behind them, and the mood vanished abruptly. Kristina jumped back, and regretfully, Tucker did the same, turning toward the new voice. Its owner was a tall, genial-looking man wearing pajamas and a flannel bathrobe, with his white hair rumpled and standing on end. The man, who could only be Nick, extended a hand holding a mug of something.

"Tucker Bennett, I presume?" he asked, with a mischievous twinkle in his mild blue eyes.

"Nick," Tucker responded, in a less-than-enthusiastic tone. "We didn't think you'd still be up."

He stuck out his own hand to shake, and then waited as Nick realized his was full, shuffled the coffee mug from left to right and then finally fobbed it off on Kristina.

As his hand was heartily pumped, Tucker offered, "Nice to meet you, Nick."

"Did you children enjoy yourselves this evening?" Nick prompted eagerly.

"Well . . ." they said in tandem.

"Sort of," Kristina finished. "First the good news. He likes the workshop idea, Nick."

"Wonderful, wonderful," Nick returned, beaming.

"But then there's bad news. My mother overheard, and she's extremely upset."

"But why?"

"That's the million-dollar question," Tucker put in.

Kristina tucked her hair behind one ear and put on a studiously indifferent face. She said quickly, "It's a long story. Let's just say it's all tied up with my father and the toy business, and leftover baggage from the past."

Nick clucked his tongue. "Don't fret, my dear. I'm sure your mother will come around to your way of thinking once she's got used to the idea. It's immensely better that it's all out in the open now, don't you think?"

"I think you guys are related." She shook her head, but she was smiling. "Are you members of the same team?"

Tucker and Nick exchanged bemused glances. "No," they chorused. Tucker added, "We can't help it if we're both right."

"Dandy," she grumbled.

"Kristina," Nick cut in. "When are you going to get your Christmas tree? I cleared the space there by the stairs."

"That's not all you did, is it?" she asked as she moved to the place he'd indicated. She pointed at the evergreen branches and big red bows wrapped around the banister. "When did you do this?"

"This evening," Nick said brightly. "I thought we needed a bit of Christmas cheer."

Tucker was confused. "What's this about a tree?"

"Nick's just dying for me to get one, but so far I've resisted," she explained. "So I guess this is a hint, hmm?"

"Perhaps," the older man admitted. "I hate to push, but..."

"You? Hate to push?" Kristina raised an eyebrow. "So it wasn't you who sent Tucker to the Austins' party, then, was it?"

"Oh, no. He did that all on his own. I simply happened to mention that you might be there."

"I see." She shook her head at him. "What am I going to do with you?"

"You could get a Christmas tree," he offered.

"Nick—" she started to say.

"What have you got against Christmas trees?" Tucker interrupted, putting himself back into the conversation.

Kristina said stiffly, "I don't like them. But it's really none of your business. Or yours, either," she directed at Nick.

"My dear child, I think you're overtired. Why don't you go up to bed now? Don't worry," Nick added, "I'll stay and talk to Mr. Bennett."

"Oh, no, that wouldn't be right," Kristina said automatically.

Silently, Tucker seconded her words, willing Nick to go to bed himself, and leave them alone again. It had been much nicer before he interrupted.

"Kristina," Nick went on, in a more severe tone, "you have to work early in the morning, don't you?"

"But tomorrow's Saturday," Tucker said helpfully.

"I, uh, work on Saturday." She shrugged self-consciously. "The store's so busy, I could work eight days a week and still not catch up."

"Now, now, young lady—off to bed," Nick instructed.

"I really am exhausted." She paused, chewing her lip, drawing Tucker's eyes, reminding him of the kiss they'd shared, the kiss that her mother had effectively put to a stop. "I hope you don't mind waiting for your cab by yourself."

"Oh, but I do," he murmured.

"But you're not alone. I'm here," Nick reminded them.

Tucker gave the man a black look, and apparently the message got across. Murmuring something about a mess in the kitchen, Nick made himself scarce, leaving them at least partially alone.

"Good night," Kristina said softly, edging closer to the stairs.

Watching her tactical retreat, Tucker shook his head. "You know, I don't know if you're crazy or I am."

Gently he caught her hand where it lay on the banister, and he entwined her fingers with his own. Under his touch, she trembled slightly, and he was inordinately pleased. She was as vulnerable as he was, and he'd needed to know that.

"You already have one strange man staying in your house," he said lightly, carefully, "and now you're leaving another one down here. We could get into all kinds of trouble."

She smiled suddenly, releasing a soft laugh. "Don't be silly, Tucker. You're not going to do anything."

"How do you know?"

"I trust you," she said simply. And then she slipped her hand out from under his and sped upstairs. "Good night," she offered again, peeking her head around the corner before disappearing completely.

"She trusts me," he muttered in disgust. "Whoever said I wanted to be trusted?"

But there was no answer. Kristina had gone to bed.

And Kristina in connection with beds was not something he needed to be thinking about. With frustration uppermost in his mind—and his body—he decided he'd better look for the phone. The night wasn't getting any younger, and he still had to retrieve his car and get himself home to a warm bed.

Of course, the warmest bed was right here....

He grinned and shook his head as he realized Kristina was right; he *was* trustworthy.

Damn it, anyway. What a time to find that out.

"Well, then," Nick said jovially, strolling in from the kitchen with a deck of cards. "How about a hand of gin rummy while we await your taxi?"

"Gin rummy?" he echoed woefully. It wasn't quite what he'd had in mind.

"TUCKER?" Kristina poked her head around the door into the playroom. "Are you here?"

No answer.

Sliding into the big, crowded room, with toys and games overflowing from every possible surface, she experienced again the mixed feelings of awe and belonging this place generated. She caught the tail of a kite and swung it back and forth, smiling to herself like a giddy fool.

Lord, but she loved this room, and every bit of its chaos.

"Tucker?" she called out again, just in case he was puttering underneath the worktable or inside a cabinet and hadn't heard her the first time. Still, only silence greeted her.

"Kristina?"

She jumped and spun back toward the door, batting away the kite tail. "Oh. Trey. Hi. You scared me."

He grinned, looking very young and very glad to see to her. "What are you doing here?"

"I, uh, was looking for Tucker. I thought by now he'd be done for the day, and that he might help me put together my proposal for the board."

"I could have helped you," Trey said peevishly. "Why did you ask Tucker instead of me?"

Good grief. What could she say without sounding like she was passing him up in favor of his older brother? She *was* passing him up in favor of his older brother.

"Trey," she ventured, "I don't want this to seem like a competition between you and Tucker for my, uh, friendship. I'd like to be friends with both of you. But as far as anything else, which is what I think you may be hinting at, like the two of us..." She peered into Trey's face. Was she misinterpreting his motives? He'd certainly seemed like he was flashing "interest" signals her way. " ... the two of us dating or something? I mean, I like you, Trey, but..." There was simply no polite way to put it. "You're so much younger than I am."

"Are you trying to tell me something *is* going on between you and Tucker?"

"No, of course not," she hastened to assure him. "Although I don't know exactly what might happen." Good Lord, this was awkward, trying to sort out subjects she didn't even trust herself with.

He clenched his jaw. "I see. Well. Far be it from me to interfere." His hands in the pockets of his expensive suit, Trey retreated out the playroom door. At the last moment, he announced, "By the way, Tucker is in a meeting. Another crisis. You may be waiting a long time." And then he ducked through the door without looking back for her reaction.

Well, that had been unpleasant, hadn't it? Instead of her usual path of least resistance—letting things slide until they resolved themselves—she'd done things Tucker's way. She'd come right out and told Trey the plain, unvarnished truth. So why did she feel like such a jerk?

From what Trey had said about a meeting and a crisis, it didn't sound like Tucker would be arriving anytime soon. But now that she'd driven all the way out to St.

Charles, she wasn't leaving without a chance to see him. Determined to wait him out, however long it took, Kristina hung up her coat, stuck her briefcase near the door and climbed up on one of the stools at the worktable.

"Hi," Tucker said cheerfully, ambling into the room.

She glanced up in surprise. "Tucker."

Oh, it was definitely him, all right, with his white dress shirt rumpled and his tie half-undone.

"You were expecting the Ghost of Christmas Past, maybe?"

"Hardly," she said with a laugh. "I'm not that big a Scrooge. Besides, I don't think he knows a thing about toys."

"So you're only romancing me for my brain?" His grin widened. "I can handle that."

"I'm not romancing you for anything," she returned quickly. "I came by after work to see if you could help me with my proposal, you know, tell me what should go in it to make the best impression. I—I don't know how long it will take. I guess I should have scheduled an appointment."

"No, that's okay." He rolled up his sleeves and tossed himself onto a stool opposite hers. "Where do you want to start?"

She was definitely surprised by his easygoing manner. "Are you sure you have time for this?" she asked doubtfully. "Trey made it sound like you were kind of busy."

"Oh, it was just another dumb meeting. Some foreign company has been selling counterfeit Zappers and Spinners, and my sister Tegan got all fried about it."

"Well, I can come back another time, if you need to get back to your meeting."

He smiled. "Are you nervous about something?"

"No, of course not. Whatever gave you that idea?"

"You keep fooling around with your collar, and sticking your hands in and out of your pockets," he noted. "You seem kind of fidgety. But it's no wonder, dressed like that."

She gazed down at her suit, a long, straight navy number, worn with a lace-edged white blouse, buttoned to the top and accented with a pretty pearl collar bar. Her standard work attire was complemented by sensible two-inch navy pumps. "It's what I wore to work," she said warily. "What's wrong with it?"

"You'll suffocate, all buttoned up like that."

Frowning, he came around behind her, while she tried to spin around to see what he was doing. She didn't trust him as far as she could throw him—which was about an inch and a half.

"I can take off my jacket," she began as a concession, but Tucker was already lifting it up at the shoulders and sliding her arms out.

Carelessly, he tossed it at a coat tree on the other side of the room, successfully catching the lowest hook possible. Apparently satisfied with his throw, he shocked her completely when he leaned over and around her to fiddle with the pin at her collar.

"How can you breathe?" he muttered.

With his long, nimble fingers brushing her neck and his face so close to hers, she couldn't breathe. Except for maybe panting a little.

"Ahem," a female voice said near the door. "Excuse me."

This could only be Tucker's sister, since the young woman clearly bore the stamp of the Bennett features and coloring. Light brown hair hung in a pageboy about chin length, emphasizing large, soft blue eyes, and a rather perplexed expression. At the moment, she was turning about fifteen shades of pink.

"Oh, hi, Teeg," Tucker offered nonchalantly. "Have you met Kristina?"

"No," they both murmured, and he provided quick introductions.

"Nice to meet you," Kristina offered. Quickly, she tried to refasten the pin at her collar, but it wouldn't go. Finally she gave in and pulled it out all the way, awkwardly sticking it in her pocket.

But if she felt uncomfortable getting caught with Tucker's hands on her blouse, Tegan seemed far worse off. A paler, less focused version of her brother, she showed none of the spark that made Tucker so appealing, but she did look about as ill at ease as was humanly possible.

"So what's up?" Tucker asked.

"I, uh..." Tegan stumbled over her words. "Could I talk to you for a minute? It's the fake Zappers thing, and the guy from Customs wanted an answer right away."

"Do we have to do this right now?"

"Well, it would be nice," Tegan said tartly. "This is your company, you know."

"Tegan..."

"*Now,* Tucker," she persisted.

"Okay, okay."

He disappeared after his sister, leaving Kristina feeling even more guilty about barging in on him at a moment's notice. And when he got back, he didn't look any too happy, either.

"Everything okay?" she asked gently.

"Yeah, sure." He shrugged. "It's just, every once in a while, I wonder whether I'm cut out for this job." He pulled off his tie with a vicious jerk, sending it sailing at the coat tree near her jacket.

"You seem to be awfully concerned about clothes today," she commented, casting a nervous eye at the disarray he was making.

"I hate the stuff," he muttered. "Look, I've had a hell of a day, and I don't think I can take another iota of work without some fun first."

"Okay, well, I can talk to you about this some other time."

"That's not what I meant." Abruptly he stalked to the other side of the room and bent over a huge, brightly lit jukebox stuck in one corner. "A new acquisition," he told her with a grin. "It got here yesterday."

She trailed over to the jukebox to peer over his shoulder. Picking tunes? This was beginning to seem more like a date than a work session. "This may be a dumb question, but what are you doing?"

"I need to loosen up a little. I think you do, too."

"No, really, I'm fine," she protested.

"It's for your own good," he insisted. "Come on. Let's have some fun."

"If we're not going to discuss my proposal, then I think I should—"

"Oh, come on!" he said in mock horror. "We'll have some tunes, we'll relax and we'll get more creative. Then we'll talk about your workshop presentation. Music is the food of life, you know."

"Oh, my God, he's quoting Shakespeare at me," she moaned under her breath. She'd always wanted to meet a man who would quote—even misquote—Shakespeare.

"See if you like this," he told her, as he pushed a button and an honest-to-goodness record twisted around inside the machine, finally dropping flat onto the turntable.

The jukebox sang out a snappy old tune, "The Locomotion." Kristina remembered it from sock hops in high school. Even then, it was a golden oldie.

Tucker joined in for the chorus, singing way off key, something about dances and taking chances.

"Tucker," she said firmly, trying to rein in her wayward companion, "you aren't suggesting we—"

"Dance?" He grinned and took her hand, dragging her out into a clear space of floor. "What a great idea. How clever of you to suggest it, Kristina."

"I didn't suggest it. And I'm not going to do it!" she protested, digging in her heels as he tried to pull her. "I came here to get your ideas for my proposal, not to fool around."

He winked broadly, spinning her around, fitting her backside right up against his front and then coaxing her forward a step at a time to the music. "It helps productivity," he whispered in her ear.

"But..."

Oh, God. She could feel him back there, strong and warm, swaying slightly from side to side, as if her perceptive powers were switched onto the supersensitive setting. It was like every atom in her body was different and discrete from its brothers and sisters, and she could tell exactly which ones Tucker was touching.

She had no choice but to follow where his hands, gently riding her hips, were sending her.

"Wait a minute. I do have a choice," she mumbled, and stopped dead in her tracks.

Tucker was in the middle of some "locomotion" movement, and he didn't notice that she'd stopped so abruptly. As a result, his whole, long body bashed into her from behind, almost knocking her over.

"Whoa," he said, catching her as she stumbled, snaking an arm firmly around her waist. "That's not the way you do it."

"I don't do it," she returned. "At all."

"You don't dance? You're kidding."

"Not with..." Not with men? Not with Tucker? How about not with anybody? She felt her face flame with warmth. "No. As a matter of fact, I don't dance."

She tried to walk away, very calmly, back to her stool, but once again Tucker caught her.

"Come on," he coaxed, in a lower, huskier voice that sent tingles racing in loop-the-loops around and around her body. He took both her hands in his and pulled her in very close, paraphrasing the song, whispering that she might start to like dancing with him if she gave it a chance.

I just bet I will, she thought, as her palms began to sweat and her mouth went dry. She fixed her gaze at a point on Tucker's shoulder and tried not to be so anxious, so edgy. But how could she help it, when he was holding her like this?

"The Locomotion" ended then, and Tucker slowed their rhythm to the new song—an old ballad in the mellow tones of Nat King Cole—moving her back and forth, with one hand at the small of her back, gently, forcefully pulling her into him, and the other clasping her hand tightly between them.

Who needed to dance? At this point, she felt like a rousing success for staying upright on her own two feet.

But then, who needed feet, for that matter? As close as Tucker was holding her, they could have managed nicely with only one pair.

"Relax," he said warmly, breathing in her ear. "Relax."

Relax? She was melting into a puddle, like the Wicked Witch of the West after her run-in with the bucket of water.

Nat King Cole sang on about how unforgettable his love was, and Kristina actually began to hear the music. She closed her eyes and snuggled in closer, feeling Tucker's smile brush her hair as she did so.

Suddenly a new song dropped into place, and a fast, sassy beat kicked in. It was "Rescue Me," a song she'd heard on a TV commercial not too long ago, and practically adopted as her theme song. There was something about its lyrics—about being rescued, about being taken in some mystery man's arms—that really appealed to her.

As if obeying the music's command, Tucker spun her around inside the circle of his arms, and then whipped her back out again in a fancy turn of some sort. It took her breath away—it was like feeling the wind on her face on a roller-coaster ride—and she laughed out loud with sheer surprise.

Tucker laughed, too, whirling her so fast she forgot to be nervous. One moment she was jammed up against him, and the next they were tangled in some complicated maneuver even he didn't seem to be sure of. But it never lasted long, because Tucker was racing into another turn, another spin, faster and faster.

Kristina found herself calling out the song's title, even after it ended. "Rescue me," she said happily. "I like that."

Tucker chose that moment to try a dip, bending her back over one knee and pretending he might drop her. Suspended in midair, she was helpless.

"Rescue me," she whispered in earnest.

"Anytime," he murmured, ruffling her hair with his soft words. Still holding her securely in this impossible position, he leaned in and pressed his lips to the hollow of her neck.

"Oh, Tucker..." Closing her eyes, she tightened her grasp around his neck, and pulled her head up to meet his kiss more fully.

"Tucker!"

This time he wasn't pretending; as they both jumped to attention at the sound of a visitor, he really did almost drop her.

He managed to stand up and carry her with him, albeit a bit awkwardly. "Trey," he said with a certain amount of hostility. "What do you want?"

One look at Trey's face told her he was furious. Hadn't she told him that nothing was going on between her and Tucker? And now Trey had stumbled over what must look like an intimate embrace.

"We were... dancing," she managed, brushing imaginary dust off her skirt.

"I could see what you were doing," Trey said snidely.

Tucker crossed to where his brother stood, and grabbed the younger man's arm. Speaking firmly but quietly, he spent several moments on some sort of tirade meant for Trey's ears only.

Kristina caught phrases like "rude interruption" and "nothing to do with you," but most of it was inaudible.

"I don't give a damn what you two do," Trey retorted, knocking Tucker's hand off his arm. "This is business. I have more Christmas season figures, and you told me to bring them to you the minute I had them. Do you want them or not?"

"Get out of here," Tucker said angrily. "I'll look at the figures in the morning. During regular business hours."

"Fine," Trey snapped.

"Fine," Tucker shot back. As Trey bolted from the room with fury darkening his face, Tucker turned to Kristina. "I guess this was a bad idea."

"I guess."

"Do you still want to talk about your proposal?"

"Well, I don't know. This wasn't the best timing, and maybe it would be better to—"

"No, wait," Tucker said suddenly. "Look, I'm starved. What do you say we discuss this over some dinner?"

"Dinner?" she echoed.

"Yeah. Come on upstairs. I'll make you dinner at my place."

"Your place? You live upstairs?"

He nodded. "I have the whole fourth floor. It's great. You'll love it."

He headed out of the playroom before she had a chance to object. "Your place," she repeated, trailing after him. "Oh, dear."

Chapter Eight

Behind a funny little door at the end of the hall, an equally funny little staircase led up to the fourth floor.

"Is this the attic?" she asked.

"Not really."

He ushered her up the stairs and into his apartment, his usual cocky grin on his face, and she was even more confused. He seemed to have recovered his equanimity from the argument with Trey with no problem whatsoever. Maybe he really was starving, and now that food was in sight, he was feeling more chipper.

It seemed rather farfetched. She was musing on that possibility when he picked up his story.

"Originally, this was a kind of dormitory floor, for the maids, I guess, back in the old days when they had a whole fleet of servants. Mom and Dad made it into an apartment for me when I got out of college and came back to Toyland."

The whole place simply screamed "Tucker." An apartment, to Kristina, meant a certain number of recognizable rooms, with doors and hallways and interior walls. But there was no definition to this space, just a flow of exposed beams and brick under sloping ceilings, giving it the feel of a loft, where you could roller-skate if you had a mind to.

A basketball hoop with a life-size poster of Michael Jordan behind it decorated one wall, while a low-slung electric blue couch, heaped with red and yellow pillows, took up most of the opposite side. The rest of the furnishings were a hodgepodge of styles and colors, with sports posters and framed prints of modern art hovering over Victorian pie-crust tables and a beautiful Persian rug.

Magazines cascaded off the sofa and over the edges of the coffee table, a monstrosity composed by sticking a sheet of thick glass over some kind of preserved tree stump, while bits and pieces of sports equipment littered the floor.

And toys—well, there were toys everywhere. Six or seven race cars in metallic blues and greens graced the big, round kitchen table, and there was a pile of blocks built into an elaborate spaceship in front of an overstuffed chair. Sketches of toy designs were taped to every available wall.

No question what the man who lived here did for a living. Tucker wasn't neat, but he sure had personality to spare.

"Well," she said, gazing around, wondering what to say. In the end, she had to be honest. "I love it. It's wonderful."

"I just stick whatever I like in here." He shrugged. "It seems to work out."

He strolled over to the refrigerator and peered in, leaning well inside the door. As he bent, pulling the fabric of his expensive wool slacks tight against his backside, Kristina held her breath.

Rescue me, indeed.

Extracting himself from the refrigerator, Tucker turned around expectantly. "Kristina?"

She attempted to look innocent. "Uh-huh?"

"Dinner," he reminded her. "What should I make?"

"What can you make?" she asked tactfully. Somehow, he didn't seem the type to be whipping up veal Prince Orlov for two on the spur of the moment.

"Well, I was thinking of ordering a pizza," he admitted. "I'm a terrible cook."

"Me, too."

It struck her as humorous that they were stuck here with no food when he'd invited her up for dinner, and she let a smile sneak over her lips.

Tucker answered the smile with one of his own. When their gazes intersected and held, it was hard for her not to imagine that they understood each other very, very well.

"You have a way..." she began, but she didn't know how to finish the thought.

"A way of what?"

"Of getting around me." Exasperation edged her voice. "Of making me like you even though you are all the things I shouldn't like."

"Me?" He seemed astonished. "What's not to like about a nice guy like me?"

"Oh, right. A nice, overpowering, pushy bulldozer who forces me to tell him about my most private fantasy—"

"If Santa's Magic Workshop is your most private fantasy, darlin', we have some work to do," he interjected.

She gave him a severe look, and continued. "Who never gives me or anyone else a straight answer, who tries to flirt with me all the time when I keep telling him not to, who happens to be in the one profession my mother despises."

He shook his head. "I know I'm pushy." His smile widened. "It's part of my charm. I can't help the fact that your mother hates the toy business, and I sure can't help what you call flirting." He shrugged, and once more rammed his hands into his pockets. "I . . . like you. A lot. There's something between you and me that I can't exactly explain."

She knew how that felt. "Go on," she murmured.

"But whatever it is, I feel it. I keep feeling it. And it's making it almost impossible for me to keep my hands off you when we're in the same room."

The comment seemed simple and honest, but it carried the payload of a ballistic missile, sneaking around her protective barriers and slamming straight into her heart.

His eyes were so blue, and his voice wrapped around her like a net of silken threads. What was she going to do?

"I like you, too," she said breathlessly. The feeble offering seemed terribly inadequate.

But at her words, he crossed the big, open room within the matter of a few seconds, leaving the refrigerator door wide open behind him. Bracketing her shoulders in his arms, he just stood there, gazing down at her for a long pause.

His voice dipped even lower, with an uneven note to it. "If you like me and I like you, what's wrong with a little . . . flirting between friends?"

"Nothing," she murmured.

And then he lowered his lips to hers.

It wasn't at all like the first kiss, that sweet, unthreatening gesture under the mistletoe. This one was hungrier, harder, more desperate, as if he'd been waiting a long time to really let go.

She wound her hands into the soft, tousled hair at the nape of his neck, pulling him closer, wanting more of him.

It was the first time she'd touched his hair, although she'd wanted to before, but it was so silky and smooth between her fingers that it surprised her.

"Kiss me back, Krissie," he whispered, and she didn't even fuss about him using her childhood nickname.

She just kissed him back.

As his mouth covered hers, she opened to him, tipping her tongue against his, returning measure for measure as the heavy, sweet, demanding pressure of the kiss deepened. His lips, his tongue, whatever unique current there was flowing inside Tucker Bennett, claimed her and seared her deep inside.

Kissing had never felt like this.

"Maybe it did and I forgot," she murmured against his lips.

"What?"

"Nothing, Tucker," she breathed, letting the feel of his name drift over the lips he'd just kissed so thoroughly. "Tucker."

"Krissie," he whispered back, and then he swept her up into his arms and carried her to the outrageous blue sofa.

He set her down carefully, but she felt herself sinking into the big, soft pouf of cushions. Tucker spilled pillows every which way as he edged onto the couch beside her.

She tried to sit up a little, but the couch simply wouldn't allow it. "Oh, my."

"Shh," he murmured, and slid a long leg in between hers to fit their bodies together more securely.

Wrapping his arms around her, holding her tight, he framed her face with his long, elegant, inventor's fingers, and then he waited, watching her with a mysterious expression on his face.

What was he waiting for? Some signal, some message she didn't know how to send?

Just when she could stand it no longer, when she planned to pull him down and find his mouth all by herself, he resumed the wonderful kiss. She sighed with pure bliss.

And then his mouth danced across the curve of her cheek and down the line of her jaw, nibbling her ear, teasing the tip of her nose. His tongue traced the outline of her lips, before he began a slow trail down her neck, down to where her buttons lay undone.

Alarms were sounding in her brain. *I don't know about this. Should I stop him?* But the answer from her heart was clear: *I don't want to stop him.*

And then the phone rang.

"Message machine," Tucker mumbled against her mouth. He made no move to leave her. His hand slipped down to her next button, and he pressed a gentle kiss on the warm, tingling expanse of skin already revealed.

Even as he spoke, the machine kicked on, and in the periphery of her consciousness, she heard Tucker's recorded voice ramble on about being unable to come to the phone and waiting for the beep. But then another voice broke in.

"Tucker?" Tegan's voice spilled out, sounding very panicky. "Are you there? If you are, you have to pick up. This is important! It's the Customs thing again. If you don't answer, Trey is threatening to call Mom and Dad. Tucker? Tucker, answer the phone!"

Kristina tried to disentangle herself. "You can't ignore that."

"No?"

"No," she said regretfully, pulling farther away.

He scowled. "I hate being responsible."

"Tucker, answer the phone."

Reaching over her, he knocked the phone off the tree-trunk coffee table and almost pitched off the couch himself as he tried to catch it. Grabbing the receiver from the floor where it lay, he said, in a muffled voice, "Hi, Teeg. I'm here."

Kristina could now only catch his side of the conversation, but it didn't sound pleasant.

"Okay, okay," he said, and then, "I'll be down as soon as I can. Yeah, okay. Thanks, Teeg."

Carefully, she slipped out from under him, attempting to rearrange her clothing enough to look a little more presentable. She knew that the little interlude on the couch was over, and she knew she should be glad they'd been interrupted. It hadn't been smart to lose control like that.

Trying to give him some privacy, she made her way to the tiny kitchen area, where the first thing that caught her eye was the refrigerator door, standing wide open. How embarrassing that neither one of them had noticed.

She shut the door, and then yanked open the freezer compartment, just long enough to give herself a good blast of frigid air in the face.

Finally, Tucker hung up, and she ventured back into the main area. "Sounds like you have to go back to work."

"I'm afraid so. Life's no fun when you're president." He managed a half-hearted smile. "I still have time for that pizza, though, if you're game."

"Are you sure?"

"Quit asking me if I'm sure about things, will you?" He shook his head. "It's fine. Tegan's not going to die if I take time to eat. On the other hand, I may die if I don't."

"Okay, if you say so." She knew what it was like to be torn in different directions, and to make difficult decisions. If he'd made up his mind, who was she to disagree?

He poked around the bottom of the coffee table's tree stump, emerging with a phone book eventually. "Here," he said. "For the pizza. You choose."

"I don't want to deci—" she started, but as he held it out to her, a whole stack of little white sheets of paper, the kind that come on memo pads, slipped out from under the phone book's cover and spilled to the floor at Tucker's feet.

"Whoops," she said, and she knelt near him to pick up the scattered memos.

"No, don't," he told her, but she paid no attention, retrieving three or four of the nearest sheets.

"Rikki's Car Repair," she read, handing it over. "Wouldn't want to lose that number. And here's Tracy Butler, paperboy. And how about..." But when she saw the name, she stopped. "George Castleberry," she read slowly. "There's an address and a phone number. What are you doing with this?"

"It's from our files." He paused. "I thought you might want it, so I copied it. That way, I'd have it ready, just in case."

"It's none of your business." The hand holding the slip of paper was trembling, but she only tightened her grip. "You could have asked me if I wanted it or not. You could have asked."

"I thought you might be trying to forget about it."

"And what if I was?"

"You've spent most of your life leaving loose ends hanging—your father, the career you really want." His voice was even, his gaze steady. "Don't you think you should tie up a few things once and for all, and get on with your life?"

"That's for me to decide, not you," she shot back. "You've got enough problems of your own without interfering in mine."

Tucker stood there, looking confused and disappointed, but she told herself it was his own fault.

"Why won't you accept my help?" he asked after a moment.

"I don't need your help."

"Yes," he said grimly, "you do. You can't go on lying to everybody about what you feel and what you want. You want the workshop, so fine, let's get the damned thing going. You want your father, so let's find him and see what he has to say for himself."

"I don't need your help," she repeated, more for her benefit than his.

"Damn it all to hell—yes, you do! I know you want me," he told her. "*Fine.* Here I am."

"I don't want my father, and I don't want you," she said, and she dashed out of his apartment and down the narrow stairs.

"Kristina," he called after her. "You are still coming to the meeting, aren't you? To pitch the workshop to the board?"

She stopped in midflight. Turning on the stairs, she gazed up at him, not sure what she wanted to do. Finally, she sighed with resignation. It was no good this way, and she knew it. She said, "Look, I'm sorry. I didn't mean to..."

"It's okay."

"But my father is personal, okay? Off-limits."

He nodded. "I didn't mean to interfere."

"Fine." She moistened her lips. "But I will see you at the board meeting. I'm not giving up."

"Good. That's good."

And then she turned and fled down the stairs, with the piece of paper still firmly clasped in her hand.

"POLLY?" SHE ASKED, and then sighed with frustration as some underling from the clerical pool put her on hold. Again. "Finally," she muttered, as a rustling on the other end of the line indicated a live person was picking it up. "Hello?"

"Kristina? Is that you? This is Polly. Where are you? Windy's been down to your office twice, asking about you."

Kristina was not a good liar; she never had been. But today was an emergency, and she was just going to have to fib away and get it over with. With that in mind, she pinched her nose tightly between two fingers, and kept her voice very weak and slushy. Her words came out, "I'b hobe sick."

"Gee, you sound terrible."

"Yes, I dow. I hab a code." Behind her, she heard Nick click his tongue with disapproval. She stuck her tongue out at him and faked a hollow, rolling cough for Polly's benefit. It sounded more like a hyena than a person in the throes of a rotten cold, but she thought it was probably close enough to fool Polly. "I dode think I'll bake it in today," she said, carefully nasal and thickheaded. "Sedd a bessage up to Bister Austid, okay?"

"Yeah, sure, Kristina. Hope you're feeling better soon."

She made another polite little wheeze or two before getting off the phone and wheeling around to face Nick. "Don't say a word. I had to do it."

"I didn't say anything, my dear."

"Yes, but I can tell you're dying to." She lifted her hands in supplication. "I don't have a choice, Nick. I had to call in sick if I wanted to make it to the Toyland meeting. It may take all day, so another fake doctor's appointment wouldn't have been good enough.''

"It's your decision, my dear," he said mildly. "But untruths have a way of rebounding upon a person.''

"I know, but I don't have time to worry about it right now." Hands on hips, she stood and surveyed the chaos in her living room. It was difficult to judge how much time she had against how much more remained to be done.

"I'm fine," she decided. "Fine." A few tiny touches on the drawings of the Magic Workshop were really all that was left to do, and then she'd be ready for the drive to Toyland, to pitch her idea once and for all.

"Well, my dear, you'd better get a move on if you're planning to arrive promptly." He leaned over to peek at her sketches. "Lovely, my dear. Simply lovely. Couldn't have done better myself.''

"Oh, really?" As she gave the top sheet the once-over, double-checking it, she fiddled with the markers in their carrying case. "Do you do artwork, Nick?''

"Oh, no, no. I have been known to tinker a bit with toys, however. I was referring to the..." He twirled his hands in the air. "The, uh, technical portion. If you see what I mean.''

"No, I don't.''

"I meant that it's a very lovely design, and Toyland will certainly snap it up.''

As Nick smiled down at her with an expression of genial pride, she slid the first of the sketches into a large, flat portfolio. And then the phone rang.

"Can you get that?" she asked hurriedly. "I have to get packed up and out of here.''

"Certainly," he responded, and he leaned over her to pick up the receiver. "Hello? Yes, that's right. You've reached the correct home, and yes, she's here."

She waved her hands frantically. "No! No!" she mouthed. "I can't take it!"

"Yes, Mrs. Austin. She's right here." Beaming at Kristina as if he hadn't just committed an unpardonable offense, Nick proffered the phone.

Mrs. Austin? Her mother or Mirabel? Either one was a disaster.

But what could she do? As she hesitated, Nick explained, "It's your mother. I didn't feel it was quite the thing for me to fabricate something about your imaginary illness." With obvious distaste, he added, "It wouldn't be right. Not to your mother, Kristina."

"No, of course not," she muttered, fighting down the urge to smack his well-intentioned, conscientious little face.

She was somewhat surprised to be hearing from her mother, even though they *were* once more on speaking terms. As a matter of fact, the two of them had reached a tentative peace days ago, right after Mirabel's party.

Of course, to get to that point, Kristina had been forced to call her mother first thing the morning after the party, apologize abjectly for her behavior, blame it all on drinking too much champagne and promise to rid herself of any connection to toys, Toyland, or Tucker Bennett.

It was all lies—more sins laid at her doorstep—but it kept the peace for the time being, and that was the important thing. A niggling little voice whispered, *It's a house of cards, and it's all going to come tumbling down around you,* but she did her best to ignore the niggling little voice.

She was simply not the kind of person who could stand being on the outs with her mother, and that was that.

Letting Nick foist the phone into her hand, she manufactured a dutiful, interested tone of voice. "Hello, Mother. How are you?"

"Fine, darling. Windy called to tell me you weren't coming in to the store, that you're not feeling well, and I thought I'd better check in. It's so seldom you're ill." Bitsy paused before announcing, "But you know, you sounded fine just now."

Damnation. She'd forgotten she was supposed to sound like she had a cold. "It's the flu." She improvised. "I may sound okay, but I'm feeling really awful. As a matter of fact, I was on my way to lie down when you called, and I think I'd better—"

"Who answered your phone, dear?" Bitsy's tone had turned very suspicious. "That man, I mean?"

Kristina was not in the mood for an inquisition. "It's not Tucker, if that's what you're thinking."

"I didn't say it was," Bitsy returned sharply. "You told me you weren't going to see him again, and I believed you."

Actually, she hadn't seen him for several days, not since the night she'd left him in his apartment without a pizza. But that didn't mean she hadn't thought about him.

All she'd done was think about him.

When she should've been concentrating on Austin's problems, which continued to mount, or finishing up her proposal for the workshop, which simply had to get done, she found herself daydreaming instead about Tucker Bennett's narrow, clever lips or mischievous blue eyes. Or even the high-top sneakers he'd worn to a black-tie affair.

"Kristina?" her mother demanded, and the visions of Tucker regretfully vanished. "Who was that man?"

"No one," she answered vaguely.

"He had to be someone. I've never known you to have a man answering your telephone at eight o'clock in the morning before."

"His name is Nick, Mother. He works at Austin's."

She was certainly not going to get into the story of Santa Claus and her unexpected stay-over guest of the male variety, even if Nick was as harmless as they came. Bitsy would never approve.

A convenient explanation occurred to her, and she seized it. Maybe she was better at this dishonesty and deception stuff than she'd thought.

"We carpool together," she said, in a flurry of inspiration, "and he stopped by to pick me up. I was telling him that I wouldn't need a ride, that I was staying home sick today, when the phone rang. And since I was feeling absolutely wretched, and I wasn't sure I felt strong enough to talk just then..." She finished up cheerfully, "I asked him to pick it up."

"Oh, someone from Austin's," her mother murmured. "Well, that's fine then, isn't it?"

"Of course."

"Kristina," Nick whispered loudly in the background. When she edged around to see what he wanted, he gestured at his watch. "Time to go, my dear. Don't want to be late for your meeting."

She nodded, and made her voice pitiful and sickly for the mouthpiece. "Look, Mother, I really have to go. Thanks for calling. I'm sure I'll be fine after I get some rest, so I think I'll turn the answering machine on and go to bed. Wouldn't want to miss another day of work.''

"No, no, heavens no," Bitsy agreed. "You lie down. Take an aspirin or something."

"Right," Kristina said, and prepared to hang up.

"Kristina?" Bitsy ventured, pulling her back to the phone. "Darling, I know you really are sick, and I'm sure the way you're feeling has nothing to do with that unpleasantness last week, but I just wanted to tell you that I'm awfully glad we've patched things up. You really are doing the right thing, you know. Austin's is the job for you. You forget about the toy nonsense and that odious young man and you'll be ever so much better off."

"Right. Goodbye, Mom."

Overwhelmed with guilt, she dropped the phone back into its cradle with a soft thud. "I'm no good at this, Nick. Why did I lie to her? Tucker would've said, 'I'm off for Toyland to pitch my idea, and you can like it or lump it, Ma.' But I'm not Tucker, and I couldn't tell her. Could I?"

"Later, my dear, later," Nick fussed, handing her the briefcase. "Time to be on your way, out the door, quick, quick, quick."

"You're the one who made me talk to her."

"Well, I didn't say you had to chat with her all bloody morning, did I?"

Struggling to push her arms into her coat while she held on to both cases and opened the front door, she laughed at the tangle she was in. "Oh, Nick, are you sure I'm doing the right thing?"

"Absolutely. Positively."

"I wish I was as sure as you are. I'm kind of nervous," she admitted.

"I'd be happy to go with you," he said quickly. Without being asked, he took her parcels while she buttoned up her coat. "Moral support and all that."

"No, that's okay." It was bad enough she was risking losing her own job if all these lies got uncovered; she wasn't going to put Nick in jeopardy, too. "You have to work this afternoon, remember?"

"Ah, yes." He brightened. "You know, I'm quite enjoying my Santa position."

"I'm glad." All ready to go, she took back her briefcase and the artist's portfolio and brushed a quick kiss on his cheek. She was gratified to note his tickled expression. "Wish me luck."

"Certainly, my dear girl. Best of luck!"

She couldn't have said which of them was counting on this more. Whichever, the butterflies only got worse the nearer she got to Toyland. Maybe she should've brought Nick along after all, to keep her attitude positive and her morale boosted high.

But Tucker was waiting for her, lounging on the bottom steps of Toyland's wide front staircase, looking very spiffy in a navy double-breasted suit with a striped shirt and a natty dark red tie. One glance at him, and she decided that perhaps Nick's presence wasn't really necessary.

Tucker looked wonderful, but then, he always did. She couldn't have missed him—it had only been a few days since she'd seen him—but she had. Oh, Lord, how she had.

But now that she looked more closely, she noticed a distinctly uncomfortable expression on his face. "You don't look so hot," she said slowly. "Is something wrong?"

"No, of course not," he said quickly, hoisting himself to his feet and taking her portfolio and briefcase without even asking if she needed help.

Without her arms full, she felt even more nervous. What was she supposed to do with her hands?

And why was he so jumpy? "Are you sure nothing's wrong?"

He gave her a dark look as he slung the baggage under one arm and began to pull at his collar with the other hand. "No, but something's going to *get* wrong if you keep asking."

Now she knew something was definitely up, or he wouldn't be denying it so vehemently. What did he know that she didn't? And why was he fussing with his tie like that?

She narrowed her gaze at his furtive movements.

"It's the damn clothes," he grumbled. "You know I hate suits. Makes me feel like a buttoned-up old fuddy-duddy."

Silently she removed her coat, revealing a severely cut gray suit, complete with white silk blouse and discreet pearls at the neck.

"I meant on me," he said hastily. "You look great in suits. Really."

She nodded. "This is all wrong, isn't it?"

"No, you look fine. Better than fine. Beautiful."

"I didn't mean my clothes. I meant being here, doing

this. I'm going to make a fool of myself, Santa's Workshop will go up in flames and I'll never live it down."

"Calm down," he said sternly.

"I hate it when people tell me to calm down."

"Well, you'd better do it anyway."

As the grandfather clock in the first floor hallway began to bong the hours, loud and clear, Tucker sprinted up the stairs ahead of her, still hauling her cumbersome portfolio and briefcase.

At the top of the landing, he turned to her with an unreadable expression. "Get ready, kiddo. It's show time."

Chapter Nine

Tucker held open the door to the boardroom, expecting Kristina to go on in. But before she could, Trey came barreling out, acting like he was a bull and Tucker was waving a red flag.

Tucker stifled a groan. Just what he didn't need was another squabble with his power-hungry younger brother.

"Kristina," Trey acknowledged, clearly intent on cornering Tucker rather than wasting words on her. "Tucker, can I talk to you?"

"We're on our way into the meeting. Can it wait?"

"No," his brother replied. "It can't."

Tucker frowned. He'd been avoiding this kind of showdown all morning, trying to forestall Trey until after Kristina's meeting, but it looked like he was fated to fail. "Why don't you go on in and get set up?" he asked her. "I'll be there in a few seconds."

She looked none too happy that he was abandoning her at the door, but Trey wasn't taking no for an answer, either.

"All right," she said softly.

"I'll be in to get things started ASAP," he promised, and she nodded.

"It's okay. I'll see you inside."

She took a deep breath, squared her shoulders and plunged through the doorway. Tucker couldn't suppress a smile. He loved it when she was being brave.

"There's nothing to smile about," Trey snapped, bringing Tucker back to grim reality. "The preliminary figures are not good, and you're going to have to do something about it."

"I am," Tucker shot back. He was, in a word, furious. Coldly, calmly furious with his brother for behaving like such an idiot. "*I* am. Not you. Your job is design, and that's it. So leave it alone."

"But you're not doing your job," Trey protested. "If I don't call you on it, Toyland will go down the tubes!"

Tucker had had just about enough of this nonsense. He ought to be inside, helping Kristina sell the workshop idea, not retreading tired arguments with his brother.

"Look," he said tersely, barely resisting the urge to shove Trey up against the nearest wall. "Toyland is fine. Got that? *Fine.* I'm going to go through this with you once, and once only. You can either listen, or I can smash your face."

"Go on," Trey mumbled.

"Okay." Impatiently, Tucker state, "No, the Christmas sales are not great. We're in a recession. Nobody's Christmas sales are great. Even if they were horrendous—which they're not—it wouldn't be my fault. Dad put this year's Christmas strategy in the works a year ago, which you well know. All I can do is wait it out and use the information to plan for next year." He finished up, "And I'm not going to do that until after the numbers from this year are complete."

Trey's face was flushed by the end of the speech, but he refused to give up. "So after all the figures are in, you'll consider my proposals for the direction the company should take?''

''Consider, yes. But that's all.''

He already knew he would never agree to market the upscale, yuppie toys Trey wanted, but he supposed he'd have to at least look at the proposals.

''We'll see,'' Trey muttered.

''Are you two fighting again?'' Tegan asked, as she came running up to the boardroom door. ''At least I'm not late for the meeting. I thought sure I was late, and I haven't even made the coffee yet.''

''That would be a disaster.'' Tucker managed a smile for his sister, who was in a dither as usual. ''Why are you late?''

''This.'' She stuck a yellow envelope at him, clearly marked TELEGRAM.

''A telegram?'' He couldn't recall ever getting a telegram before. ''What is it? Did you read it?''

''Of course not. I don't read other people's mail,'' she said archly.

Tucker ripped it open without further ado. ''It's from Dad.''

After a quick look at the contents, he decided not to read it out loud.

What the hell is going on there?
Straighten things out with your brother, or I will.

Love, Dad

''Great,'' Tucker mumbled. He knew how this had started. Narrowing his gaze at his brother, he demanded, ''What exactly did you tell him?''

''The truth,'' Trey insisted.

"Or your version of it." Tucker felt anger and humiliation rise up and burn in his chest. He couldn't remember ever being so provoked by another human being in his life. Even the seven-foot center from an opposing team, who'd slugged him on the basketball court, hadn't made him this mad. "What in the hell did you think you were doing?" he asked savagely. "He's sick, Trey. He could have another heart attack with you playing these kinds of games."

"Baloney," Trey scoffed, and Tegan interceded.

"Come on, you guys," she told them both sternly. "Enough of this. We're supposed to be in a meeting, and you're fighting out in the hall. Let's get our act together, okay?"

Tucker nodded curtly, but he was still fuming. What was he, some kind of little kid, being taken to task by anyone and everyone who felt like it? The hell with that noise.

"Just remember who's president of this company." Yanking open the door to the boardroom, he gestured for Tegan to pass, and then strode purposefully in ahead of his brother.

Let the little jerk bring up the rear.

KRISTINA HAD HAD PLENTY of time to set up her illustrations, stack the notebooks with the details of her proposal neatly on the long, dark board table and twiddle her thumbs, waiting for the Bennett portion of the Toyland board of directors.

The other three board members were present, but they were chatting with one another on the far side of the room. She smiled pleasantly in their direction, but figured she should wait to be formally introduced. If Tucker ever got there.

She could hear raised voices out in the corridor, indicating a heated argument was brewing, but she couldn't make out the particulars. She just hoped it wasn't about her.

Get a grip, she told herself. *Why would they argue about me?* She couldn't think of any reason why they would, but she was feeling rather paranoid at the moment, with the future of her Magic Workshop on the line, and a major battle raging in the hallway.

Finally, Tegan came tentatively into the room, with Tucker and Trey close behind. All three of them looked tense and unhappy, and her heart sank. This was not going to be a receptive audience.

Unclenching his jaw, Tucker announced, "Everyone's here, so we might as well get started."

"An introduction might be nice," she said under her breath.

"What? Oh, right. Everyone—this is Kristina Castleberry. She has a proposal for us that I think you'll be very interested in."

Still looking glum, he shuffled into one of the tall leather chairs around the board table, and motioned to the others to take their seats, too.

"Kristina, you know Trey," he said, as the young man in question sat down opposite him. "And Tegan, of course."

Tegan nodded and smiled wanly, mumbling that she was happy to see Kristina again.

"Frank Dundee is next to Tegan," Tucker continued. "Frank heads up Production."

Kristina smiled at the rather steely-looking man Tucker had indicated. Frank seemed to be sizing her up. She pegged him as gruff, but accessible, as if he were willing to hear her out.

That only left a vague, slender man chewing on a pencil, whom Tucker quickly introduced as Pete Carpenter, their "numbers" man, and a very attractive woman who happened to be sitting next to Tucker at the board table. Kristina waited to find out who the mystery woman was, but Tucker hesitated.

She glanced at the woman and back at him, prodding him to finish up, so they could get on with business.

"And this is Vanessa," he said after a moment. "Vanessa heads up Sales."

"Vanessa Bennett," Trey added meaningfully.

"Oh." So she was a Bennett, was she? Well, it was a family-owned and operated company; Tucker, Tegan, and Trey were evidence of that. But still . . .

Kristina regarded the other woman with curiosity she hoped didn't show. Vanessa might be a Bennett, but she sure didn't look like the other ones. And her name didn't begin with a *T*, either.

Unlike Tegan, Vanessa Bennett made a vivid statement in a striking purple wool suit. She had dark hair, darker even than Kristina's, swept smoothly into some sort of complicated knot on the back of her head, and dark eyes that sparkled with intelligence.

"Tucker's ex-wife," Trey added slyly.

Kristina hadn't even been aware Tucker had an ex-wife, let alone one who worked at Toyland. Her gaze flashed to Tucker's extremely uncomfortable face. His jaw was clenched tighter than ever, and he looked like he wanted to strangle Trey with his bare hands. She didn't blame him. She wasn't feeling particularly charitable toward that young troublemaker herself.

"Trey," Vanessa Bennett chided. "This is probably not the best time to spring that on her. Sorry," she offered

Kristina. "But don't let it bother you. It's really no big deal."

No big deal? If she'd felt paranoid before, she was absolutely thunderstruck now. How did one react to meeting the ex-wife of a man one was sort of, maybe, interested in?

She wasn't all that sure she'd have wanted to meet Tucker's ex-wife *ever,* but especially not ten minutes before she pitched her beloved idea to the Toyland board of directors.

Questions crowded her brain, but one was blaring louder than the rest.

Why didn't he warn me?

It was almost as if he'd wanted to hide the fact that he had an ex-wife. But how could he, when the woman worked at Toyland? And damn it, Vanessa even seemed like a nice person. She was certainly a snappy dresser. He could hardly be embarrassed that he'd been married to the woman.

So why didn't he warn me?

As far as Kristina was concerned, it was unforgivable to let her stumble over this when she was already in the midst of an anxiety attack over Santa's Magic Workshop.

She had a pounding headache, she couldn't remember one thing about the workshop she was supposed to be so enthusiastic about and her confidence level was hovering around zero. And it was all his fault.

"Ready to go?" he asked, as the others settled in and started to thumb through the folders in front of them.

Ready to club you over the head with my briefcase. But she smiled sweetly and tried to look like the soul of professionalism.

"Santa's Magic Workshop," she began in a less-than-inspiring tone. Her stomach was doing flip-flops, and she was afraid she was going to throw up. "This is a toy for the discriminating child or the adult who never grows up. It's intended to be beautiful to look at, fun to play with and involve hours of quality time.

"Yes, it will be expensive," she admitted, wondering why she'd decided to put that up front. It felt more like flirting with disaster than staking out a gutsy game plan. "But it will be worth it, like the Victoria's Dollhouse and Lancelot's Castle sets that Toyland already markets."

Nods of agreement met her reference to two items in their current product line, and she felt more encouraged. If she concentrated on the prepared words of her speech and didn't look at Vanessa or Tucker, she might be able to salvage this.

"The emphasis of this toy is on the magic and charm of Christmas, and hopefully, spreading those feelings into other seasons, as well."

Again, she got glimmers of approval from the Toyland board members. *Maybe it's going okay,* she decided, and the words began to flow on their own with a little more enthusiasm and energy. After all, this was Santa's Magic Workshop she was talking about, and it was a darn good idea, no matter what.

It was only when she came to the conclusion of her remarks some twenty minutes later that she realized she had no idea what she'd said or what they thought.

"Any questions?" she inquired.

"Thank you, Kristina," Vanessa said sweetly. "You've done a wonderful job presenting this."

She managed a smile in return, even if she did not appreciate being complimented by Tucker's too perfect ex-wife.

"It's a rather complete proposal," Pete, the numbers man, added in a low rumble. "I'm sure we can find answers here if we need them."

"Are you ready to vote?" Trey popped up with. "I'm ready."

"Well . . ." Pete said doubtfully.

Frank, head of Production, tapped his forefinger on the front of Kristina's report. "There are a few things in here I'd like to go over if Ms. Castleberry doesn't mind excusing us for a couple of minutes."

"Not at all." She shifted her glance from face to face, but no one looked confused or otherwise in need of her services. Was that good or bad? She really couldn't read their expressions, to gauge how well she'd done, or if she'd convinced them. Wishing she knew what to think, she began to gather up her materials. "Okay, well, I guess if that's all . . ."

"You can wait in my office," Tucker suggested. "I'll walk you down there."

"Fine," she said evenly. But as soon as they were safely out in the hall, she demanded, "How could you let me come here to pitch my idea to the Toyland board without mentioning that your ex-wife *happened* to be on that board?"

He was looking decidedly gray around the gills, and she almost felt sorry for him. Almost.

"Well?"

"I don't know," he muttered. "It didn't seem important."

"Oh, Tucker, please. How did you think I would feel when I found out?"

"Look, I don't want to get into this right now, okay?" He ushered her into his office and then turned to leave, but at the last moment, he relented. "For what it's worth, you did a great job in there, even, uh, under the circumstances. I don't think there will be any problem with the preliminary approval."

"Thank you," she said softly.

But as he left her to go back to the boardroom, she was very troubled. Not about Santa's Magic Workshop. She trusted Tucker enough to believe him if he said its approval was in the bag.

No, she was worried about Tucker. He hadn't seemed like himself at all, and she didn't know why. Her anger evaporated as her misgivings increased. Why was Tucker so grim?

"OKAY, EVERYBODY. Good job," Tucker called back into the boardroom. "And thanks."

He glanced at his watch, noting that only twenty minutes had elapsed since he'd left Kristina by herself in his office.

Jeez, he berated himself, *you didn't even offer her a magazine.* He'd been too consumed with anger and guilt—over Trey and his father and who exactly was in charge here—to think about what his behavior would seem like to Kristina.

Well, at least the meeting had gone smoothly, even if the rest of this rotten day had to be chalked up as a total loss. Tucker ambled down the corridor, his hands in his pockets, fingering the crumpled telegram that was still haunting him.

"Hi," he said casually, angling his head around the door into his office. He was determined to be more cheerful, and not to share his bad mood with Kristina. He grinned when he saw she was leafing through a copy of *Sports Illustrated*. He should've known Kristina would be resourceful.

When she saw him, she stood up awkwardly, dropping the magazine. "What's the news?"

"You got it," he said with a spark of triumph lighting his voice. "The Toyland Board of Directors has voted, unanimously I might add, to approve the creation of a prototype of Santa's Magic Workshop. Once we see the genuine article, we'll make our final decision on whether to proceed into production with the workshop."

Kristina said slowly, "So now I go ahead and create a prototype, right?"

He nodded.

She brightened so quickly that he was dazzled. With her hands at her mouth, she laughed out loud. "I can't believe it! I mean, I can, but still . . ." Her eyes were shining when she danced over to him and threw her arms around him. "Tucker, this is wonderful. I'm so excited! Aren't you excited?"

"Well, sure, but . . ." *But I've had a truly awful day.* Somehow it didn't seem fair to spoil her fun. "Congratulations, sweetheart."

"Thank you." She took a deep breath, clearly trying to contain her exuberance. "So now what? What's our schedule?"

"Well, we set a date for the demo—to show the board your model. The earlier the better."

"Okay." She laughed again. "I can't wait. A real-life model of Santa's Magic Workshop. Well, it will take their breath away!"

"Great."

"Tucker," she ventured, "I want to thank you for all your help, and to make up for, you know, giving you a hard time the other night."

He nodded, remembering that little skirmish. *I don't want my father, and I don't want you,* she'd said. It was not a pleasant memory. He still thought she was wrong; he wondered if she did.

"I don't know if you'd want to or anything," she went on, "but I was wondering if maybe you'd like to go somewhere tonight and sort of..." She paused, but then finished. "Celebrate. You know, that the workshop went over so well. With me."

"I'd love to," he said, and he meant it. Maybe this was Kristina's way of apologizing, without actually coming right out and saying it. He'd accept that.

And what a relief it would be to put aside the damn suits and ties and all of Toyland's lousy problems long enough to go out and engage in just plain fun.

"You don't play hockey, do you?" he asked, thinking of the best way he knew how to blow off some frustration in a hurry.

"Hockey?" she asked in a horrified tone.

"Just kidding."

"Okay, well, hockey is probably not the best idea," she admitted. "But I am free the rest of the day, so if you want to go right now, that's okay with me. I just have to get my stuff from the boardroom, and I'll be all set."

The weight of his responsibilities settled back around him like the cloak of doom. "I can't," he said finally. "I have too much to do to leave now. There are some administrative hassles going on with Toyland that I'm afraid can't wait."

"Okay. Well, later then?"

He nodded, noting the puzzled expression on her face. It wasn't too hard to guess what was bothering her. *You seemed like such a fun guy, Tucker,* he could imagine her saying. *But now you turn out dull and boring and responsible, just like everybody else.* "Sorry," he said softly. "Sometimes duty calls."

"Oh, I know. Believe me, I understand." She tilted her head to one side and looked at him for a long moment. "But it's funny. I never picked you as the nose-to-the-grindstone type. You keep telling me to loosen up, and now I'm thinking you need that advice yourself. Am I wrong?"

"No. I'm not the nose-to-the-grindstone type." He forced a smile. "But I'm trying."

"Well, you keep trying. And I'll see you later."

"Right," he said. "We can do something fun and stupid and not related in the least to Toyland or toys."

"Or department stores," she added mischievously.

"Or department stores."

He helped her get her portfolio together, offered his congratulations again and then stood thoughtfully, watching her walk down the staircase and out of Toyland.

Now if he could only get through the rest of the afternoon without bolting to Kristina's to beg her to let him play hookey with her.

"Tucker?"

It was Vanessa, and he turned to see what she wanted.

"May I speak with you?" she asked, in an ominous tone.

"Why not?" His voice was low and mocking. "Everybody else has thrown potshots at me today. You might as well join the crowd."

"Aren't we feeling sorry for ourselves?" With a raised eyebrow, Vanessa led him down to the employee kitchen on Toyland's first floor. "So," she said, installing him at the small, round table and glaring at him. "Why didn't you tell her about me?"

"How do you know I didn't tell her?"

"What do you think I am, stupid?"

He smiled fondly. "Never, Van. That's the one thing I would never accuse you of."

"Don't smile at me, Bennett," she returned. "I'm immune to your charms. Anyway, I saw the look on the girl's face, and I could tell she was shocked. So why were you keeping me a secret?"

"You know, it's weird," he said, trying to elude her question. "She asked me the exact same thing, and I didn't appreciate it from her, either."

"I'm not surprised she asked you, you nitwit!" Vanessa had never been one to stifle her feelings, and that, at least hadn't changed. "She could hardly be thrilled to trip over me like that without even knowing I existed."

Stubbornly silent, he crossed his arms over his chest and slid down in his seat at the table.

"Are you ashamed of me or what?" Vanessa demanded. "Is that it? You're embarrassed you were married to me?"

"Of course not."

"Then what?"

He stared at a coffee stain on the table. "This really isn't my day."

"Out with it, bucko," she commanded.

"If you really *have* to know..." He could feel himself starting to lose his temper.

"I do."

"Damn it." Tucker's gaze narrowed at his ex-wife. "I hate parading my failures in front of people, okay?"

Vanessa chewed her lipstick, considering. In a less hostile tone, she asked, "And that's what I am, a failure?"

"No, of course not, Van." He stood up from the table impatiently. "*I'm* the failure. My parents have been married for forty years, and I can barely make a year and a half. That's a failure in anyone's book."

"Oh, Tucker, sometimes you're such a moron." Vanessa shook her head. "I think I'm getting a handle on this. You wanted Kristina to think you were this big success story who never made a mistake in his entire life, right?"

"You make it sound really stupid, but, yes, that's basically it."

"Spare me from wounded male pride," she said with a sigh. "Tucker, you're a great guy, and I love you dearly, but we should never have gotten married, at least not to each other. You know that better than I do."

"I suppose."

"We were hardly the love story of the century."

"I know."

"So what's the big deal? We were young and stupid and we mistook friendship for something more." She patted him kindly on the arm. "We made a mistake and we fixed it. End of problem."

Rehashing the end of their marriage was about his least favorite topic of conversation. "I hate feeling like a quitter."

She smiled cynically. "I don't recall giving you a choice."

"Can we please talk about something else?"

"Darling Tucker, I should've known you'd hide the fact that you'd been married, just on general principles. Deny, ignore, sidetrack." She sighed. "You're very good at clamming up."

He arched an eyebrow. "Are you saying I'm uncommunicative?"

"Heavens, no, not as long as it's someone else's problems you're discussing. You love to dissect everybody else." She examined her purple polished nails. "Maybe it's because you're an oldest. I've heard that's a pattern.

Anyway, you always want to jump in and fix things for other people, while remaining Mr. Perfect yourself."

"So?"

"So it's a big lie." Vanessa started to make exaggerated hand gestures, a sure sign she was getting into her little speech. "I'm doing you a favor telling you this. But somebody has to."

"Tell me what?"

"Santa's Magic Workshop."

"What about it?" he asked warily.

"It's going nowhere, and you'd better tell her that before she gets her heart set on it."

"What?" The vote at the board table had been unanimous. "You voted for it, Van! What the hell is going on?"

"I voted for it out of loyalty to you," she said primly.

If he'd ever understood women, he hadn't a clue at this moment. "Jesus, Van, what kind of line are you feeding me? You hate her idea but you voted for it because you think I want you to?"

"Tucker, this is the first proposal you've brought before the board since Harley retired. With just a preliminary okay like this, I knew you'd want it to be unanimous, to feel like the board is behind you, like we were always behind your dad."

He ran his hand through his hair so roughly that it hurt. "I don't care if it's unanimous or not," he argued. "All I wanted was for Kristina to get the chance to get her workshop made. It happens to be a great idea."

"It's also an extremely expensive idea," Vanessa replied stubbornly. "The kind of thing Trey keeps proposing and you keep telling him doesn't fly. And you're right."

"But Kristina's idea—"

"Is Kristina's," she finished for him. "And you love it because you're bananas over the girl. Well, sooner or later you'll learn that running a company means making hard choices. Maybe then you'll learn to say no, even if it hurts someone's feelings."

"Why do you think I can't say no if I need to?"

"What did you say when I asked you to marry me?" she inquired calmly.

"Yes."

"My point exactly." Without further comment, she marched for the door.

"Vanessa!" he shouted. "Don't you dare leave...."

But she had already swept out of the kitchen, and he could hear her heels clicking smartly on her way down the hall.

"Damn that woman," he muttered.

As far as he was concerned, Vanessa was being completely unfair. He wasn't being swayed by his feelings for Kristina; it was a damn good idea. After all, he'd been around the toy business his entire life, and he knew a good idea when he saw one.

Didn't he?

Damn right, I do, he told himself fiercely.

But a tiny, wispy, ghostlike figure of doubt—something with which he was quite unfamiliar—began to dance around the edges of his mind.

What was he going to do if Vanessa was right?

Chapter Ten

"Stop that, Nick," she complained. "Stop peeking around the drapes. He'll see you when he pulls up."

"Isn't he late?"

"Well, yes, a little, but he said he was busy with Toyland business, so he's probably just running a little behind schedule."

"Hmph." Nick didn't look pleased. "If this was to be a celebration, he should have made the effort to appear in a timely manner. I didn't judge Tucker to be the sort of person to let a mere job interfere when something really important called."

"His job *is* important."

"I suppose," Nick muttered. "But I'm still disappointed in that young man—"

His words were interrupted by the doorbell, and she threw an I-told-you-so smile at Nick. When she opened the door, Tucker beamed back at her, looking a lot more like the carefree renegade she expected than the cranky corporate type he'd been today. He was wearing a bulky sweater and disreputable jeans, with an orange-and-black letter jacket tossed over one shoulder. In the other hand, he was holding a single, long-stemmed white rose.

"For you," he said, offering it.

"Thank you." As she took the rose, she smiled at him, enjoying the moment and the soft, warm look in his blue eyes. "It's beautiful." And it was, far more beautiful than six dozen of any other color.

"Ahem," Nick interjected. "Perhaps you ought not stand there with the door open."

"Oh, right."

But Tucker declared, "It's starting to snow," and he tugged her halfway out the door, pulling her hand inside his, palm up, to try to catch wayward snowflakes.

They were the fat, fluffy kind, terrible for snowmen or snow forts, but the absolute best kind to create a fairy-tale Christmas mood. As the snowflakes danced lazily in the air outside Kristina's front door, one landed right in the center of her outstretched palm.

"Wonderful," she murmured, gazing down at the intricate, lacy little thing melting in her hand. It had been such a dreary winter so far, but this coating of snow seemed to make everything new and bright.

Tucker turned his face skyward and stuck out his tongue, catching a snowflake neatly. "Come on—get your coat. I have a surprise planned."

"A surprise?" She envisioned dinner in a posh restaurant or dancing at Chicago's trendiest club, and neither of them were dressed for that. In his outfit, he looked ready for a football game, and she wasn't all that much better, in her hand-knit sweater and corduroy pants. "What kind of surprise?"

"You'll see," he said, holding the rose as he helped her into her long wool coat. "Do you have mittens or a hat?"

"Well, yes, but..." She grabbed her mittens and a set of earmuffs, before narrowing her gaze at Tucker. "Are we doing something outside?"

He didn't answer, saying goodbye to Nick instead, and pulling Kristina along out to his Jeep. As he opened her door, the light hit two pairs of ice skates lying on the back seat.

"I thought you were kidding about the hockey thing," she said warily.

"Those aren't hockey skates. Can't you tell the difference?"

"Does this mean we're going ice-skating?" she asked doubtfully.

"Well, that was the plan. Unless you don't want to."

"I guess it's okay." She settled into the passenger seat, wondering what she was in for. "But I don't think I've ever done it before."

"No problem." He grinned and put the car in gear. "I'm good at it. I'll help you."

"Somehow I knew you were going to say that," she muttered under her breath.

AND TRUE TO FORM, he *was* good at it. A pro, it looked like to her untrained eyes. As he tried to con her into coming out on the ice, he slid backward easily, etching fine lines with the blades of his skates. He did a little loop, raced around for a quick lap, speed-skating-style and then shot her the sunniest smile this side of the equator.

Was there anything that made her feel that good? Her face flushed with warmth as her mind furnished the answer. *Kissing Tucker. Holding Tucker...*

"Are you coming out here?" he called.

"Where are we, anyway?" she asked, grabbing on to the wrought-iron base of a nearby street lamp for dear life.

"Park," he said breezily, spinning back in her direction with a flourish.

"I know it's a park." She gazed around at their surroundings, at the tall, dark trees, the impressive white pavilion behind them and the pretty little lake they were on, spanned by a curvy bridge that looked magical enough to have trolls underneath it. "You don't usually see lakes and trees and pavilions just standing around without a park."

"It's not a lake, it's a lagoon. This is Lord's Park, we're in Elgin and you're skating on a lagoon." His lips curved into a wry smile. "Or you would be skating, if you'd let go of that light pole and get out here."

Luckily, there were few skaters at the park tonight; perhaps the experts preferred indoor rinks when it was snowing. In any event, there would be hardly any witnesses when she fell down and made a fool of herself.

"Come on," he coaxed, holding out a hand. "You'll like it."

"That's what you said about dancing."

"And I was right, wasn't I?"

"Well, sort of," she admitted. Gingerly she let go of the streetlight long enough to stick her mittened hand carefully in his bare one. "Is the snow going to complicate this?"

"If you're Peggy Fleming, it may screw up your triple jump, but otherwise I think we're okay."

"Very funny." Before she noticed, he'd pulled her out onto the edge of the lagoon. The ice wasn't completely smooth under her faltering feet, and the light cover of snowflakes didn't help, but she supposed this halting, choppy thing she was doing was actually sort of like skating if you weren't too picky in your definition.

"See," Tucker said helpfully, "you're doing it."

As he kept an arm around her waist, holding her steady, she realized she was getting better at it. She began to look at Tucker instead of at her feet, to glide a little as she moved, to enjoy the feeling of frosty air nipping her nose and cheeks and the look of delicate snowflakes dusting the evergreens and piling up on the frozen grass. Instead of feeling like a total klutz, now she was only a bad skater. She laughed out loud at that idea.

"You're having fun, aren't you?" he asked smugly.

"Yes, I am, but don't look so proud of yourself." She brushed a snowy mitten against the top of his head, ruffling his untidy hair and working snow into it.

"Hey," he objected, catching her hand and pulling her almost off her feet. And then, "Hey," in a different, more intimate tone, when she circled her arms around his waist, and turned up her face to be kissed. "Kristina, Kristina," he murmured. "We're in the middle of a pond and people are watching. Are you starting what I think you're starting?"

"You said it was a lagoon, not a pond. And nobody's looking at us. Besides," she declared, "I think this is a very romantic place, and I didn't want to waste it."

"So you like this place, huh?" he inquired softly.

"I like the company," she added.

He smiled as he bent his head to hers, and his lips were as cool and surprising as the breeze around them. He linked his arms over hers, edging closer, and the temperature began to soar.

If his lips were chilly, the inside of his mouth was warm and willing, and she pressed closer, kissing him harder and longer.

"I'm not sure I've ever been kissed in the cold before," she said breathlessly.

"There are so many things you haven't done," he whispered. "Why don't you make a list, and we'll see how many we can hit?"

"Okay."

"Okay." And he smiled again, that reckless, naughty smile he did so well.

With the snowflakes falling, dancing and spinning around them, nothing seemed quite real except the strength of Tucker's arms.

"This is wonderful," she murmured.

He kissed her cheek, near her earmuff. "Uh-huh."

The outside world began to come into hazy focus. "But there's a whole family watching us."

"Yeah, I know."

"You knew?" She batted at his shoulder. "You saw all those people staring at us, and you kept...nuzzling me?"

"You started it."

"They weren't there when I started it!"

He held up his hands. "What could I do?"

"You could've told me," she persisted.

"You're impossible," he told her, as he gently detached his arm of support, so that she had to manage under her own steam.

"So are you," she returned, and she skated off just fine by herself. It was a little shaky at first, but then she got her feet going the right way, and she took a few nice strokes, gliding over the ice like a champ.

Showing off his athletic grace, he skated around behind her, but she kept going. "Hey, Krissie, you're getting good at this."

"What am I, your personal reclamation project or something?" she grumbled. "So you feel personally responsible for filling in the holes in my résumé?"

He glided farther away, daring her to follow. "I'm just trying to make up for your stunted adulthood—no dancing, no skating—sheesh!"

"It's not just my adulthood." She stuck out her tongue at him as she slipped serenely past and then spun back in his direction, feeling like she was ready for the Ice Capades. "I didn't do this stuff when I was a kid, either."

He stopped. "Why not?"

"The question, my dear Tucker, is why?"

She wasn't quite sure how to put on the brakes, so she just sort of drifted into him, knowing he would catch her. And he did. As he braced her hands in his, holding her at arms' length, she finished her thoughts about her less-than-exciting childhood.

"I was brought up," she said as she caught her breath, "to do things for a reason. I learned to roller-skate because I could get a Girl Scout badge for it. But ice-skating came with no badge, so it was worthless in my household." She shrugged. "And after I got my roller-skating badge, I never did it again, so I guess it doesn't make much difference one way or the other."

"But that's no fun. In fact," he decided, "that's downright un-American, subverting fun into work like that."

"I'll bet you did every sport imaginable," she teased. "I'll bet you were a seventeen-sport jock in high school, when you earned your letters." She tapped the intertwined *S* and *C*, for St. Charles High School, on the front of his jacket. "And all the girls swooned, didn't they?"

He scowled and shoved his hands in his pockets. "I don't want to talk about it."

"Tucker?" She was frankly surprised. "If you weren't an athlete in high school, there's nothing to be ashamed of. I was just kidding around."

"I was a jock, okay? Four sports. Not seventeen." His scowl grew darker. "Nobody can do seventeen, even if

there are that many sports, because the seasons overlap.''
And then he pushed off and skated away.

"Tucker," she called after him, "four sports is fine.
Really!" When he didn't respond, she muttered, "Now
what did I do?"

By the time she caught him, he had his unconcerned
face on again, and she knew she wasn't going to find out
what was wrong. But she decided it was worth a try, anyway.

"You know," she said, grabbing his jacket, so he'd pull
her along in his wake if he skated off. "You know, you're
really a pain sometimes. What's with this silent treat-
ment?"

His face was a study in unconcern. "I don't know what
you mean."

"Oh, yes, you do." She shook her head, tossing the
long waves of her hair back over her shoulder. "You have
these taboo subjects, and when I hit one, it's like this
curtain comes down. And what could be taboo about your
high school sports career?"

"Nothing," he insisted. "I just don't want to talk about
it."

"But why?" At his enigmatic shrug, she swore under
her breath. "You did the same thing earlier today, when
I asked you about why you were so grumpy, and when I
asked why you hadn't warned me about your ex-wife."
She mimicked him, "'I don't want to talk about it.' Well,
I deserve some answers, you know!"

"This is the second time today someone has accused me
of clamming up," he muttered.

"So are you beginning to see some truth in it?"

"Do you really want to know?" he demanded.

"Yes, I really want to know."

"Okay, come on, then."

With her hand in his, he raced off the ice, towing her along behind him. He sat down on a bench and began to work at the laces of his skates.

"So what do you want to hear first?" he asked bleakly.

"You don't have to act like this is torture."

His gaze came up slowly. "It is torture."

She tried not to smile, and she bent to remove her own skates. "Okay, well, why don't we start with the sports thing? That can't be too revealing."

"It's embarrassing," he contended.

"Try me."

"Well, you were right. I was a big jock in high school."

She couldn't tell if his pink cheeks were due to the cold weather or a hot blush, but she could make a guess. "Go on."

"It was what you said about the girls swooning." He sighed. "They did. But it had nothing to do with me—the person I was—just with how many points I scored on the field. And I hated it."

"You hated all the attention?"

"Well, yeah. The girls used to leave stuff in my locker—like underwear. Classic bimbo games, and I got really tired of it." He clenched his jaw. "Which leads to your next question—Vanessa."

She sat forward, shocked. "Vanessa left underwear in your locker?"

"Of course not." He laughed out loud at the very idea. "I met Van in college, where I was doing a lot of sports, and running into the same problems with these dumb girls. Van and I became friends, and having her around kept the bimbos away, so we sort of stuck together. And then we got married because everybody expected us to by that point."

"You got married because everyone expected you to?" Kristina stared at him, completely astonished. "Did you ever think about love or commitment or anything?"

"No, and we should have." He shook his head gloomily. "It was a major mistake."

"So, Tucker, tell me..." She took his hand in between her mittens. "Why didn't you warn me about Vanessa before the board meeting? It really would've been the best thing to do."

"I know. She told me that, too."

"She told you, too?" She didn't want to hate his ex-wife, but she was getting close. He'd discussed it with Vanessa, but brushed Kristina off with "I don't want to talk about it." It was truly irritating.

"And I'll tell you what I told her—I don't like parading my failures in front of people." Abruptly he stood up and looked out at the skaters on the lagoon.

"You act like nobody ever got divorced before." She said lightly, "There are a lot of failures running around out there if divorce is all it takes."

"Yeah, well, I take marriage seriously." His jaw was a hard, firm line. "And I don't like failing at anything."

"Tucker," she ventured, beginning to see where this was leading, "have we gotten to Taboo Number Three now?"

"Huh?"

"You know—why you were in a bad mood at Toyland today—why you and your brother and sister were fighting in the hall." She chewed her lip thoughtfully. "Something's wrong at Toyland, isn't it?"

"No," he said tersely, "it isn't."

She rose to stand next to him, trying to get him to meet her gaze. "I saw what kind of mood you were in today, and I think I've got it figured out. Things are going wrong at Toyland, and you feel like a failure—Tucker's taboo.''

"I really don't want to talk about this.''

"You always say that," she mocked. "I'm not paying any attention to it anymore. And you know, this is one case where I might actually be able to help, if you told me what was wrong.''

That got his attention. "How?" he asked cynically.

"You may not realize it, but I am a good manager. A damn good manager.''

"Is that why you're always running away from Austin's?''

"No," she said coolly, "it's not. I like what I do, but not where I do it. I happen to be a good manager stuck in an impossible situation. My mother is married to my boss, who didn't want to hire me, but my mother forced him. So he dislikes me, plus all the other managers spy on me because they think I got my job unfairly. It's lovely.''

"So why do you stay?''

"It's complicated," she mumbled.

"Isn't it always?''

"We weren't talking about my job," she reminded him. "We were discussing yours. And I could help you, if you'd let me. If it's the workload that's bothering you, you can learn to prioritize, make lists. Have you ever heard of the One Minute Manager?''

"That's not the problem.''

"Then what is?" When he didn't respond, she started to ponder the issue for herself. "It's Trey, isn't it? Every time I've been at Toyland, Trey's been on your back. So he's making trouble, maybe ratting on you to your dad or something, like he was threatening that night in the playroom, and now you're mad at him, and he's mad at you, and everybody's crabby.'' The look on his face told her she'd hit the nail on the head. "I told you I was a good manager. One of the primary skills is ESP."

"I believe it," he muttered, jamming his hands into his pockets.

"So what to do about Trey?" she mused. "Well, I'd start by letting the whole board hear Trey's proposals, so it's not just you passing judgment and setting up this adversarial thing. And then I'd—"

"Look, Kristina," he interrupted. "I appreciate your suggestions, but I don't really need this."

"So I'm wrong?"

"Actually, you're mostly right." He kicked at the light snow covering. "But I can handle it. By myself."

"You're a fine one for handing out advice, but you can't take it, huh?"

"What's that supposed to mean?"

"It means," she returned smartly, "that you keep harping at me to do what I like, follow my dreams, ignore the pressure to conform, when you haven't got the guts to do it yourself."

"That's nonsense."

"Oh, yeah?" She didn't like her ideas being rejected out of hand, and she didn't appreciate being told she was spouting nonsense. "Well, I think you aren't a good president because you don't like being president, and you're too chicken to admit that maybe you should be in a different job."

"That is enough," he said angrily. "You stand there and call me chicken when you're scared of your own mother?"

"I am not!"

"Have you told her?"

"Told her what?"

"About Santa's Magic Workshop. About your father." Grimly, he added, "About me."

She was too stung to reply.

"Yeah, that's what I thought." He said softly, dangerously, "Until you get your own house in order, maybe you'd better lay off mine."

Kristina pressed her lips together firmly, but said nothing. Although she was furious with him, she knew there was truth to what he said. And that made it all the more aggravating.

She crossed her arms over her chest. "Could you take me home now, please? I'm freezing. I always did hate winter sports."

"Fine."

"Fine."

She refused to be the one to break the silence. It hung there all the way home, like an extra person in the car with them. When Tucker pulled to a stop in front of her house, she got out and sped up the walk before he had a chance to move. Behind her, she heard his car squeal away into the night.

"I take it your evening didn't go well?" Nick asked, as she raced past him up the stairs.

"You take it right," she said savagely.

AUSTIN'S WAS IN the full euphoria of the Christmas season. The decorations were lush and beautiful, the music sweet and sentimental and thousands of shoppers were taking advantage of the last week and a half before Christmas by piling up debt on their Austin's credit cards.

Kristina was late. Monday morning, ten days before Christmas, was no time to come in late, but she'd stayed up last night fussing with the chimney on the Magic Workshop, and now she'd overslept. Arriving with the customers, she found no parking space and jam-packed elevators.

As she raced down the hall in her tennis shoes, juggling coat, briefcase, purse and shoe bag, her secretary came running out of the office, frantically signaling her.

"Thank God!" Polly cried, awkwardly taking the coat and the briefcase while Kristina struggled to change shoes. "Finally! I thought you were never going to get here. Windy, er, Mr. Austin, that is, and your mother have been calling for the past hour, trying to get a meeting ASAP. I told them you were on the floor, checking a shipment in Gourmet or something, but Windy is—"

"Okay," Kristina interrupted calmly, before Polly could overflow with more words. "Where are they? Windy's office? I'll get right up there. You take all this stuff in, okay?"

"Right." Laden down under a pile of Kristina's personal belongings, Polly headed back for the office. "Oh." She wheeled back toward Kristina. "I almost forgot. I think Windy said it was about the windows."

"Windows?"

"The big ones—the displays. Charles Dickens, you know."

Of course it was about the big window displays on Michigan Avenue. Where was her head? "I'll just grab the file and be on my way."

"Thank God," Polly muttered.

The executive offices were up one more floor, but made use of the same elevators that shoppers and store staff rode on. Rather than spend extra moments waiting for the elevator to disgorge and take on passengers at every retail floor before it got up to the offices on six, Kristina decided to take the stairs up to what was euphemistically called the "Garden Level."

It had originally been a real rooftop garden, and in the old days, they'd had a fashion show and given away free Easter lilies every year to celebrate the store's anniversary.

But the garden and the Easter extravaganza went the way of nickel candy bars; they got to be much too expensive to keep up. So the Austins rebuilt the garden level into elegant offices for a handful of company bigwigs . . . including, of course, chairman of the board Mirabel and her president son, Windy.

Quickly getting past the obstacle of two guard-dog secretaries, Kristina approached the big glass doors to Windy's inner sanctum with more than a hint of nerves. She'd never really felt comfortable with her mother's new husband, even though Bitsy constantly tried to pretend they were all the best of pals.

She raised her hand to knock, and then withdrew it, unsure. There was, after all, no need to announce herself, since the glass doors gave away the presence of visitors.

"Come in," Windham Forbes Austin IV barked, and she forced herself to march in.

Windy was a small, slender man, always dressed to the nines, and yet always rumpled-looking somehow. Today, his monogrammed shirtsleeve hung too far below the sleeve of his expensive jacket, and his silk tie was just a tad askew.

"Hello, dear," her mother murmured beside him, in the quietly respectful tone she always used around Windy. Tastefully dressed in a pink cashmere suit, with just the perfect note of expensive perfume, Bitsy strolled over and brushed a kiss in the general area of Kristina's cheek. "So busy, darling?"

Windy wasted no time on chitchat. "Is there some catastrophe I don't know about in the gourmet department?" he asked, referring to Polly's excuse for Kristina's whereabouts.

"All taken care of," she said quickly. Once this lie business got started, the lies really began to pile up, didn't they?

"All right then, let's get down to business." Windy braced himself on his huge desk. A button popped off the front of his shirt and went sailing out into his extraplush carpet, but he ignored it. "What's the meaning of those windows?"

"The Dickens windows, sir?"

"Exactly."

She waited for further explanation of the problem, but Windy only frowned and said nothing.

"Windy doesn't care for the theme, dear," her mother offered helpfully. "He thinks perhaps something more modern would be nice."

"I see." How did one diplomatically tell the president of one's company that he was being utterly and completely ridiculous? "I understand your feelings, Mr. Austin, but there are a few..." She paused, searching for inspiration. "A few complications. As I'm sure you're aware, we are featuring a Victorian Christmas theme store-wide, and I'm afraid something more modern wouldn't really fit."

Windy glared at her, and her mother pressed her lips together, looking dismayed.

But she had no choice. "We do our Christmas windows in three-year cycles," she explained. "The Dickens windows are on their last year... their last few weeks actually. Next year we'll have something you like, I'm sure, sir."

"Next year is a long way away, Miss Castleberry."

Technically, next year was less than three weeks away, but she wasn't foolish enough to mention that.

"I wish I could help, Mr. Austin, but I feel my hands are tied." Maybe he would respect a little honesty. Lord knew he got precious little of it from the rest of the yes-men at Austin's. "Even if we redesigned the displays, we couldn't possibly get them together in the time left before Christmas. We normally have those windows mapped out years ahead." She hated to remind him, but... "As a matter of fact, sir, you okayed the designs for next year's windows several months ago."

"All right then, we understand," Bitsy said brightly. "I'll walk you out, dear."

As soon as they'd cleared the double glass doors, Bitsy demanded, "Where were you this morning? We were waiting for over an hour."

"Didn't my secretary tell you I was down in Gourmet, trying to fix a problem?"

"Darling, I wasn't born yesterday. I know a secretary covering for her boss when I hear one." She pushed Kristina toward Windy's outer office, away from his line of vision. "Not that it matters where you were," she continued, in an acid tone. "What matters is that you were not here when you should have been, and from what Windy says, you're neglecting your job responsibilities terribly."

"I am not!" she protested.

"Well, Windy says the other managers are complaining that you come in late and leave early, and that you pay no attention when they tell you about matters that need to be taken care of."

The Austin's spy network was out in full force, as usual.

"Plus," Bitsy added, "Windy tried to get hold of you several times last week to discuss this windows thing, and you were never available! What kind of work ethic is that?"

"I had several doctor's appointments." Kristina quickly improvised. "You know, that flu bug I had. But I was here all day Saturday, trying to get through my paperwork, and part of Sunday, too."

Bitsy waved a negligent hand. "I know, I know. But darling, appearances are everything. If it *appears* you're being lazy, that's all that counts, even if you're working your little tail off in reality." She draped a small, cashmere-clad arm around her daughter. "Now what you need to do is put in lots of hours between now and Christmas, so you don't give the other sharks any ammunition. And make sure you see Windy several times a day, just in passing, so *he* sees *you* looking busy. Appearances are everything," Bitsy repeated.

"Yes, but..." But she had to get the workshop prototype finished by December 24, and she had no extra time to give to "being seen" at Austin's.

"No buts, darling. You'll do as I tell you if you want to keep your job here."

"Yes, Mother."

Her toy design was a mess anyway, so how could she risk her job by continuing to concentrate on Santa's Magic Workshop?

The job at Austin's might be all she had to hold on to by the time Christmas rolled around. She couldn't afford to lose it.

Chapter Eleven

She concentrated completely on work all day, and even though she felt like a slime, she made sure anyone who was anyone saw her acting busy and competent.

The floor manager in Children's put in a call a few minutes before three, and Kristina hustled right down there to see what the crisis was this time. She sincerely hoped it wasn't Nick.

"Some kid tried to get on the rocking horse with one of the singing teddy bears," the supervisor explained. "He fell off, and the mother said she'd sue. Do you think we should replace all the rocking horses with something else?"

What else? she wanted to scream. Why had these people chosen today to suggest dumping half the Christmas decorations?

"No," Kristina responded, "I do not think we should get rid of the horses. Why don't we set up some ropes, like the ones around Santa's area, to cordon off the displays so kids can't jump on them?"

This less drastic solution was acceptable to the floor manager, and Kristina scribbled a note to herself to find more red velvet cord before the day was out.

As she walked back through the children's department on her way to the elevator, she had to maneuver around the lines of children waiting to see Nick.

She smiled fondly. At least Nick had worked out. In fact, he was wonderful. At the moment, he was sitting cozily on his velvet wing chair, wearing his dark maroon robe and a holly wreath on his head, and he looked the very picture of Saint Nicholas.

Watching Nick chat amiably with a small girl in a hideous red taffeta dress, Kristina crossed her arms over the file folder she was carrying. She hadn't had a chance to tell Nick about her run-in with her mother and Windy, or her newfound determination to make Austin's her first priority at the expense of Santa's Magic Workshop. Nick was not going to be pleased.

If only she could perch on Nick's lap and get a few Christmas wishes. Or maybe a little reassurance that she was doing the right thing.

"Checking up on Santa?" a deep, haughty voice asked at her elbow.

She glanced down to see Mirabel Austin's beady eyes giving her the once-over.

"Uh, yes," she said. "He seems to be working out rather well, don't you think?"

"Until he made that child cry," Mirabel put in dryly.

"What child?"

"The one on his lap right now."

"But she was fine a second ago," Kristina noted.

Mirabel raised a very thin eyebrow. "She's wailing. I don't like wailing in my store. I suggest you take care of it."

"Right away," she murmured.

Under Mirabel's watchful eye, Kristina skirted around the crowd of anxious children and made her way to the front of the line. She had no idea what she could do to stop a child from crying, but she'd give it her best shot.

As she approached Nick's chair, she heard the little girl howl, "But Mommy won't let me! Even if you bring the Down 'N' Dirty Dump Truck set, Mommy won't let me play with it."

This child did not look like someone who needed a Down 'N' Dirty Dump Truck. In her overdone ruffles and bows, she seemed more suited to a toddler beauty pageant.

"Is the dump truck what you really want, Brandee?" Nick asked kindly.

"Yes, Santa." The little girl sniffed. "I wanted it my whole life."

"Your whole life? My, my."

"But Mommy says girls don't play with dirty toys."

"Oh, my." Nick clucked his tongue sympathetically.

"My Uncle Buddy drives a dump truck," Brandee said eagerly, swiping at her tears with one grubby little hand. "He let me ride in it. It was my favorite thing in my whole life. I want to grow up and drive a dump truck, too, like Uncle Buddy."

"And so you shall." Nick beamed at his small charge. "Santa Claus will bring you the very Down 'N' Dirty Dump Truck you desire, and for this very Christmas. When your mommy sees how much you like it, I'm sure she'll let you play with it. Everyone should have a dream, Brandee, and if your dream is to grow up and drive a dump truck, then Santa will help you make your dream come true."

"Promise?" Brandee asked solemnly.

"I promise."

Kristina felt like crying herself.

"Thank you, thank you, thank you, Santa!" Brandee stuck her chubby arms around Nick's neck and gave him a big smack on the cheek before tumbling to the floor and racing off to find her mother.

"Nick," Kristina whispered. "Do you think that was wise? What's going to happen when she doesn't get the dump truck?"

"But she will get it," he said placidly. "I promised."

"Nick, even if you talk to her mother, you can't promise that."

"Certainly I can."

As usual, she was getting nowhere with Nick. For all she knew, he was planning to buy the Down 'N' Dirty Dump Truck himself and hand-deliver it to Brandee's chimney. She wouldn't have put it past him.

"So you're in the business of making dreams come true, huh?"

"Well, I suppose so." He smiled wistfully. "There's nothing that makes me sadder than unrealized dreams."

"Me, either." Suddenly it seemed they were talking about *her* dreams again, as always. "Nick, there's something I have to tell you."

"Yes?"

"About Santa's Magic Workshop..."

"Going great guns, I hope," he offered cheerily.

There was no way; she simply couldn't tell him. And why not? Because she wasn't ready to give up on the workshop yet. The hell with her job at Austin's if she couldn't let it slide long enough to do what she knew in her heart she had to do.

"Yes," she said brightly. "It's going great guns. Brandee has her dump truck and I have my dream, too. Let's hope we both get them."

"Indeed." He motioned for the next child to come up, and Kristina waved goodbye.

She bypassed the elevators and took the stairs instead, in too much of a hurry to negotiate all those people and packages.

Ignoring Polly and the handful of message slips she was waving, Kristina barged right into her office and began to dial the phone.

"Mother? I'm glad I caught you. It's Kristina. Can you have lunch with me tomorrow? There's something I need to talk to you about."

SHE WAS NERVOUS, but ready. For the eleventh time, she pulled out the list and went over it again.

Things to tell Mother:
1—Santa's Magic Workshop is important to me and I want to pursue it.
2—I know where my father is, and I want to contact him.

And then there was number 3.

I want to see Tucker again.

She'd sort of scratched that on at the end, after the other neatly typed parts. She wasn't quite sure why.

It was strange how wound up in all this Tucker had become. She didn't think of him as part of her dream, but in a way, he was inextricably entangled, part and parcel of the whole toy design thing. Her thoughts kept returning to him, whether she wanted them to or not.

She'd tried to work on the model by herself since that fatal ice-skating date. But it hadn't gone very well. And she knew in her heart that he was right; she did need his help. She needed his know-how with toys, but she also needed his laughter and his jokes, his way of making things seem okay even when they weren't.

Maybe it wouldn't be so bad to be rescued.

"Hello, sweetheart. Sorry if I'm late."

Kristina hastily stuck the list in her lap, as Bitsy breezed in and tossed her alligator bag and fur coat over the empty chair at their table.

"Love this place." Bitsy picked up her lace-edged napkin. "I'm so glad they decided to redo it."

Bitsy said that every time they came to the Tea Room, Austin's delicate, feminine fourth-floor restaurant. It was right next to Posh, the ultraexclusive boutique where Bitsy had spent her retail years, so Kristina could understand her mother feeling a proprietary interest in the pretty little place.

Kristina had chosen the Tea Room for their lunch with Bitsy's goodwill in mind. Plus, it was in the middle of Austin's, surrounded by people who knew Windy Austin and his wife, so Kristina's mother wouldn't be able to shriek too loudly.

After setting her napkin ever so carefully in her lap, Bitsy began to examine the pale lavender menu. "They're no longer offering the cucumber soup. Isn't that distressing?"

Kristina was in no mood for cucumber soup talk. "Mother," she said, strengthening her resolve, "I asked you to meet me for a reason. There's something I need to tell you."

Bitsy closed her menu. "It's that Tucker Bennett, isn't it? You're still seeing him."

Blast it, anyway. Tucker was number three on the list! Things were out of order, and she hadn't even begun.

"Well, actually I'm not seeing Tucker. I did, but we argued, and now I haven't for..." She counted quickly. "Four days." It seemed a lot longer.

"So you've been lying to me."

"In my heart, Mother, I've been lying to both of us for years."

"Kristina, how could you?" Bitsy hissed under her breath, darting glances at the other tables to see if there was anyone she knew.

"Mother, we're getting sidetracked. I had an order I wanted to keep to, so that this would be, you know, orderly."

"There's nothing orderly about a daughter lying to her mother." Bitsy sniffed. "Why did you decide to tell me now? Guilt? Or are you planning to marry the man, or something equally dreadful, so you didn't have a choice?"

Kristina began to get angry. "You won't give me a chance to talk."

"So talk. Talk away. It won't make any difference." Bitsy sat back and pretended to gaze around the Tea Room, as if she hadn't a care in the world.

"Mother, listen to me. This isn't about Tucker. It's about Daddy," she said flatly.

"What?" Bitsy choked. She leaned forward angrily. "You'd better explain yourself, my girl."

"Mother, I'm not your girl anymore. I think we'd better get that straight. I'm twenty-nine years old, and I make my own decisions." Immediately, she cringed at how harsh she sounded.

"Kristina! This isn't like you at all. I knew that horrid Bennett person would be a bad influence."

"Let's drop Tucker for right now, okay? I'm not ready to discuss him."

"No, you want to discuss—" Bitsy dropped her voice as if to even mention him were scandalous "—your father."

Kristina folded her hands in her lap. "You can't expect a person to go for nineteen years without seeing her father and not even be curious."

"So be curious. So what?"

"Let's start at the beginning. You remember the Toyland contest over ten years ago, right?"

"This has been going on for ten years?"

"Mother," she warned. "The Tuesday before Thanksgiving—this Thanksgiving—I found out that Toyland, Tucker's company, liked the idea I had entered in the contest. I went to Toyland and I told them about it." She said softly, "That's when I met Tucker."

"Wonderful," Bitsy said sarcastically.

"My idea—it was called Santa's Magic Workshop. Do you remember?"

"No," her mother said curtly. "I try very hard to forget things like that."

"Look, it isn't my fault that he left you!" she said passionately. "And it isn't my workshop's fault, either. Now you know why I keep things from you—because you snipe at me and insult me. I hate it."

Her mother sat very stiffly. "I beg your pardon. Please continue. I'm most anxious to hear what it is you've been keeping from me."

"The Toyland people like my idea," Kristina declared, with only a hint of defensiveness. "They're going to decide if they want to market it."

"I'm still listening."

"It's important to me, to know if it can be something. All my life, I wanted to design toys, and this is my chance." She swallowed around the constriction in her throat. "You were right yesterday when you said I'd been taking time away from Austin's. I have. To work on my design. I know you don't want me to have anything to do with toys, because of Daddy. But I have to."

"Even if it breaks my heart?"

"Mother, this isn't fair."

"I don't care." Bitsy threw her napkin down on the table, almost overturning her water glass. "I hate that man. I hate him. I won't let you have anything to do with him."

"I know where he is."

"I knew it." Bitsy's mouth twisted in a bitter grimace. "You're going to see him, aren't you?"

"He's my father."

"And a terrific father he was, too," Bitsy said with a sneer. "Where was he when you needed him? Where was he all those years?"

"I don't know."

"You bet you don't know. He couldn't have cared less whether you were alive or dead." She stood up and reached for her coat. "And now you're going to find him and stage some Hallmark Hall of Fame reunion. Well, go right ahead. But don't ask for my approval. I won't be there."

Without another word, Bitsy Austin marched out of the Tea Room, drawing curious glances from the other diners.

"Well, now I've done it," Kristina whispered.

She had avoided conflict her entire life, and now here she was, striding right into it like a prizefighter. It was no wonder her stomach felt queasy and her head hurt. Arguing like this, with claws unsheathed, was her worst nightmare.

She crumpled her unused list of things to tell her mother and tossed the little ball onto the table.

"The good news is," she said out loud, "that part's over."

And the bad news? The bad news was that there was no taking it back. Maybe Mother would come around, and maybe she wouldn't.

When she got back to her office, Kristina told Polly to hold all her messages.

"I have something I have to do," she said quietly. "I'll be gone the rest of the afternoon."

THE CAR DROVE ITSELF to Toyland. It wasn't her fault.

Right inside the front door, she stumbled over Tegan, who was headed in the other direction. Tucker's younger sister was looking even more frazzled than usual.

"Kristina, hi," she offered gloomily.

"Hello, Tegan. How are you?"

Heaving a heavy sigh, Tegan said, "Don't ask."

She started to walk past, but Kristina stopped her, laying a tentative hand on Tegan's arm. "Look, Tegan, it's none of my business, but you don't seem very happy here."

"I hate it," Tegan announced. "Detest, abhor and despise it. I hate toys, and I hate Toyland."

Kristina was astonished at her companion's vehemence. "So why don't you leave?"

"Because Tucker would kill me."

"No, he wouldn't." Kristina smiled, thinking of Tucker's lectures on deciding for yourself, doing what *you* want. "It's your decision, not his. If you're clear in your own mind that you don't want to work at Toyland, then you should leave. It's as simple as that."

"You really think Tucker would be okay with it?"

Kristina nodded. She wasn't all that sure, because after all, he was a pushy kind of guy, and he always seemed to think he knew what was best for everyone, especially his family members. But she had to put on a brave face for Tegan. The poor girl was miserable!

Tegan seemed to consider the idea for a moment. Then she said, with a note of surprise in her voice, "I just may do it."

"Go for it, kid."

"Thanks, Kristina!" Tegan went skipping away with a positive spring in her step. She called back, "Oh, by the way, if you're looking for Tucker, he's upstairs in his apartment. Do you know where it is?"

She knew only too well, especially the blue couch that swallowed you up if you weren't careful. "Is he, uh, mad at me, do you think?"

"He's pretty grumpy, but that's nothing new." Tegan shrugged. "I never have understood Tucker, to tell you the truth."

Me, either. But now was her chance.

Four flights of stairs had never seemed so long, especially the last one, that funny, curvy set of steps between the third floor and Tucker's apartment.

She hesitated there in the narrow passage, deciding whether or not to knock, when Tucker's voice trapped her where she stood.

"Come in," he called out. "Door's open."

Like the first time she'd heard it, his voice sounded deep and rich, a little mysterious, a little dark. She remembered thinking then that his voice had the power to undress her, to seep in under her clothes and physically touch her.

She remembered.

"Tucker?" She pushed the door open a few inches, so that she could talk to him without actually having to see him yet. "It's me. I know you might not want to see me after the other night, but I need to talk to you."

"Kristina?" He yanked the door open the rest of the way from the other side. "What are you doing here?"

He didn't look thrilled to see her. His face was flushed, his jaw was clenched and his hair was a worse mess than usual, as if he'd been raking both hands through it in opposite directions. He was wearing a gray Mickey Mouse sweatshirt with gym shorts and untied black high-tops, and he was carrying a basketball under one arm. His shorts were dangerously short, scooped up on the sides well into his thighs, and in the front... Well, the front was something she wasn't going to look at or think about, not even on a bet.

She focused on a spot near the laces on his left sneaker. It seemed the safest spot. "I need to talk to you," she repeated.

"What about?"

"Can I come in?"

He stepped back, silently answering her question as he allowed her to come inside his crazy apartment.

Like his hair, the apartment looked as though it had been roughed up since she saw it last. Even more debris littered the floor, and the elaborate spaceship built out of blocks was now only rubble.

Carelessly balancing the basketball on the tips of his fingers, Tucker remained near the door. He seemed to be waiting for her to speak.

When she didn't, he bounced the ball exactly twice, and then sent it careening all the way across the room, arcing as it neared the hoop, catching nothing but net as it swished through.

"Nice shot." She wished she knew how to whistle.

"Thanks," he said as he jogged over to retrieve his ball. "Want to try?"

"Ah, no. Tucker?"

"Yeah?" He half turned toward her as he put up a lay-up.

"I did it."

"What do you mean?"

"I told my mother everything. Came clean, so to speak."

He dropped the ball. "That's great. I'm glad for you."

She shrugged. "Maybe. The jury's still out." She managed a wan smile. "But you were right. I do, uh, need you." Lord, this was hard. Harder even than confessing her sins to her mother. "If you're still willing to help me."

"Of course. What is it you want me to do?"

His eyes were full of warm concern. *Of course,* he'd said, without hesitation. At that moment, gazing into the blue of his beautiful eyes, she knew she'd done the right thing by coming here.

"What is it I want you to do?" she echoed. *Rescue me?*

She chose to begin with the easiest part. "First off, there's the Magic Workshop. It's not going so well, and I thought maybe I could bring the pieces over to the playroom, if you wouldn't mind helping me put it together."

"Actually, I'd love to," he admitted. "I haven't had the chance to really put something together from the bottom up since back in my Design days. It would be great to get my hands on a project like that."

"Good. That's a relief."

His gaze was curious. "Is that it?"

She took a deep breath, and carefully picked her way through the debris in his apartment, to perch on the edge of the big blue sofa. Then she fished a very crumpled piece of notepaper out of her coat pocket, smoothing it out and setting it square in the middle of the tree-stump coffee table. "I've decided I want to contact my father. Will you help me?"

"What can I do? Write the letter? Dial the phone?"

"Either," she admitted. "Or maybe just hold my hand?"

The spark of mischief she recognized returned to Tucker's eyes. "Hand-holding is available."

"Great," she said with heartfelt relief.

He joined her on the couch, settling in with a whoosh of cushions. "So what are you going to say to him?"

"I don't know. Hello? How are you? Nothing seems appropriate for someone I haven't seen in almost twenty years."

"You could ask him about his toy designs," he suggested. "We know he's still doing those. That way, you'd have something in common."

"Right." It all came back to toys, one way or the other. "You know, he might be more likely to come back if you asked him," she said suddenly. "Toyland is everything he's always wanted." Extracting herself from the depths of the couch far enough to turn toward Tucker, she thumped his bare knee with the excitement of this brainstorm. "A job with Toyland! Tucker, it's perfect!"

"You want me to offer him a job?" he asked slowly.

"Could you? For me? I know his ideas have always been crackpot, but maybe if he were here, under supervision, he'd improve." Was it so very much to ask?

Tucker carefully removed himself from the sofa. "Is this the real reason you came here and apologized? So I could hire your father?"

"No," she insisted. "I wouldn't do that. Besides, I just this minute thought of it."

"I don't know if I can." He picked a tennis ball up off the floor and pitched it at a bucket of balls. He missed.

"If it's the money, I could pay his salary for a while." This was getting more preposterous by the second. Where would she get that kind of money? "Don't you see? I want to get him here. Seeing me isn't enough. I've been here for nineteen years and he hasn't come back. But if he had a job at Toyland..." She plucked at the sleeve of Tucker's sweatshirt. "Please?"

"Okay," he said tersely. "I'll hire him. For now. But if he doesn't work out, he doesn't work out, and he goes. Understood?"

She nodded eagerly.

"And Kristina?"

"Yes?"

"I don't want to think that you're using me for the favors I can do for you." His voice was soft, unsure. "That's not it, is it?"

"No." She took his long, narrow fingers in between both her hands, and fixed him with her most sincere expression. "If you want to know the truth, I was hoping this would be a two-way street. That I'd ask for your help, and you'd ask for mine."

There was a pause. "I think I'd like that," he said finally.

"Whatever I can do—all you have to do is ask."

"So maybe I should start making lists and using the One Minute Manager, huh?" He didn't look thrilled at the prospect.

"All in good time," she said with a smile.

"Okay, but there's one thing I want you to know." His gaze dropped to their clasped hands. "It means a lot to me that you came to me with this. I've...I've never felt about anyone the way I feel—"

"Tucker, you don't have to—"

"No, I want to," he insisted. "I want you to know how I feel." He brought his free hand up to her cheek, and he brushed it lightly with the edge of his thumb. "I've never wanted anyone the way I want you."

"Me, too," she whispered. "And it scares me."

"Me, too."

Now that she'd started this total honesty business, it was impossible to stop. The truth was spilling out all over. "After the argument with my mother, the only person I wanted to talk to was you."

"God, I missed you," he said roughly. He pulled her over into his lap and held her, hard, for a long moment, cradling her head on his shoulder.

"Can we start over?" she asked.

"There's something we need to get out of the way first."

Without another word, he plucked the small white sheet of paper off the coffee table, and then hauled the phone up into his lap. He punched out the numbers so fast, they were a blur to Kristina.

"I'm calling for George Castleberry," he said into the receiver, and Kristina's heart stood still.

Tucker waited, she assumed for some kind of response on the other end. And then he squeezed Kristina's hand, and gazed at her with silent support.

"Mr. Castleberry? There's someone here who wants to talk to you."

Tucker handed her the phone.

She met his gaze, tried to be brave and failed. Her hand was trembling, and the receiver felt slick and sweaty in her fingers.

"Hello, this is Kristina," she said quietly. There was only silence on the line, but she made herself say the rest. "Your daughter."

Chapter Twelve

"What do I call him?" she wondered out loud. "I used to call him Daddy when I was little, but that seems too cutesy for someone I hardly know. 'Dad' is all wrong, like somebody with a pipe and slippers. And 'Father' sounds like a priest. I could call him George, but..." She shuddered with distaste. "How can I call my own father George?"

"Calm down," Tucker said kindly.

But the questions kept rattling around in her brain. "Why do you think he wanted to meet me here?" she asked doubtfully. "Why not at my house? Why do you suppose?"

As he guided her along the corridor to the tiny design department conference room, Tucker gently put his arm around her shoulders. "He said he wanted to get right to work," he told her. "Plus I guess this is more neutral, less pressure."

"Believe me, there's plenty of pressure wherever we meet."

"It'll be okay."

She nodded, but she was preoccupied. A crush of memories had suddenly overwhelmed her.

For the first few years after her father left, she had been consumed with the imaginary details of his homecoming. Every night before she went to bed, she'd picture just how it would be.

When he came back for her, he'd be weighted down with packages, but he'd drop all the presents the moment he saw her, because he couldn't wait to catch her in his arms.

The contents of the fantasy parcels had changed over the years. At first, she had envisioned a pair of red leather cowboy boots and a giant stuffed giraffe she'd seen once at the mall. Over time, those items gave way to an ID bracelet with her name inscribed on it and a complete collection of David Cassidy records.

But the sentiment was the same. The important part was that, without a word from her, he would've brought all the things she wanted the most.

Every nuance of that fantasy was still so clearly etched in her memory, she could almost smell the leather of the cowboy boots. She had hugged her dream closely, night after night, and she could still feel it now.

Now, of course, the reality would be nothing like her childish dream. She no longer wanted or needed stuffed animals and ID bracelets, and she was too big to be swept off her feet by her daddy's embrace.

At her side, Tucker said quietly, "We're here."

She nodded, but stopped a few feet short of the conference room. "Is he already in there?"

"He should be. He's been at Toyland for over an hour."

"He was an hour early?"

If he was that anxious to meet her, perhaps there was hope for this reunion after all.

"He said that before you got here he wanted to see the place where he'd be working."

"Ah." She smiled with cynicism she didn't want to feel. "The job is the attraction, not the long-lost daughter."

"Don't give up before you even see him." Tucker's blue eyes blazed with concern, and perhaps a touch of annoyance. "Enticing him with the job offer was your idea, you know."

"I know." Somehow, she managed to push herself forward the last few steps. And then Tucker slid open the door, and she had to go in.

A gray-haired man with a slight droop to his shoulders rose from the far end of the conference table.

She had remembered a tower of strength, but he was no bigger than her own five-ten. She had no clear recollection of his face, but she saw now that his features were strongly etched, and his eyes dark under narrow brows. He had the myopic squint of a person not quite of this world. The eyes of a dreamer, her mother had always said.

He cleared his throat clumsily and stuck out a slender, time-worn hand. "You must be Kristina."

She took his hand, and shook it limply, wondering what she should feel and how she should behave. Finally, she dropped his hand, sticking both of hers in the pockets of her dress.

"You don't look like your mother," he commented, cocking his head to one side. "You're so tall, and your hair is dark. I expected you to look like Betty."

"She's called Bitsy now," she answered. "I, uh, never looked like her. I thought you'd remember that I took after you."

He shook his head, and for the first time, his eyes met hers. "I remember a little girl in pigtails who wanted to know how the toys worked. But it's all so long ago."

Funny. She'd wanted to see him so badly that she hadn't realized how bitter she'd feel. But here, facing him, she had to tamp down the urge to shout at him, to demand to know why he didn't even remember the color of her hair.

Instead, she asked, "How was your trip from Cleveland?"

"Fine, uneventful," he responded. "And you? How are you?"

"Fine," she echoed. Lord, this was painful. "Are you settled in?"

"Oh, yes. Yes," he murmured. His eyes lit up, and he stood a little straighter. "I've always been a one-man band, so to speak, so this notion of working for someone else is new to me, but the tools and the facilities here— well, it's fantastic." Excitement threaded his words. "I already feel the sap starting to flow."

"The sap?"

"Ideas!" he said impatiently. "Schemes! Plans!"

"I'm glad you like it."

"I don't just like it." The eyes of a dreamer became the eyes of a zealot. "I'm raring to go."

"That's . . . good." Suddenly, she couldn't think of anything else to say. Well, he was clearly keen on getting started at his new job, so maybe it was best not to keep him. It was a relief to contemplate being done with this conversation. "Do you have a place to stay? I still have the old house, and you can stay with me if you'd like."

"The house? Is my old workbench still in the basement?"

"No, I'm sorry." She shrugged. "Mother cleared it out years ago."

"I have good memories of that little lab of mine in the basement." He rubbed his chin thoughtfully. "Why, that's where I had the idea for Thor's Flying Hammer, and that was one of my favorites. Never did figure out the answer to the rebounding problem that thing had. What a shame—it was a good little idea."

"I remember Thor's Flying Hammer."

"I expect you got hit in the head a few times when I was testing it." He sighed. "Used to make your mother so mad when I let you help in the lab." He glanced up from under his brows. "And how is your mother?"

Kristina noted that he seemed to have a lot less trouble discussing Bitsy than Bitsy did him.

"Still a big wheel at Austin's?" he went on.

"Uh, no." She took her hands out of her pockets, clasping one inside the other. "She remarried last year, and left the store. Her new husband is Windham Austin."

George Castleberry smiled fondly. "Good old Betty. She always did set her sights high. And she certainly seems to have done a fine job with you."

"Uh, thank you." She backed toward the door, and hopefully Tucker, who should be waiting in the hall. "I'll just let you get back to work. About staying with me...?"

"Oh, no, that won't be necessary. I'm planning to find something out here, closer to Toyland."

"Right." She'd counted on some time at her house, where they could relax and get to know each other again. But maybe it was better this way. "Whatever suits you. I'll leave my number, so you can reach me."

Her hand found the doorknob behind her, and she turned to leave.

"Kristina?" She stopped to listen. "I'm glad you arranged this."

"I'm glad, too." After a pause, she completed the thought. "I'm glad you're here, Dad."

And then she was out of that stuffy little room, and Tucker was holding her in the embrace she'd always wanted from her father.

"That bad?" he asked.

"No, it was okay. Awkward, you know, but it was bound to be." She put on a brave face. "It will take some time, I think. It's just . . . new."

"Right."

SHE WAS GETTING BETTER and better at putting her job on the back burner without experiencing guilt. What with the steady progress she and Tucker were making on Santa's Magic Workshop and her new preoccupation with reserving a certain amount of space on her schedule for her father, she didn't have time to worry about Austin's or her own shaky future there.

"Too bad," she muttered as she let herself into Toyland's design department, with its rabbit warren of cubicles. "I deserve this time. I deserve it."

Peering over the divider into her father's carrel, she saw the top of his head bent studiously over a stack of papers. Déjà vu, she thought. It was just like peeking down the basement steps to catch a glimpse of him at his workbench.

There were drawings of odd vehicles pinned to the walls, and tons of crumpled-up paper around him in the cubicle. She didn't spy anything that looked like a hopeful toy design, but that didn't mean anything. Did it?

"Hi, Dad," she said cheerfully. "Ready to break for lunch?"

"Hmm? What's that?" He glanced up briefly, clearly distracted. "Oh, Kristina. Hello."

"Dad?" she tried again. "Lunch?"

"Lunch? Oh, no I couldn't. Busy," he said with a frown, tipping his head to one side to study the crazy looking drawing he was making.

Déjà vu again. *Dinner time, Daddy,* she'd been sent to announce too many times to remember. *Mommy says come right now or it will get cold.*

And then, if he bothered to answer at all, he would say, *I can't come right now. I'm busy.* Yeah, well, Daddy was always busy, wasn't he?

"Dad," she prodded, "you have to eat."

"Oh, all right," he responded, in a muddled sort of voice. "But not for very long. I have to get back."

She took him to a small Chinese restaurant not too far from Toyland, a favorite with the employees from the office according to Tucker. In fact, she saw several other members of the design staff in the restaurant's red plastic booths.

"So, what looks good to you?" she asked brightly, determined to make it a nice lunch.

"Hmm? Oh, I don't care. Anything is fine."

He kept tapping a chopstick against his paper place mat, and it was driving her crazy. She wondered what he would do if she leaned over and took it away from him. And then he started to whistle tunelessly.

"Dad," she prompted, trying to remind him she was there. "How are things going at Toyland?"

"They seem rather thick there to me," he said peevishly.

"Thick?"

"Yes," he complained. "They wouldn't recognize real creativity if it jumped up and bit them."

"I'm sorry to hear that."

"Here, let me show you what I mean...." Pulling a mechanical pencil from his shirt pocket, he flipped over his place mat to the blank side and began to sketch some sort of blob. "You'll see how good this is," he muttered.

She couldn't believe what her eyes told her he was drawing. "Dad, that's Thor's Flying Hammer. That's the same thing you were working on years ago."

"No, no, it's different," he asserted. He kept puttering with the pencil and the place mat, adding new lines and scratching out the old ones, and she started to panic.

But she took a short breath and tried again, hoping to keep the note of alarm out of her voice. "Why don't you put the hammer aside for the moment?"

"But it's not the hammer," he insisted.

No, it just looks exactly like the hammer. "Dad, I asked you to lunch so we could talk." She reached across the table and covered his hand with hers, blocking the frantic motion of his pencil. "I thought we could use the time to get to know each other again."

He blinked several time. "I'm, uh, not very good at that kind of thing."

"But, Dad, couldn't you at least try?"

Managing a weak smile, he told her, "You wanted your old man to be *Father Knows Best,* but all you got was George Castleberry. Not much, is it?"

"Please don't say that."

His dark eyes filled with dismay. "I never wanted to disappoint you, Krissie. But I don't know how to do anything else."

"You didn't disappoint me, Daddy." But she remembered what it felt like to be ten years old, and to wonder why her father had gone away. It felt awful. "Did I disappoint you?"

"Never," he murmured. "Never."

"Okay, well, let's try to cheer up here, all right?" She brushed at the tears threatening to swamp her. "We're both trying our best, and that's all we can do."

He nodded, but she knew his heart wasn't in it.

"Waiter," she called out. "I think we're ready to order."

At least it filled the silence.

"Hi, Dad." Tucker pulled the phone over to the coffee table, setting it next to a roof section from Santa's Magic Workshop.

"Hello, son. Things going any better there?"

"Not really, Dad." He could hear the frustration seeping into his voice. He propped the receiver on his shoulder and fiddled with the roof, fitting it together as he talked, feeling better if his hands were busy. "I'm still not doing so well with Trey, and the thing is, Dad, I'm wondering if maybe the handwriting isn't on the wall."

"You want to run that by me again?"

Tucker paused. "I mean that maybe I should step down."

He heard the deep sigh echoing from his father's end of the line. "Son, I'm disappointed to hear you say that."

"I know, Dad."

"I wouldn't have picked you for the job if I didn't think you could handle it," his father said sternly.

"I can handle it," he answered roughly. "But I'm not sure I want to handle it. I think . . ."

"Yes?"

"I think it's crazy for me to stay in a job I hate."

"Well, I agree with you there. I'm just surprised to hear you say that, since the last time I talked to you, you were so gung ho on being president, nothing short of dynamite was going to dislodge you.'' Harley Bennett added gruffly, "What happened to change your mind?"

He thought of Kristina, of counseling her to be honest with herself, of hearing his own words rebound on him. He looked down at the Magic Workshop, and he saw the pieces that needed to be put together, pieces he and Kristina had cut out by hand, treated so delicately, sweated over.

This was what he should be doing; he felt it in his gut.

"I've been working on a new design project," he said finally. He picked up the small Santa Claus figure from where it lay next to the Workshop. Kristina had given it hair and a beard last night, but it still didn't have any clothes. Tucker smiled, balancing the naked Santa in his palm. "I remembered what it felt like to be a designer again. Dad, the thing is, I miss it."

"You always were a damn good designer, Tucker."

He didn't know quite what to say. "I've never been a quitter, Dad. You know that."

"Yep."

"I can't stand the idea that by going back to Design, I'd be letting you down."

"It doesn't matter, Tucker. If I'd been any good as a designer, maybe I'd have stayed there myself. Who knows? Your Uncle Pete might've been president. God forbid." He chuckled. "So you want to step down and go back to Design, huh?"

"That's the basic idea."

"But that leaves us with a big problem. Who's going to take the helm?"

"I don't know. Tegan, maybe, except I don't think she'd do it. Or Trey." He hated to even think it. "He's hungry enough."

"But he's not ready for it," his father remarked shrewdly.

"No," Tucker said honestly, "he's not."

"Then who?"

"I don't know."

"Look, son," Harley Bennett declared, "I think it's time to cut this cruise short. It's driving me crazy, and your mother is getting weepy thinking about not being home for Christmas. So what I think we should do is fly home right away. We'll get the whole family together and hash it out. Deal?"

"Dad, if you shouldn't—"

"Don't start in on the heart attack, will you please? The doctor says I'm fine, and I feel great, and I'm damned sick of this ship."

Tucker smiled to himself. *Now* he sounded like the father he knew. "Yeah, okay." He added, "But don't think you'll talk me out of this. I'm going back to Design."

"We'll work it out," his father promised. And then, in a muffled voice, he announced, "Thelma—get packing. We're going home for Christmas."

Tucker's smile widened when he heard his mother's whoop in the background.

WHEN SHE WANTED TO SEE Tucker, she knew where to find him. In the playroom, working diligently on Santa's Magic Workshop. Sometimes she thought he was more caught up in it than she was.

His back was toward the door, and he was bent low over the long center table, frowning over some aspect of the Workshop. When she tiptoed closer, she could see more of it, and she smiled. Since the last time she'd seen it, he'd put the walls up. Wonderful!

Feeling mischievous, she crept up behind him and slid her hands over his eyes. "Guess who," she commanded, in what she hoped was a low, sultry voice.

Instead of answering, he whipped around on his stool, trapping her between his thighs and holding her there. Before she could say a word, he pulled her forward by the lapels of her suit jacket and hungrily covered her mouth with his own.

At first she was stunned, and she didn't really react. She just stood there under the onslaught. But it was a devouring kiss, hot and dangerous, and the effect of it began to burn through her veins like tequila. She couldn't stop her arms from wrapping around his neck, or her mouth from slamming back against his and giving as good as she got.

She moaned into the kiss, and the greedy sound of it was shocking to her ears. *Not me,* she thought, but she knew it was.

When she began to see stars, she knew she had to breathe or pass out, so she detached herself enough to gulp down some air, still bracing herself on his broad shoulders for support.

"That's some welcome. Much better than a boring old hello," she managed. Holding the full weight of her hair off her neck with one hand, she wondered if she looked as overheated and frazzled as she felt. "I guess you must have missed me. But I just saw you last night."

The flames were still burning in his eyes as he rubbed a thumb down the curve of her cheek. "But every time we're together, all we do is slave over Santa's Magic Workshop. I thought maybe we could both use a diversion."

"But not for long." Regretfully, she broke away from him to gaze down at the bits and pieces on the table.

Thank goodness Tucker had the frame together, but there was still a ton of tiny fixtures to hook up, and the interior pieces to arrange.

"There's a lot left to do," he told her, "and not much time."

"The meeting's not until ten tomorrow. I planned to pull an all-nighter if I had to."

Tucker raised an eyebrow. "I'm not sure even an all-nighter will do it. Before you got here, I was trying to figure out what we could afford to lose."

"We're not losing one thing!" she cried.

"How about the shingles? The roof will go a lot faster if we paint it in one piece."

"But what about my color-coded chart to show exactly how the shingles should be attached?"

"Electricity?" he tried hopefully.

Her mouth fell open. "But the fireplace won't have flames, and there won't be lamps in the living room. Or sconces in the elves' workroom, or a glow in Mrs. Claus's stove, or Christmas lights that spell NOEL in the window! No," she moaned, "we have to have the lights."

"We may not have time, Krissie," he warned.

"Let's get to it," she said with determination. She stripped off her jacket and rolled up her sleeves. "You start the lights right now, and I'll finish the rest of the miniatures."

"I'll start the lights, but you aren't doing anything dressed like that. Go upstairs and change your clothes," he said sternly.

"You are so picky about dress codes," she complained, but she relented, figuring it would take less time to give in than to fight about it. Besides, she probably would be more comfortable out of her Austin's wardrobe. She had to admit, it was going to feel good to get out of panty hose and heels for once.

"Here's the key," Tucker said casually, and tossed it to her across the table.

Key in hand, she raced up the stairs and into his den of outrageous taste. Her pace slackened immediately inside the door.

It felt very weird to be roaming through Tucker's apartment all by herself, especially with Michael Jordan staring at her from behind the basketball hoop. She caught herself humming "Who's Afraid of the Big Bad Wolf" to fill the eerie silence.

And now that she was here all alone, she realized that she didn't know where the bedroom or the clothes closets were. It was only when she poked around behind what looked like a brick wall that she found one step up into a cozy little bedroom niche.

What she had thought was a wall wasn't. From the bedroom side, it was actually a fireplace that faced Tucker's huge bed. His bedroom contained nothing more than a king-size bed, heaped with quilts and Teenage Mutant Ninja Turtles sheets.

"Since when do they make Teenage Mutant Ninja Turtles sheets in king-size?" she muttered.

Because the bed was huge and the space was small, she had to stand or kneel on the bed to get to the closet, which was really nothing more than a deep indentation in the brick, with shelves on one side, and a hanging rack on the other. With this scenario, all Tucker had to do was reach over and grab fresh clothes on his way out of bed in the morning.

Nonetheless, she was absolutely amazed to find that his clothes were carefully folded into separate stacks of T-shirts, sweats, shorts and jeans. She couldn't imagine

Tucker putting things away so neatly. Maybe he had maid service. Tegan, probably.

Quickly she picked out a purple Northwestern Wildcats football jersey, and a pair of black sweatpants that still had the tags on. Wearing his pants didn't seem nearly as intimate if said pants still had the tags on.

After several glances around, to make sure no one was going to sneak up on her, she tore off her suit and blouse and threw on the huge T-shirt and sweatpants. It was an interesting look for her, she decided with a frown. At least the drawstring waist on the sweatpants pulled them up to a respectable fit, even if the football jersey did hang to midthigh.

Since shoes were out of the question, she rummaged around till she found where he stored his socks. Tucker seemed to have extensive supplies on hand, keeping spares of the things he wore all the time—she found about fifteen pairs of tennis shoes, several of them unworn, and a whole pile of brand-new cotton crew socks.

After folding down the socks, she realized time was getting short, and she raced back down to the playroom.

She came skating in, sliding in the too-big socks, expecting Tucker to make fun of her outfit. But he wasn't there.

There was, however, a large note taped prominently to the center of the train set. Flapping from the water tower in Whoville, it said, ''Tucker—I quit. Tegan.''

Kristina's heart dropped to her knees. Had he seen this yet? Did she have a chance of hiding it before he got back?

She knew she couldn't hide it, because he really ought to see it. But darn it anyway, the timing couldn't have been worse. She sagged to a stool and tried to figure out what she was going to tell Tucker, but all she managed to do was knock over a pile of Workshop props. As she bent under the table to pick them up, she heard voices.

"There's nothing I can do," Tucker argued.

Trey's voice followed hard upon his brother's. "But, Tucker, it's not fair to the others."

"Give it some time. If he doesn't get any better, we'll get rid of him. Okay?"

"What are you talking about?" Kristina inquired, easing herself up from under the table as she piled the tiny sleds and bicycles back on top. She had the sinking feeling her father was the one who was going to be gotten rid of.

"Nothing," the brothers said in unison.

"What are you doing hiding under the table?" Tucker asked hastily. "And what's that?" He plucked the note off the Whoville water tower. "Tegan quit?" he sputtered. "She can't!"

"Well, there's always a chance she'll change her mind later," Kristina offered kindly.

"Where did she go?" Trey demanded.

"The note doesn't say." Tucker handed it over. "Just that she quit."

Kristina avoided his eyes, trying hard to look uninvolved.

"Why do I get the feeling you had something to do with this?" Tucker asked quietly.

"I'm not sure if I did or not," she said weakly. "I did have a chat with her once about, you know, the same things you and I always talk about—following your dreams, not letting other people push you around. So in a way, Tegan took *your* advice, didn't she?"

He raised an eyebrow. "Oh, so it's my fault now?"

"Damn right it is," his younger brother said heatedly. "Tegan hated her job because you made it so unbearable. And without Tegan here, things are going to get even worse. I can't believe this!'' Muttering dire imprecations to himself, Trey stomped out of the room.

''Oh, hellfire.''

''Tucker, I'm sorry you're upset, but I'm not sorry Tegan's gone. She felt trapped, in the wrong job for her.''

''Actually, I understand better than you probably think,'' he said cryptically. Kristina was about to ask him what he meant by that when he continued. ''There's just one problem. With Tegan gone, we lose a vote on the board, and I'm not sure there are any to spare at the moment.''

She framed his face with her hands, pulling him toward her, until they were almost as close as they had been before, when he'd kissed her. She whispered, ''It's going to be so gorgeous, they'll have no choice but to vote for it.''

''Okay,'' he murmured, dropping a soft kiss to her lips. ''But if you start this . . .'' He kissed her again for good measure. ''We'll never get the model done.''

With regret, she pulled away. ''Okay, where do we start?''

''Shingles,'' he told her grimly. ''You and your color-coded chart. If we're going to be here all night, you'd better get a move on.''

''FOOD,'' KRISTINA MOANED, as she sewed the last piece of lace on Mrs. Claus's apron. ''I need food. Real food.'' Her gaze swept the stack of candy wrappers and soda bottles lining the floor. ''If I see another M&M's, I'll die. Good grief, Tucker, it's almost nine o'clock. Can we stop long enough to get a pizza delivered?''

"Yeah, okay," he said, but he sounded so distracted, she wasn't sure he'd heard her. "Let me know when it's here. I almost have the flames in the fireplace working."

This was a fine how-do-you-do. He was the one toiling so hard he barely noticed her presence, and she was the one begging for breaks. If she had an ounce of pride, she told herself, she'd stay where she was and gut it out until *he* cried uncle.

Too bad. She was starving. Shameless, she left him and his minifireplace long enough to go down the hall to Design and use the phone to order pizza. Funny, her father's cubicle looked almost empty, as if all the drawings and paper wads had been cleared out since the last time she'd seen it.

"He probably took stuff home to work on," she muttered, and then she forgot about it because the thought of food made her mouth start to water.

When the pizza finally got there, Tucker managed to venture far enough away from his project to eat, but then it was back to work.

As the hands crawled around the clock, and the time to finish grew shorter and shorter, the exact placement of the little Christmas cookies on Mrs. Claus's cookie tray suddenly seemed unimportant. After slaving over the tiny fixtures of the Magic Workshop for so long, her eyesight was blurring and her fingers were uncoordinated. Worst of all, the most commonplace things had begun to strike her as howlingly funny.

She glanced over at Tucker, unfazed and still working like a drone in a beehive. He'd put music on hours ago— Christmas carols, for the proper mood, he'd told her— and he had the gall to hum along with "Rudolph the Red-Nosed Reindeer" at whatever ungodly hour it was.

Not really paying attention, she gave one miniature gingerbread man three eyes and dribbled paint across the crotch of another one, making him into a very studlike little guy.

One look at his crotch, and she started to giggle. And then she couldn't stop. "Oh, God," she said between peals of laughter, "I just cement glued four half-inch gingerbread men to my hand. And one of them is the most macho gingerbread man *I've* ever seen."

"Krissie," he said meaningfully, heading around the table. "I think you've lost it."

"I know. I know. I have."

He spun her around on her stool and lifted her hand up near his face, patiently ripping the gingerbread men off one at a time. "Okay, you're free."

Dropping an arm over his shoulder to keep him there, she tickled the edge of his jaw with one finger. "Did you see that gingerbread man?" she whispered. "The one who was rather, ahem, well endowed?"

"I think you're getting hysterical."

"Uh-oh." She leaned in, as near to his ear as she could get, and spoke very softly. "Is this the part where you spank me and then I say, 'I needed that'?"

Something flashed in his eyes, something dangerously close to desire. "I think that's slapping, not spanking." He reached around her, cupping her bottom through the layers of football jersey and sweatpants, drawing her close up against him, so that her knees rode his hipbones. "But I'd be willing to spank you. If you like that kind of thing."

"Oh, Tucker." She sighed. "It's so late, and I'm so tired. If you go around touching me like that..."

His hand ventured under her shirt, and his fingers began to play with the drawstring on the sweatpants.

"Oh, dear," she said breathlessly. "And like that. And that. Heavens, Tucker." She leaned forward and nipped at his ear with her teeth. "Tucker," she whispered, "if you keep this up, I may be forced to seduce you."

"Fire away," he said lazily.

Chapter Thirteen

"You don't mean that," she murmured. Whatever he was doing to her, it was wonderful. She wiggled closer on the stool, arching against him. Her body felt like hot molasses, and of its own accord, it kept draping itself all over him.

"I mean it," he whispered back, ruffling her hair with his hot breath.

"But the workshop..."

"So we'll take a little break. You wanted a break."

She followed the line of his bottom lip with the tip of her finger. "But you didn't."

"I changed my mind," he said roughly, and his hold tightened.

She felt sure she had a snappy reply waiting somewhere, but his warm, tingling hands slid farther up her back, unhooking her bra, and her mouth became incapable of anything more than a slow, tortured moan.

"Upstairs," he whispered.

"No," she said on a sigh. He was licking her ear and drifting his fingers, inexorably, closer and closer, to the sides of her breasts. She couldn't breathe. "Don't move. Please don't move."

"Upstairs," he repeated more firmly, and then he hauled her up off the stool, plastering her body next to his. She had no choice but to wrap her legs around his waist, and let herself be swept away.

How he maneuvered the stairs she'd never know. He couldn't have been able to see, cradling her against the front of his body, gazing into her eyes and raining hungry little kisses across her cheeks, the corners of her mouth, even her eyelids.

"God, I want you," he whispered, kicking the apartment door closed behind them.

She had visions of all those golf and tennis balls underfoot, and she feared they'd both be rolling on their heads before long, but she held on tight and took the ride. Tucker navigated like an admiral, until he stopped, right next to the brick wall that hid the entrance to the bedroom.

His hot gaze met hers as he slowly released her, sliding her down his body and to her feet. "Are you sure?" he asked.

"Don't ask me that. Don't ask me anything," she breathed. "Just kiss me. Please?"

She tangled her arms around his neck and thrust her fingers into the silky strands of his hair, trying desperately to reconnect them, to take away his reason and his common sense until he was as driven as she was.

Pressed up against the lean, muscular length of him, she realized she knew every angle and curve of that hard body, although they'd traded no more than a few kisses. But she remembered, and her mind filled in the rest—Tucker spinning to shoot a basketball, his clothes gapping to reveal a hard, flat stomach and long, firmly sinewed legs; Tucker in softly molded jeans, or formal black-and-white;

Tucker in skimpy gym shorts that took her breath away, leaving almost nothing to the imagination.

"I want to make love to you." His voice was a soft, husky whisper, and it melted every nerve-ending in her body. "But it has to be right."

"Maybe I'll force the issue," she told him wickedly. "How about if *I* make love to you? Would you like it on the floor, maybe?" Her brazen words shocked her, but she slanted her mouth up next to his and nipped at his lip, sliding her tongue into the warmth and wetness of his mouth.

"God, Kristina, don't do this to me. Not if you don't mean it."

"Mean it?" Angrily, she shook him by the shoulders. "Mean it? I'm about ready to die from it!" Embarrassed by her outburst, she dropped her hands away from him, linking them together tightly behind her back, so that she couldn't touch him. "What more do you want from me?"

"I want you to be happy."

"I can't be happy right now."

"Why not?"

"Because..." Her deepest secrets were hovering on the end of her tongue. "This kind of thing is not something I'm very good at," she confessed.

"Kristina—"

"No, really," she said, trying to sound light and amusing. It didn't come out that way. "I'm scared, Tucker, scared that I'll be awful and you'll think I'm stupid or bad at it or..."

"Krissie," he started, reaching out to reassure her, but she wasn't finished yet.

"I just want to do it and get it over with, okay?" She saw the question in his eyes, and she felt like an idiot, like an inexperienced teenager. "I mean, I've done it before, but not," she added fiercely, "with anyone like you."

The light in his blue, blue eyes grew hotter than a forest fire. "Kristina, you and I, we're not doing it just to get it over with, no matter what you do to me."

"No?" she asked, in a small voice.

"No. It's going to be slow. Real slow. And I doubt it will ever be over."

A heavy sweetness coursed her limbs. She took his hand, lifting it to the side of her face, leaning into his touch.

The pad of his thumb was uneven as he traced a faint line down her cheek, around her jaw, up to the edge of her bottom lip. "I want you, more than you can imagine, but that's not all."

"What do you mean?"

"Kristina, I want you so much..." He paused. "Because I love you." Looking confused, a little bewildered perhaps, Tucker added, "I don't know how and I'm not sure I know why, but I fell in love with you before the first time I kissed you."

"Did you say you love me?" It was hardly more than a breath.

"Yes." He clasped her hands in his and drew them up between them. "That's why it's not going to be fast, and it's not going to be easy, for either of us."

"No?"

"No way, Krissie."

She swallowed. "I think I love you, too. But I'm afraid."

"I know."

"I think if we..." She moistened parched lips. "If we make love, I won't have a choice about loving you."

"There's already no choice."

She held him at arm's length, watching him, taking the measure of the man, whom she knew, in her heart, she loved. "You have a way of getting under my skin, and I don't think I can lose you, no matter what," she said honestly.

"You won't lose me."

Without another word, he gathered her in his arms and carried her to his bed. And right there, in front of the Teenage Mutant Ninja Turtles and everybody, Tucker set her down gently, and began to disrobe.

He slipped his black T-shirt over his head, revealing a long, beautiful torso—all sleek muscle and sinuous curves. And then his hands moved to the top snap of his jeans. Pop. And the zipper began to zag, tooth by tooth.

"Uh, maybe I'm not ready for this," she said in a funny, uneven voice, and she half sat up, crumpling the front of her shirt in one nervous hand.

"What's wrong?" He stopped there, with his pants beginning to gap at the top. Her eyes were riveted to that spot. "You said you were sure a minute ago."

"Well..." She swallowed. "That was before I saw you...you know."

"Is there something wrong with my body?"

"Oh, heavens, no," she whispered, feasting her eyes on his gorgeous chest, on the light feathering of golden hair that led down to his...button. She tried to remember to breathe. "You're absolutely perfect."

He arched an eyebrow. "Wait till you see my birthmark." And then, still partially dressed at least, he slid into the bed next to her, wrapping her in his arms and finding her mouth with his before she could raise any more objections.

Underneath him, she was melting. She forgot to be anxious or self-conscious; there wasn't room in her brain for anything except these wonderful, mesmerizing sensations.

His hands, his mouth, his skin... She was consumed with him, and it had barely begun.

His mouth was hot and soft, moist, achingly sweet, and he opened it wider, making the kiss fuller, deeper. She moaned, a tiny pleasure-filled sigh, and tested his smooth shoulders under her palms. She liked the feel of him, so sleek and rangy. She couldn't get enough of him under her hands, and she slid them down his chest and up his back, exploring, claiming, pulling him nearer.

He nibbled her lips, unsettling her when he framed her face with his clever hands and brushed her lips with a series of small, chaste kisses. It made her restless, edgy; it felt too remote after the more intimate kiss of a moment ago. Yet when he held back, slowing the pace even further, tracing the curve of her bottom lip with the tip of his tongue, she felt it echo deep inside.

"Tucker," she tried, finding her voice with difficulty. "Do you really have a birthmark?"

"Uh-huh."

"Where?"

"Hide-and-seek," he whispered mockingly.

A reckless smile curved her lips, and she took the dare, slipping one hand to the top of his jeans. Delicately, she touched the snap, and then the rough edge of fabric next to it. "Am I warm?"

"Hot. Very hot," he murmured, easing aside the loose neckline of her football jersey to nuzzle her neck and dip his tongue along her collarbone.

"How hot?" Her finger pressed on, finding warm, velvety skin where the zipper separated.

"Too hot," he said, catching her hand. "I promised slow, remember?"

She evaded him with her other hand. "No."

"Kristina..."

"No," she whispered. "I'm dying. I can't breathe." She raised the lower half of her body enough to press it against him. "Yes?"

"No." He cupped the roundness of her bottom through the thick, soft sweatpants, cradling her so close that her hand couldn't fit between them anymore, putting a stop to her exploration of his jeans.

Her eyelids fluttered as he moved against her, slowly, tantalizingly, with a rhythm she found fascinating. She was so tangled up in this bewitching dance they were doing, she barely noticed it when he bunched up her football jersey and tossed it aside.

Cool air drifted across her breasts and shoulders as they were bared to his eyes, and he trailed his lips and his hands across her passion-slick skin. Twisting tendrils of her long, dark hair around his fingers and across her body, he played the strands of her hair out like a web of black silk.

It was the most erotic thing she'd ever seen.

She wanted him with a primitive longing that jolted her, shamed her. Who was this wild woman, writhing under him, curling into him, pushing away his clothes, begging him to touch her? No one she knew. She hungered for him, ached for him, yet she had never felt such intense and conflicting emotions in her life.

"Don't stop," she murmured, as he edged away to discard the remnants of their clothing. "But, oh, that feels wonderful, too," she whispered when he returned.

He refused to pick up his excruciating pace, caressing her, teasing her, barely grazing her with kisses, until she simply couldn't endure another instant of this mindless, agonizing desire.

"Please?" she tried again. "Please?"

His face was dark and dangerous, not at all the Tucker she knew.

She squeezed her eyes shut, past the point of no return. "What are you waiting for?" she asked, in a voice that got caught in her throat.

"You," he said simply. And then he slipped inside her with a smooth stroke that took her beyond reason, beyond desire, beyond anything.

"Tucker," she breathed.

He moved inside her, against her. It was slow and sweet, steady. The cadence reined her in and set her free. Her body tightened until it had nowhere else to go and she arched off the bed, so near to blessed release she could taste it with every particle of air she breathed.

But he rolled over onto his back, breaking the rhythm, holding her steady and still with his hands riding her hips.

"Damn you," she swore, as her hair fell down around them, brushing across his chest. She thrust against him. "Damn you. I had it. I was there, and you..."

And then, there it was. Soaring over the edge, she cried out with pure pleasure. And Tucker's low moan told her she'd brought him with her on the roller coaster ride into oblivion.

No one moved for a long moment.

"I love you," he whispered into her ear, pulling her down onto his chest. "Kristina. I love you."

She smiled, propping herself up on his shoulder. "Tucker, you don't have a birthmark."

"Keep looking," he said gruffly.

Her smile widened. She planned to do just that, even if it took all night.

MORNING INTRUDED ITSELF into Kristina's consciousness little by little. There were no windows in Tucker's bedroom nook, so the light of daybreak only crawled in, as gray and gentle as spring fog.

But eventually, the soft, cool unfamiliarity of her surroundings sent signals to her hazy brain, and she sighed, realizing she was going to have to leave behind the wonderfully sweet dream she was having. Time to wake up. Probably time for work, she decided, trusting her unfailingly accurate inner alarm system.

Still luxuriating in the memory of the fantastic dream—something erotic about Tucker and her, laughing and playing in a big bed without a stitch of clothes between them—she opened her eyes a tiny crack, hoping to make out the numbers on her bedside clock. But under her right eye, a green blob wearing a mask brandished a sword at her.

"Yikes," she yelped, and sat up. With relief, she realized that the green blob was only a cartoon character, a design on her pillowcase. "Cartoons on my pillowcase?" she mumbled. "Since when?"

"Kristina?" Tucker murmured, half raising himself next to her. He was wrapped in a sheet with similar green blobs running rampant over it. "What's wrong?"

"Oh, my God." She was with Tucker. In his bed. And she wasn't wearing a stitch! The dream... She yanked the nearest cover up over her breasts, but it was a lacy-looking white afghan, with big holes in the pattern.

"Nice," he said, propping himself up on one elbow, and raising a naughty eyebrow.

"Tucker! You shouldn't look," she protested, casting about for something else, and coming up with the other half of the Teenage Mutant Ninja Turtles sheet. When she pulled on it, he obliged by rolling out of it, leaving her protected, but himself *very* exposed.

"I've already seen it, sweetheart," he said kindly, pulling her over on top of him, sheet and all.

Her hair, long, dark and unbound, spilled down next to him, as she braced herself on his chest. "Well, at least now you're covered up," she murmured, unable to stop the smile dancing on her lips. "With me."

"Uh-huh."

"Tucker," she said mockingly, as he rocked her back and forth gently above him, letting her feel very clearly through the thin sheet that he wanted her just as much this morning as he had last night. She began to tingle deep inside, ready for another round, even as long-unused parts of her body sent up warnings that they were a little stiff, a little sore, after last night's fun and games. "We were very bad last night."

"Nope." He grinned and moved her hair far enough out of the way to nibble her neck. "We were good. Very, very good. Spectacular, I might say."

"We said some things last night...." she ventured, hoping he'd pick up on her thought.

"Uh-huh." Catching a long tendril of her hair, he ran his fingers through it from beginning to end, tugging her closer with this silky rein. "Like 'I love you'?"

"Yeah. Like that." She knew she sounded far too solemn, but she'd had no practice at lighthearted "day after" repartee. So she came right out and asked, "Did you mean it?"

Swiftly he flipped her over, trapping her neatly, and exposing his perfect backside to her startled gaze. He had an athlete's body from stem to stern, all lean muscles and strong angles, and he didn't seem to mind if she looked her fill. She might have drooled on him if she hadn't been on the bottom.

And then he moved above her, rubbing against her in a very sensuous, rather obvious motion. "Want me to prove it?"

"That's not how you prove it."

"How then?"

She smiled. "You could tell me again."

"I love you. I love you. I love you. I love you."

His eyes shone and his arms tightened around her, and she couldn't remember ever feeling happier. "I love you, too. I really do."

"Now can I prove it?" he asked slyly.

"I'm sure you'll think of something." Of that she was certain. Tucker was nothing if not inventive.

"I could kiss you like this," he improvised, brushing his lips against her collarbone. "Or like this." His mouth trailed lower. "Or this."

He was just tasting the soft flesh at the top mound of her breast, when she suddenly sat straight up, nearly wounding him.

"Oh, my God! The Workshop!" She grabbed him by the shoulders and cried, "We didn't finish last night. Tucker, the Magic Workshop! What time is it?"

Scooting out from underneath him, she began pawing around in the scattered clothing at the foot of the bed, looking for her watch.

"And why exactly did that occur to you at this moment?" he inquired, looking a little peeved.

"Oh, no, Tucker," she moaned, holding up the thin strap of her watch. "We're dead. It's after seven! We're supposed to show it at ten, and we didn't finish."

"Don't worry." He leaned over into his closet and pulled out a pair of gym shorts and a sweatshirt. "We'll go down right now and finish it."

"There was too much left to do," she argued. "We'll never finish it now."

"All we can do is try. Put on some clothes," he ordered, "and let's hightail it down to the playroom."

"Oh, all right." But, as she slipped back into the Northwestern jersey and sweatpants she'd worn last night, she was far from convinced.

"Why are you so negative?" Tucker demanded, from right behind her as they made their way downstairs.

"I'm being realistic," she said stubbornly. "There's a difference."

He ran an aggravated hand through his hair, and pushed open the door to the playroom. "At 9:50 you can be realistic. Now is the time for optimism."

"Yeah, okay," she grumbled, heading directly for the table where the unfinished Magic Workshop had sat last night. She wanted to see it for herself, to get a handle on the depth of the dilemma. "Well, the outside looks good," she admitted. "Huh. I didn't think we'd gotten that far."

"I didn't, either," Tucker said slowly. "What gives?"

Gingerly Kristina lifted the lid to look inside. "Look!" she exclaimed. "The stove is together, and the cookie trays are in. And Mrs. Claus is sitting at the kitchen table, just like I wanted her." As she checked through the other rooms of the Magic Workshop, she began to rush her words with excitement. "The rug and the chair—Santa's in place—even the toys. Tucker, everything is here! But who did it? I don't think Trey would have, do you?"

"Don't look at me. You know where I was."

"Or I guess it could've been my father," she mused. "But I'm having a hard time believing it."

Tucker lifted the workshop by its new handle, testing it out. "Great," he told her. When he hoisted it up, they both saw a note of some sort lying on the table where the workshop had been. Setting the workshop aside, Tucker pounced on the note before Kristina could get to it.

"Well, well, what do you know?"

"Nothing! Tell me, what is it? Who's it from? Does it say who finished the Magic Workshop?"

He looked up with a curious smile. "It was Nick, believe it or not."

"Nick? But why would he . . . ? Give me that," she said finally, taking the small sheet of paper, and scanning the lines for herself trying to decipher the funny, cramped, old-fashioned writing.

Dear Kristina and Tucker,

I popped by to see how things were progressing, but found you absent. As the deadline loomed so very close, I took the liberty of finishing it off myself. You may consider it a Christmas gift if you like. Best of luck at the meeting.

Merry Christmas to all.

Nick

Kristina let the note dangle from her fingers as she found Tucker's gaze. "But how? How did he even get in here, let alone do all the work that was left, all by himself?"

Tucker laughed. "Maybe he really is Santa Claus. You know, finishing the shoes while the other guy slept?"

"That's the shoemaker and the elves," she said dryly. "Wrong legend."

"Santa's an elf, right? That jolly old elf?"

"Forget it, Tucker." She stretched up to kiss his cheek. "The important thing is that the workshop is done, and done beautifully, from all appearances. It looks gor-

geous to me, anyway." She shook her head in amaze-
ment. "Every last gingerbread man, every last doily... I'd
kiss Nick if he were here, I'll tell you that."

"I'm here. You could kiss me again instead."

"Can't," she said briskly, checking her watch. "If I
leave now and speed the whole way, I have just enough
time to get home, take a shower, change my clothes and
get back here for the presentation."

"I don't know," Tucker said doubtfully. "That's cut-
ting it awfully close."

"Well, if I'm a few minutes late, you can either stall, or
start without me." He still looked dubious, so she added,
"Please? I can't do this without a shower, and I really
wanted to wear my lucky red suit. Please?"

"Yeah, okay." He relented. "But no more than fifteen
minutes late. Or they'll get restless, and probably crabby,
and I can't guarantee how well it will go."

"I'll be here!" She kissed him again, and pulled away,
catching his hand. "I love you!"

"I love you, too." He blew her a kiss. "See you soon."

With his last "I love you" firmly in mind, she was
humming "Rescue Me" all the way back to her house. It
was a cold, gloomy morning, overcast and drizzly, but it
couldn't touch her good spirits. Hurrying, she squealed to
a stop, threw open her car door and raced up the walk to
her house.

She hummed, as she turned her key in the front door.
But the door wasn't locked. "Nick?" she called out un-
certainly. It was after eight; he ought to have left for
Austin's ages ago. "Nick, are you here?"

"No, Kristina. It's me." Her mother rose from the
lemon-striped chair and stood there, nervously fingering
her leather bag.

Kristina stopped in her tracks inside the front door, dropping the bundle of clothes and shoes she'd worn yesterday. Her mother was the last person she'd expected to see.

Immediately, she felt self-conscious, of the fact that she was wearing Tucker's clothes, and even more that she was obviously coming home after spending the night elsewhere. The word *sin* must surely be written on her forehead.

"I've been trying to reach you since yesterday morning, but no one seemed to know where you were," Bitsy said stiffly. "A person named Nick—who I understand has been living here—let me in this morning. He said you'd be home eventually, and I guess he was right. Because here you are."

"Mother, I don't have time to argue with you," she pleaded. "Can we discuss this later? I have to get ready. I have a meeting at ten."

She was halfway up the stairs when her mother's next words caught her.

"Nine-thirty," Bitsy announced. "The meeting is at nine-thirty."

"It's at ten."

"Nine-thirty. Windy and Mirabel are going to fire you."

Kristina shut her eyes against the finality of it. "Fire me?" she asked, incredulously.

"Oh, yes. However, I have convinced them to give you a chance to speak in your own defense. Nine-thirty."

"But I can't. I have to be at Toyland at ten."

Bitsy's pale blue eyes were cold with disbelief. "Then that's it? You're going to throw your job away?"

"I guess I don't have a choice."

"What?" her mother demanded. "I've just given you a choice. Meet with Windy and Mirabel and ask for your job back!"

"I told you, I can't. I have to be at Toyland."

"Does Toyland plan to make the mortgage payments on this house? Or your car payments?" Her voice shook when she said, "Do you think your Magic Workshop will pay the bills?"

The fantasy of the last few days began to pale. Even if she sold it today, the Workshop would not bring in hard, cold cash. She had flirted with the idea of losing her job at Austin's, but it had never seemed real. Until this moment.

Sometimes the truth was hard to face, she supposed. And what exactly would she do if they fired her? Sell hamburgers at McDonald's?

"No," she admitted finally. "The Workshop will probably never pay the bills."

"Then get dressed and come with me," Bitsy urged. "You can still save your job, Kristina, but you have to try. Do the Workshop, too—invent all the toys you want—but remember where your bread is buttered."

"I suppose you're right."

"You bet I'm right. Get dressed." Her mother crossed slender arms over her chest. "I'll be waiting."

Damn, damn, damn, she repeated to herself, all the way to Austin's in her mother's luxurious car, as the windshield wipers scraped against an icy gray rain.

In her heart, she was almost sure she had made the wrong choice. Old habits were hard to break. *Mother says jump, and Kristina jumps.*

How could it be wrong, the practical side of her argued, to try to insure bread on the table?

On the other hand, her sentimental side shot back, how could it be right to leave Tucker high and dry, and let all her hopes for the workshop go down the drain?

It will be okay, she told herself. Tucker would be all right. He was Toyland's fair-haired boy. If he had to, he could go ahead and present the Workshop without her, and everything would be fine.

She'd dash in and out of this meeting with Windy, reassure him, keep her job and get to Toyland before any damage was done.

And pigs could fly.

She had come to the conclusion that, maybe this time, there was no right choice.

"Mr. Austin will see you in a moment," the receptionist announced, using a respectfully hushed voice.

"Could I use your phone, please?"

The receptionist turned her telephone around sourly, making a point of eavesdropping on Kristina's conversation.

"Yes," she said into the receiver. "This is Kristina Castleberry. Is Tucker Bennett there, please?"

"No, I'm sorry," came the reply. "Mr. Bennett is in a meeting."

"The Santa's Magic Workshop meeting? It's started already?"

"No, I'm afraid that meeting has been delayed. *This* meeting is an emergency of some sort, with Mr. Bennett, senior."

"Tucker's father?" Heavens, that was some emergency. Tucker's father was supposed to be on a cruise ship somewhere near Aruba. But at least *her* meeting had been set back, and that was good.

"Yes, that's right. Mr. Bennett, Sr., and Mr. Bennett,

Jr., are meeting right now, and they said they expect to be in there for some time. Would you like to leave a message?''

''Yes, I would. Tell him that something came up, and I may be later than I'd hoped, but I'll be there as soon as I can. Have you got that?''

''Yes, all right,'' the secretary told her. ''I've got it.''

''You can go in now,'' the receptionist at her elbow announced imperiously.

With her fingers firmly crossed, Kristina marched through the glass doors into Windy's inner sanctum.

As expected, Windy was holding court from behind his desk, standing in front of his chair. Since he was small in stature, he never liked to sit when he was trying to look powerful. And Mirabel, even tinier than her son, was fixed at his elbow like the palace guard, with her beady little eyes pointed right at Kristina.

''Mr. Austin. Mrs. Austin,'' Kristina said politely. ''Thank you for giving me this opportunity to set the record straight.''

''You're welcome,'' Mirabel returned severely. Windy pressed his lips together unhappily, as if he'd wanted to say it first, but Mirabel continued to upstage him. Pointing behind Kristina, she commanded, ''Take a seat.''

As she turned to do as she was ordered, her eyes widened with surprise. ''Nick. What are you doing here?''

Chapter Fourteen

Mirabel's voice took on an even chillier note. "Think of him as the evidence against you."

But Nick had been doing beautifully. What kind of problem could he be evidence of? He seemed his usual self; his eyes were twinkling and his smile was as kind and unconcerned as ever. In his Saint Nicholas outfit, with the maroon velvet robe and the dark green wreath in his hair, he looked the very picture of old Saint Nick.

"I don't understand," she said, moving back around to face Mirabel. "What does Nick have to do with this?"

"He insulted a customer," Mirabel sniffed, as Windy grew more and more agitated.

Kristina was irate. "I don't believe for one instant that he insulted anyone."

"It was Mrs. Someone." Windy barged in, clearly determined to reassert his position.

"Stubblebine," Mirabel hissed.

"Yes, that's right. Mrs. Stubblebine."

"Ah, Brandee's mother," Nick murmured. "That would explain it."

Windy consulted a sheaf of papers on his desk. "Mrs. Stubblebine informs us that Mr. Holiday promised her child, Brandee, age five, a toy that Mrs. Stubblebine has no intention of giving her. She says Brandee has been talking of nothing else for days, contending that Santa Claus will bring the..." He paused distastefully. "The Down 'N' Dirty Dump Truck. A toy, which I might add, Austin's does not even carry."

"But it's what the child has her heart set on," Nick informed them. "Surely that means something."

"What means something, Mr. Holiday," Mirabel said imperiously, "is that our customers leave the store satisfied. Mrs. Stubblebine is most dissatisfied."

"I do apologize. But I still feel the child's Christmas is more important."

"We don't care what you think!" Windy fumed. "You're just an employee. And you're fired!"

"You can't fire Nick," Kristina declared, even though she knew very well they could.

Mrs. Austin ignored the outburst, nodding at Nick to leave. "That's all, Mr. Holiday."

He gave Kristina an encouraging wink as he ambled out. "Don't worry, my dear," he whispered. "It will be fine."

Talk about laughing in the face of adversity. "So my job is in jeopardy because of one unhappy customer?"

"There's more," Windy said flatly. "There are your unexplained absences, including this morning, when you were nowhere to be found. Generally, Austin's managers manage, they don't disappear for days at a time."

Facing Windy and his mother defiantly, she raised her chin. "You're right. It's true that I've been neglecting my job for the past few weeks. As you may or may not know, there have been things going on in my personal life that I think would have distracted anyone, and they certainly have commanded too large a share of my attention from Austin's perspective. But for the previous six months, I was the best employee you could have asked for. I did a very good job."

"Yes, well," Windy hedged, trying to look stern.

"And I can do a good job again. I need to get a handle on a few things, and then I can concentrate on Austin's again."

"I don't think so," Mirabel began, but Windy turned to her and whispered something. Interrupted, Mirabel looked exasperated, but she muttered back at him, and the two of them continued with this heated, if restrained, conversation, for several minutes.

They were still at it when the glass doors creaked open, and the second receptionist came striding in, carrying a stenographer's notebook and a pen. "Kristina Castleberry?" she demanded.

Kristina stood, raising her hand. "Here."

"I have an urgent message for you."

Get in line, she thought, but she said, "Fine."

"It's from Trey," the woman announced, in a nasal tone. "Spelled *T-R-E-Y.* He says, 'Your father has disappeared. We've called the police.'" The woman looked up from her steno pad. "That's it."

"What do you think it means, *disappeared?* I—I don't understand."

"I'm sorry—that's the complete message."

"I have to call Trey," she whispered.

"Kristina," Mirabel called out. "If you leave now, that's it. No more chances. This is the last time you turn your back on Austin's."

"My father is missing!" she said, trying to hold down the panic. "I can't think about Austin's right now."

"You're fired!" was the last thing she heard as she went racing out of Windy's office.

"Can I use your phone?" she asked the receptionist, with a crazy sort of déjà vu.

"No, I'm sorry," the woman snapped. "I already let you use it once."

Damn Austin's and the stupid people who worked there. She fled down the stairs to her own floor, taking refuge in what had been her office. After dialing frantically and having the phone ring countless times, she finally got an answer at Toyland.

"Is Trey Bennett there, please? It's Kristina Castleberry."

"I'll see if I can locate him," the same voice she'd talked to before informed her. "Hold please."

"I don't want to hold!"

But it was too late. "The March of the Wooden Soldier" played in her ear, segueing into "Frosty the Snowman" eventually. After what seemed like an eternity, Trey's familiar voice came on the line.

"Kristina? Listen, don't get upset."

"I already am upset!"

"I know, but calm down, okay?"

"What's going on, Trey? Where he is?"

"Well, we don't know. No one's seen him for over twenty-four hours. That's why we called the police. Missing person, you know."

"No, I don't know." She rubbed her forehead with her free hand.

Trey's tone softened. "Look, I'm really sorry. When he didn't come in today, we tried calling the room where's he's been staying, and they said no one's seen him there since Sunday afternoon. Apparently his clothes and things are still there, but he's not. I thought you ought to know."

"You did the right thing, Trey." Tears pressed at her eyelids and choked her throat. She'd never had people to worry about before, and this panic, threatening to flood her, was something new.

"Don't worry, Kristina. I'm sure he's fine. We have no reason to think anything is wrong."

"Right, right." Except for the fact that his clothes were still in his room, and no one had seen him since Sunday. "It's so cold out," she whispered. "What if he's out there, hurt or something? It's so cold."

"I'm sure he's not hurt," Trey said firmly. "He probably just took off, needed some space, you know."

"Is Tucker there?" she asked in a small voice.

"He and my father are in the middle of a meeting. I don't know exactly what it's about—I'm going in there myself in a few minutes—but I think things are pretty intense." He hesitated. "Why don't you wait and talk to him later?"

"Sure." She hung up the phone, feeling drained and yet keyed up at the same time. What could she do? Her father wasn't at Toyland and he wasn't at home. Where could he be?

Her house. Maybe he'd gone to her house, or at least had left a message. Or maybe he planned to. So she'd go home, and wait for him there.

But circumstances kept conspiring against her. She'd come to Austin's in her mother's car, and now she had no way home. So, in the freezing rain, with little ice slicks forming everywhere, she walked to the train station, catching the next commuter train out to her part of the suburbs.

And the weather kept getting worse. As she caught a cab home from the station in Winnetka, the skies darkened, and the freezing drizzle kept pouring.

Didn't anyone know it was almost Christmas? *There should be snow,* she thought. *Big, puffy flakes—not this depressing downpour of ice and slush.*

Her house was cold and dark. No Dad, and no message from him, either. She rewound and forwarded the tape three times to make sure.

But inactivity was impossible. On the spur of the moment, she changed her clothes, grabbing a sweater and a pair of corduroys for warmth, and then hit the road.

It wasn't until she was behind the wheel that it hit her. She had nowhere to go.

HIS FACE FLUSHED, Trey jumped to his feet. "Why can't I be president?" he demanded.

"I think that hotheaded little display pretty much answers your question," his father replied calmly.

Harley Bennett was back in his tall leather executive chair, with the rest of his family scattered around the office. Although Tucker had very recently tried to fill that chair, he wasn't sorry to see his father back in command.

"You haven't exactly done a bang-up job where you are, Trey," Harley continued sternly, "and you're going to have to prove to all of us that you can be a team player before you go any farther."

Trey's flush grew deeper. "If Tucker doesn't want the job, and you won't give it to me, then who?"

"Well, I could step back in temporarily," the older man offered, waving off a wary look from his wife. "Don't worry, Thelma. The doctor says I'm just fine, and there's nothing about Toyland that would hurt me. Providing I get a good assistant to take over some of the load."

Tegan shuffled awkwardly in her chair. "Don't look at me," she muttered. In a black turtleneck and tights, wearing big hoop earrings and scarlet lipstick, she looked like a different person. It wasn't clear yet whether the changes were good or bad, but the difference was remarkable. "I'm not coming back, not even if you torture me."

Her father shook his head. "To find out at this late date that one of my children hates toys..."

"Oh, now, Harley," chided his wife, as she stood behind him and patted his shoulder. "Don't get all dramatic on us. Tegan has to do what's best for her."

"Exactly," Tegan chimed in. "That's just what Kristina said."

"Who is this Kristina?" Harley asked in aggravation. "That's the second or third time her name's come up, and I've never heard of the woman. So who is she?"

"More to the point, *where* is she?" Tucker murmured, glancing at his watch. "She should've been here hours ago for the Magic Workshop meeting."

"Oh." Trey sat up suddenly.

"Oh, what? Do you know where she is?"

"Now, Tucker, don't get upset...."

"Tell me," Tucker commanded. "Where's Kristina?"

"Something came up—her father kind of, well, disappeared," his brother said weakly. "I called her this morning, at Austin's, to let her know, but I really don't know where she is now. Since the call, I mean."

"Her father disappeared?" Tucker stood up, fists clenched at his sides. "And you didn't bother to tell me?"

"Well, I didn't know you'd want to know. Besides, you were wrapped up in here with Dad, and there's nothing you can do, so why bring it up?"

"Why bring it up?" Tucker growled, advancing on Trey with murder on his mind.

"Tucker!" his mother chided, taking his arm. "That won't solve anything, will it?"

And he sighed, giving in. Damn it, anyway. He never could resist his mother.

"I take it Kristina is someone important?" Thelma Bennett inquired. "And this problem with her father sounds serious, doesn't it? Harley, pick up the phone. Tucker's going to call this girl and make sure she's all right." She squeezed her eldest son's hand fondly. "Now doesn't that sound more useful than beating up your brother?"

"I suppose," he muttered. Quickly he dialed Kristina's number, but there was no answer, not even the message machine. Next he tried Austin's, but her secretary said gingerly that she didn't work there anymore. He hung up the phone with a clang. "She quit her job?" he asked of no one in particular. "What the hell is going on?"

And then he announced, "I have to go find her."

"Well, if she's not home and she's not at work, where are you going to look?" his father asked sensibly. "You said she was due here for a meeting, right? So she's sure to show up sooner or later."

"I have to go," he insisted.

"Dad's right," Tegan offered. "Where are you going to go?"

"I don't know. I'll think of somewhere."

"You're the one who wants to step down," Harley reminded him. "Running around in freezing rain after your girlfriend is all well and good, but right now, we need to solve the problem of who's going to replace you."

"But we've been at it all morning, and we're no closer to an answer."

"All right." His father sighed and leaned back in his cushy chair, pondering the question. "Let's take a break. You can try and reach the girl while we set up the...what is it?'' He consulted Tucker's appointment calendar. ''Ah, yes. The Santa's Magic Workshop meeting.''

''But that's Kristina's meeting,'' Tucker reminded him. ''Let's just postpone it until she can be here.''

''Um, you can't postpone it,'' Tegan said softly. Tucker turned to her angrily, but his sister only shrugged apologetically. ''I happened to set up the meeting originally,'' she explained. ''So I happen to know. Tomorrow's Christmas Eve, and half the company leaves for vacation, including Pete, Frank and Vanessa. Neither Frank nor Vanessa will be back until after New Year's. We scheduled the meeting as late as we possibly could to give Kristina time to make the model, but it has to be *this* year or we'll never make Toyfair with it.''

Toyfair was a huge extravaganza, held in New York each February to showcase new products. If a product wasn't ready for Toyfair, it had to wait an extra year to launch.

''Tegan's right,'' Harley said gruffly. ''We'll have to take the meeting without her, or else shelve the thing for six months or so. But you can present it, can't you? You've been working on it, right?''

''Right,'' Tucker said gloomily. He only hoped this was what Kristina would have wanted.

THERE WERE Christmas carols on the radio. ''Joy to the World'' made her angry, and ''White Christmas'' made her cry.

Swiping at the stupid tears, she switched the radio off and drove on in silence. Crying over Christmas carols. What kind of fool was she?

She was driving in circles, in a loop past the house where her father had rented a room, past the bus station, the train station and Toyland. As she peered through her

windshield, searching for some sign of her father, the day
grew darker and more dismal, and the driving conditions
continued to deteriorate. There was ice everywhere now,
crystalizing the corners of her windshield, dripping off her
headlights, turning the roads into a giant skating rink.

But she couldn't give up. Letting him slip away, not
even trying to find him, would be like admitting she'd
failed. Stubbornly, she kept driving, even though she
knew she wasn't going to find him.

Every five minutes, it seemed, she'd pull into a gas station to try calling Tucker again. She didn't know what she
planned to say once she got him, but she was getting more
and more annoyed when she still couldn't get through.
The damned secretary kept telling her that he was still in
a meeting. The same meeting, she wondered, or the one
to present the model of the Workshop?

It was well into the afternoon, and surely they'd met
and decided the fate of the Magic Workshop by now.

It was just another piece of bad news at this point.
What difference did it make?

Finally, she had to admit that her search was doomed
to failure. So she turned the car around and headed back
home. She couldn't recall ever feeling lower in her life.

As she approached her house, she saw that the lights
were on, and hope bubbled up from out of nowhere.
*Maybe he's here, waiting for me. I've been driving around
like a madwoman and he's been here all along!*

Once again, she ran up the walk and tore open the door.
''Daddy?'' she called eagerly.

But it was only Nick. She'd forgotten about him.
Wearing his dark green Holiday Courier outfit, he came
tripping down the stairs, pushing his big, funny-looking
suitcase in front of him.

"Thank you for finishing the Magic Workshop," she offered quietly.

"And did you like it?"

She tried not to cry. "It was beautiful, Nick. Just beautiful. Thank you so much."

"Well, this is good news," he commented cheerfully. "I was afraid I might miss you, and I did want to hear about the Workshop, and to say goodbye."

"You're leaving?" This time there was no stopping the tears. "Nick, you can't leave!" she sobbed.

He let his suitcase slide to the floor as he crossed to her, and then embraced her awkwardly. "There, there, my dear, don't cry." He offered her a handkerchief. "I'm afraid I haven't any choice. It's past time to be on my way."

"I know they fired you, but we can make them change their minds." She let her hot tears seep into his jacket. "I'll talk to them, Nick."

"But, Kristina, it makes very little difference one way or the other. It's almost Christmas, my dear. And I'm needed at home. I've been away much too long as it is. So many parcels to get ready." He shook his head. "And they all have to be delivered tomorrow night."

"But, Nick, tomorrow night is Christmas Eve. Why would you have to deliver packages on Christmas Eve?" The answer occurred to her suddenly, and she gulped. Poor Nick! She tried to break it to him gently. "Nick, darling, you're not really Santa Claus. It was only a job, at the store, but it's over now."

"Kristina," he chided softly. "I never lied to you. I never said I wasn't Santa Claus."

"Nick, you're not Santa Claus," she persisted.

A flicker of mischief lit his eyes. "You'll see," he told her. "It's all right to believe. What is Christmas without believing?"

"I hate Christmas. I've hated it ever since he left the first time. And now I got fired two days before this stupid holiday, and Tucker's been in a meeting all day, and I never got to present the workshop and my father is missing." Her eyes filled again, and she blew her nose noisily in Nick's handkerchief. "I drove around all day looking for him, like an idiot, like I thought I could find him. We both know what happened to him—he left, just like before. And I drove around, all day," she said, as the tears slid down her cheeks.

"I'm very sorry, my dear. It's a terrible thing to happen so close to Christmas."

"What can I believe in, Nick? Tell me," she demanded. "What's a person like me supposed to believe in?"

"And why not believe in yourself? If your father is the worst kind of bounder... Which, I might add, he is," Nick stated firmly. "Well, it simply isn't your fault."

"Thank you, Nick, for trying." She wiped her eyes and sniffled her last sniffle. "But I don't believe in Christmas."

"Kristina, all those years, again and again, you asked me to bring your father back for Christmas. Your Christmas wish never varied by one iota, until the year you designed the Magic Workshop. Then you asked me to let you win the contest. I couldn't bring your father back, and I'm afraid I failed you with the contest, too. But this year, I thought I could finally make it up." Nick's eyes were warm and soft. "Perhaps it was best left the way it was. My apologies, child."

"Nick, you're not Santa Claus."

But he gave her a quick kiss on the cheek, and sped out the door with his big suitcase. "No time to tarry," he called out. "Merry Christmas!"

"You're not Santa Claus!" she shouted after him.

He smiled and waved, and then he was gone, striding down the street to the bus stop, pushing his suitcase along.

"Wait a minute," she murmured. "How did he know what I wanted for Christmas?"

That she might have wished for her father every year was easy enough to figure out. But how had he known that she'd changed her mind at the age of eighteen, when she'd wished to win the Toyland contest instead?

"You don't suppose he really is...?" she asked out loud. "But he couldn't be."

She told herself to stop being silly, and picked up the phone to try Tucker again. But before she could dial, the doorbell rang.

"Daddy?" She flung open the door, and Tucker stepped in, looking as though he'd been through the same wringer she had.

"Thank God," he told her. "You're all right." He pulled her into his arms and hugged her fiercely, although she felt like a limp rag doll. "I was so worried when no one answered the phone."

"But the message machine..." She glanced over at it, where it was sitting next to the sofa, switched to the Listen position, instead of to Record. "Wasn't on," she finished. "Damn it. What if my dad tried to leave a message?"

"Well, *I* tried," Tucker said shortly.

"Look, I'm sorry," she offered in her own defense. "I tried to reach you all day. I must've tried fifteen times. They kept saying you were in a meeting."

"Two of them," he said grimly.

"So you had the Magic Workshop meeting without me."

He nodded, avoiding her eyes.

"Well? What did they say?"

"I don't want to talk about it," he mumbled, sinking into one of her love seats. He stuffed his hands in the pockets of his roughed-up St. Charles High School jacket.

Her heart sank. First her father and now this. "That bad, huh?"

"Look, where were you?" he asked suddenly. "I kept expecting you to show up for the meeting. I called Austin's, and they said you no longer worked there. I couldn't figure out what the hell was going on."

"But you knew about my father, right?"

"Eventually." His eyes narrowed. "When Trey decided to tell me."

"Well, that's where I was," she told him, amazed he hadn't figured it out. "After I heard about my father, I couldn't go to Toyland for a dumb meeting. I had to look for him."

"Look for him?" He raised an eyebrow. "Where did you think you could look for him?"

"I don't know. I just drove around."

"What did you think that would solve?"

"I said I don't know! But my father—" she began.

"Ran off," he finished. "Right?"

"No one knows yet. He might be hurt, or lost, or who knows?"

"Kristina, you and I both know where he is. He was having a hard time at Toyland, and he took off. Just like when you were a kid."

She swallowed. "Maybe."

"Why won't you admit it?"

Having to justify her actions was almost worse than driving around in the freezing rain. "Why are you being so ugly about this?"

"Because I want to know why you were looking for him when you should have been at Toyland pitching the Workshop!"

"Oh, so they turned the Workshop down flat, and you're blaming me for not being there?"

"They didn't turn it down flat."

"They didn't?" She came in closer. "What did they do?"

Settling his head back against the top cushions, Tucker stared at the ceiling. "I was the only one who voted for it. Everybody else thought it was too expensive to undertake during a recession."

"Goodbye Santa's Magic Workshop," she said softly. "But it was beautiful, Tucker. I—I can't believe they didn't want it."

"Oh, they wanted to play with it, just not produce it." His voice was mocking when he added, "But then my father got into the thick of things. He offered a compromise. He likes compromises."

"What compromise?"

"Make it smaller, make it plastic, sell all the accessories separately. That's it in a nutshell."

"Plastic?" she echoed, horrified. "Tucker, how could you ever think I'd agree to that? I hope you told him *no* right then and there."

"How could I? I had to run it by you first. And you weren't there," he reminded her grimly.

"You had to know what I'd say!"

"What, by ESP?"

"Are you blind and stupid? You know how I feel about that workshop!"

"Don't you yell at me, lady," he said savagely. "I did the best I could."

"Oh, I see what's going on here." Rage began to color her vision as she circled closer to him. "We're into Tucker's taboos again, aren't we? You think you failed me because they wouldn't go for my idea, so your pride is smarting. Heaven forbid that Tucker's pride should be injured."

"I didn't fail anyone!" he shouted.

"Then why are you shouting?"

"I'm not!"

"Well, at least I've got your attention." Hand on her hips, she glared at him where he sat on the love seat. "Are you going to deny that you're in a terrible mood?"

"No," he said, gritting his teeth. "But I have a right to be. Something else happened today—something you don't know about." After a pause, he announced, "I stepped down today as president. And yes, that makes me feel pretty lousy."

"You stepped down? But why?" She was horrified. The last time they'd discussed his job, he'd flatly refused to consider the idea.

"Just don't say I told you so."

"I wouldn't do that." She knelt on the floor next to him. "Does this have anything to do with your father coming back to town? Your secretary said you were in a meeting with him."

"The first meeting." Impatient, he stood and paced in front of her fireplace. "But hey, look, don't start feeling sorry for me. This was my idea. I told him about a week ago that I wasn't cut out to run the place."

Kristina rocked back on her heels, stunned. "You decided this a week ago. . . and this is the first I've heard of it."

"Dad and I had to square it away first, find a replacement."

"No, you didn't," she argued, standing up and focusing on him. "You could have told me. You said you loved me."

"I do."

"No, you don't. What kind of love is this?" She threw up her hands. "You're facing a major decision, and you don't bother to tell me. And on the other side, I have the worst day of my life, and all you care about is another blow to *your* pride."

"That's not true—" he started, but she cut him off.

"My father was missing, and I needed you."

"I tried to find you."

As her anger cooled, she could feel herself getting weepy again, and she hated it. "Don't you see? You made me need you. It wasn't my fault. I didn't want to. I wanted to depend on myself, just me, the kid herself, and nobody else.

"But no, you had to push your way into my life. You pushed me into finishing the workshop, and contacting my father and falling in love with you. Well, didn't all three of those turn out great? I got fired today, Nick left and my father pulled a disappearing act, and I feel perfectly justified in laying the blame for all three at your door."

"You got fired?"

"Yes."

"And Nick left?"

"He got fired, too," she said acidly.

"I'm sorry, Krissie." His voice was low and gruff, and he moved to put his arms around her. "I'm really sorry."

Refusing to be consoled, she pushed him away. "I needed you," she repeated. "I needed you to hold me and tell me everything was going to be okay. And where were you? At Toyland, having a little family tiff, and carrying a chip on your shoulder. Meanwhile, my life was falling apart.''

"I said I was sorry."

"I don't want you to be sorry. I want you to turn back the clock, and do things right this time. You know, I thought I wasn't angry, but I am." The burning in her eyes and her throat was back, and she pressed two fingers to the bridge of her nose, hoping to hold the tears at bay. She'd never cried this much in her entire life. What a time to turn into a human faucet. "The bottom line is, you weren't there when I needed you. It hurts. And I don't want to hurt anymore."

"So what are you saying?" he asked slowly.

She swallowed around the lump in her throat. "I want you to go away."

"You don't mean that."

"Yes," she said. "I do."

"Well, I'm not going." He said angrily, "I'm not going to walk out when we should be fixing this."

"There's nothing to fix," she said. "If you won't leave, I will."

And then she grabbed her car keys and left him standing in the middle of her prim little living room.

Chapter Fifteen

"Here we come a-wassailing among the leaves so green;
Here we come a-wand'ring so fair to be seen
Love and joy come to you,
And to you your wassail too..."

"Great," she snarled, turning the radio off so viciously it fell over the side of the kitchen counter. "Just what I need is people warbling about love and joy. Love and joy— ha!"

The unfortunate fact that it was Christmas Eve had not escaped her. Already, two clumps of carolers had come knocking at her door, and she'd had to pretend to be appreciative.

"I always did hate Christmas Eve," she muttered as she scoured out the sink. She stopped abruptly, her hand on the can of cleanser. Was it odd to be talking to herself while she cleaned the kitchen? For that matter, was it odd to be cleaning the kitchen sink on Christmas Eve?

"I don't have anything better to do." Besides, it was the ugliest, grayest, drippiest Christmas Eve she'd ever seen— a perfect day to wallow in her sweat suit and eat powdered sugar doughnuts right out of the box.

The doorbell rang, interrupting her litany of depression, and she ambled through the living room to answer it, fully expecting another complement of carolers.

But when she opened the door, Bitsy Austin stepped in.

"If you're here to yell at me about screwing up at Austin's don't bother." Kristina shut the door quietly behind her mother. "You were right, and I was wrong. Okay?"

"I'm not here to talk about Austin's," Bitsy offered. "I have a message from your father."

"You can't be serious."

"I wish I weren't," her mother said bleakly. "Why he chose to call me I'll never know. 'It just occurred to me,' he said, 'someone should tell Kristina I left.'" A hollow laugh escaped her. "Can you imagine? The jerk has been in Cleveland for days, and it only now crossed his mind that you might be worried."

"He went back to Cleveland?" she asked quietly. She couldn't believe how calm she felt. "Did he say why?"

Bitsy rolled her eyes. "Does he need a reason? Oh, he mumbled something about the pressure, that they didn't like his designs at Toyland. He said he felt like you expected too much of him, and he wasn't up to it." She shrugged. "Something like that."

"Do you think he realizes that both times he left, it was at Christmas?" She laughed cynically. "Good joke on me, huh? Let's pull a repeat."

"Darling, look—" Bitsy started, but Kristina waved her off.

"Go ahead, Mother, say 'I told you so.' I know you're dying to."

Bitsy held herself very tightly. "I know it probably seems that way to you, but I never wanted it to turn out this way. I didn't want him to hurt you again, not like the last time."

Kristina said nothing. She felt like a dead thing, all brittle and dry. *So he went back to Cleveland, and he didn't even bother to say goodbye. Well, what do I care?*

Her eyes blurred, and she raised her fingers to press against them. No more crying. Not one lousy tear.

When her mother continued, her voice was trembling. "Can you imagine anything worse than being the one left, the one who had to break the news that he was gone? When you were ten, and I had to tell you that your daddy wouldn't be home for Christmas, I thought your heart would break. I thought *my* heart would break. Can you blame me for not wanting it to happen again?"

"No," she whispered.

"He's not a bad person, Kristina. He's just never been good with people."

"You're defending him?"

"No. He's weak and irresponsible, and so self-centered it still makes me furious." Bitsy offered a mocking smile. "But hating him doesn't do any good. Take my word for it." She reached forward to smooth a wayward strand of her daughter's hair. "I'm so sorry, Kristina. I wish I could make it go away."

"You can't, Mother. I should've known better, that's all." She crossed her arms over her chest. "I should've known that men can't be trusted."

"Hmm . . ." Bitsy examined her daughter's expression. "Are we including Tucker Bennett in that condemnation?"

"He's the worst," she mumbled.

Her mother sighed. "I was afraid this would happen."

"Finally getting around to the 'I told you so'?"

"No, that's not what I mean." Brisk and efficient, Bitsy perched on the nearer love seat. "I meant that I was afraid you'd tar everyone else with your father's brush."

"Excuse me?"

"Well—" Bitsy leaned forward "—when one of them poisons the well, it's hard not to see the rest of them as toxic, too.'' Kristina was mystified, but her mother went on, ''I did the same thing. After your father left, I kept testing the men I dated, and they kept coming up short, because I kept expecting them to let me down.'' She shook her head. ''And if you look hard enough, every single person on this earth, including Mother Teresa, will let you down, because sometimes they can't be what you want them to be.''

''But that's why I broke it off with him,'' Kristina explained. ''I don't want to be let down anymore. It hurts too much.''

''But that's life!'' Bitsy rose and took her daughter's hands in hers. ''You can't make him into something he's not. He's only human, darling.''

''I know that. He's the one who has problems with the concept of imperfection,'' she grumbled.

''You have to be strong enough and secure enough to know you can do it by yourself if you have to, but sometimes you don't have to. And that's nice, too.''

''I can't think about this right now.'' Kristina squared her shoulders. ''I made up my mind, and that's it.''

''Think about it, darling. If you love him, and he loves you, you'll be able to find an answer. In the meantime,'' Bitsy ventured, ''I hope you'll forgive me.''

''For what?'' Kristina asked in surprise.

''I feel that perhaps I pushed you into working at Austin's, when maybe you would have been happier with this toy thing,'' her mother said tentatively. ''I guess, hearing your father's voice again, I realized that I didn't hate him anymore. And I felt ashamed of myself, for holding on to you too tightly.''

''I don't know what to say.''

''Say you'll forget that I thought more about what I wanted for you than what you wanted.'' Bitsy squeezed her daughter's hand. "And that you'll think about forgiving Tucker. Trying to bind someone to you—well, it chokes them, and it doesn't do a thing for you."

"It's okay, Mother. Really."

"I'm really sorry about what happened at Austin's. Windy told me what Mirabel said to you, and I was just incensed. How dare she?"

Kristina shook her head firmly. "I lost my job fair and square, Mother."

"What are you going to do now?"

"I guess I'll get the old résumé out after New Year's and start looking." Fingering the sleeve of her sweatshirt, she said lightly, "I'll find something."

"I could help. I have lots of contacts, and—"

"No, Mother." She kept her voice even, but resolute. "I'm on my own this time."

"Well, all right." Bitsy paused. "But, Kristina, you do still need me, don't you? Just a little?"

"Of course, Mother."

"I can't stand the idea that there might be this gulf between us, now, of all times." There were tears in her eyes when she said softly, "It's important to me that everything be all right between you and me for Christmas."

Kristina put her arm around her mother's slender shoulders, hugging her gently. "Everything's fine, Mama. Everything is just fine."

The doorbell rang again, and they broke apart, both brushing at their eyes surreptitiously.

"I can't believe this," Kristina joked as she rummaged around in her pocket for a tissue. "More traffic around here than Grand Central Station."

Smiling wanly, Bitsy went to the door. "Oh," she said. "It's Mr. Bennett. Should I, uh . . . ?"

"Mr. Bennett? Tucker?"

"Well, yes."

Tucker didn't give her time to decide if she wanted to see him or not; he just barged right in without an invitation. And then he stood there, staring at her, with those blue, blue eyes.

He was wearing a T-shirt and worn-out blue jeans that hugged every angle of his rangy body. Yeah, that was her Tucker. She couldn't think of a thing to say.

"Excuse me," Bitsy said behind them. "Perhaps I'd better be going."

"Mother, you don't have to leave. Tucker's not staying."

"Yes," he said firmly, "I am."

"No, you're not," she said through clenched teeth.

"I'm on my way," her mother promised. "I'll just let myself out. Will I see you tomorrow at Christmas dinner? Oh, no, I guess you wouldn't want to... at the Austins and all."

"She can't," Tucker said quietly. "She's going to have Christmas dinner at my house."

"I am not!"

"Bye," Bitsy called, slipping out the front door.

"How dare you force your way in here and push my mother out?"

"I didn't make her leave." Implacable, Tucker stood there watching her. "She just had the good sense to avoid the eye of a tornado."

"Why are you looking at me like that?"

He advanced on her. "Like what?"

She retreated. "Like...that." As she backed up, she hit something solid, and she sort of fell over the padded arm of the love seat. Collecting her dignity, she held her chin up and said, "I know I'm not dressed very well today, but there's no reason to stare."

"You look wonderful," he murmured, still moving in closer.

"I do not." From her awkward position draped over the love seat, she frowned down at her sweatshirt and pants, both splotched with water from her kitchen-cleaning experiment.

He offered a hand to help her to her feet, and she hesitated, wondering if she dared touch him. But his long, elegant hand remained there, palm up, inches from her nose, until she reached out and carefully placed her hand in his.

He yanked her to her feet, pulling her off balance so that she had no choice but to grab on to him for support. "I knew I shouldn't trust you," she whispered. But it felt so good, with his arms around her, holding her steady, with his hard, wonderful body pressed up next to her.

"I stayed away a whole day." His eyes were soft and serious as he gazed down at her. "It was the best I could do."

Reluctantly, she pulled away from his embrace. The sooner she got used to the idea that he was no longer a part of her life, the better off she'd be. "I told you I didn't want to see you anymore."

"Well, actually, you told me to go away."

"You knew what I meant."

He smiled, brushing a strand of her hair with his fingers. "But I didn't believe you."

Turning away from his hand, she twisted her hair into a makeshift braid. "I don't know why you came. Nothing has changed."

"I love you."

She closed her eyes, but it didn't block out the sound of it.

"I love you," he said again, in that husky, wicked voice of his. "I love you, and I'm not giving up. You might as well get used to the idea."

"Tucker, please—"

"I'm not your father."

Her eyes shot open, and she stared at him. "Why did you say that?"

"Because that's the real problem, isn't it?" He pulled her around so that she had to look at him, and then he traced the curve of her cheek with his thumb. "You think I'll leave you. But I won't."

"No, that's not it," she insisted. "You weren't there when I needed you, and that's it. We've been all through this—"

"You're right."

"I'm right?" she whispered.

He nodded. "I was wrong not to tell you about the Toyland thing—about the presidency." Expelling a short breath, he dropped his arms and backed away. "You were right. My pride got in the way, and I took it out on you, and I'm sorry. It's hard for me...." He slashed a hand through his hair.

"Leave your hair alone," she said softly.

He raised a hand to forestall her. "I have to say this, okay?"

She nodded.

"It's hard for me to get used to making mistakes, to realize that it's okay. I have certain standards for myself, and I hate like hell when I screw up."

"Like the divorce."

"Like the divorce. Like being president of Toyland."

"You didn't screw up," she told him honestly. "You just didn't like it. Those are different things."

"I'm working on it." When his eyes met her, they had regained some of their usual sparkle. "So, is my apology accepted?"

"I understand how you feel, but that doesn't change—"

"Look, Kristina," he said harshly, clearly at the end of his patience. "I'm sorry that I encouraged you to find your father, that I had a part in him hurting you again. Another screwup you can blame me for, I guess. But I'm not sorry that you fell in love with me, or that we made the Magic Workshop together. I loved it! And I love you, and that's not going to go away, no matter how hard you try to make it."

"I don't want to love you!" she cried. "I don't want to love anyone."

"It's too late." His eyes met hers. "You already do."

"I know," she said miserably.

"I won't lose you."

She couldn't think of a reply. She'd never been faced with an irresistible force before, not one like Tucker.

"If you say you need me," he said forcefully, "I'll be there. Whenever, whatever. I won't let you down."

She didn't want to notice how impressive he was when he got going, with his eyes blazing and his body held taut with suppressed energy. *I don't want to love you.* She squeezed her eyes closed.

"Kristina," he ordered. "Look at me. I love you. I will always love you. I won't leave you."

When she found her voice, it was barely a whisper. "Do you mean that?"

"Yes," he breathed. "Oh, yes."

Her arms reached out for him before she knew what she'd decided.

Hauling her into his arms, he wrapped himself around her so tightly she could hardly breathe. "Don't you dare scare me like that again. Don't even think of threatening to throw me out over one lousy argument."

"But—" she started.

"No buts. We can fight and squabble all you want, but you can't be threatening to throw me out at the drop of a hat."

"I hate arguments," she said vehemently.

"They have their uses," he said mischievously.

"Like?"

"Like making up," he told her with a kiss. He slipped out of his jacket, dropping it to the floor where they stood, unable to break the kiss. But she pulled away.

"Tucker, it's important to me," she said softly, "to feel safe."

"I know."

"I have to know that I can depend on you."

"You can," he promised. "Always."

"But not to the exclusion of everything else." She remembered her mother saying, *Trying to bind someone to you... it chokes them, and doesn't do a thing for you.* "I was wrong, too, about yesterday. If you say you tried to find me, I believe you. You can't know when I need you, if I don't ask."

"Listen, sweetheart," he told her, framing her face in his big hands, and grazing her lips with his own. "If you want the Magic Workshop the way it is, then we'll fight it to the death. We'll keep bringing it in front of the board at Toyland until they have to agree. Or we'll take it to another company."

Something new occurred to her. "If you stepped down as president, do you have a job? Or are we both dusting off our résumés?"

"I'm back in Design," he said with a grin. "Back where I belong."

"That's great," she said, trying to feel happy that Tucker's world was back in sync. But it only reminded her of her own unemployed condition.

Tucker read her mind. "And since you no longer work at Austin's, I could hire you in Design if I wanted to."

It was a nice offer, but... "I don't think so," she demurred. "I don't think I was cut out to be a designer. I only had the one idea, and it doesn't seem to have gone too far. No, I think I'm a born administrator—lists and pie charts and stamping out fires. So I'll just have to find another job."

He draped an arm around her, leading her to the white sofa near the fireplace. "There still might be a place for you at Toyland. My dad wants to be back in charge, but he needs help. And as a matter of fact, what he needs is someone who makes lists and pie charts and stamps out fires." He bounced down on her couch, and smiled up at her, with the familiar, impudent grin she knew so well. "Who knows? When Dad's really ready to retire for real, you could be the next president of Toyland."

"Oh, Tucker," she chastised, smacking him on the arm as he pulled her down into his lap. "Get serious."

"I am serious. Of course, Toyland presidents have to be Bennetts."

"That lets me out."

"Not necessarily." He dumped her off his lap and then followed her down into the cushions of the couch, pinning her underneath his big, long, hard body. "You could marry me," he murmured in her ear.

"Quit joking around."

"I've never been more serious in my life."

"Okay," she said primly. "Then I say yes."

He lifted his body a little. "Really? Yes?"

She laughed out loud. "You look scared, Bennett. Better run while you can."

"I'm not going anywhere." His mouth came down on hers, hot and hard, as he pressed her into the couch. "I'm planning on staying right here for a long, long time."

And then he kissed her again, until she would've said yes to anything.

"Merry Christmas," she whispered, wiggling under him to encourage him.

"Christmas," he said, and sat up abruptly. "I forgot. I brought you a present."

"What? What did you bring me?"

"You'll see. You'll see," he said mysteriously, and he bounded out the front door.

A few seconds later, she heard an odd scraping noise coming up the walk, and she peered out the door. "It's snowing! Oh, Tucker, look! The fat, fluffy kind."

"Yeah, it's great," he said, puffing. "So, what do you think?" he asked, holding up her Christmas present for inspection.

"I don't want a…" she started to say automatically, but then she saw the look on Tucker's face, and she realized she'd never had a better gift. "It's the best Christmas tree I've ever seen. It is, in fact, gorgeous."

As she helped him drag it over to the corner by the stairs, the place Nick had picked out, she couldn't keep the smile off her face. "Absolutely gorgeous." It was a scraggly little thing, covered with ice from today's storm, but it was beautiful in her eyes.

"And I have a whole bag of ornaments and lights that my mom sent along," he told her.

"Your mom? I forgot—you have a mom and a dad. And now I have to meet them. I don't know if I can handle this," she said anxiously. "Families and eggnog and Christmas ornaments handed down through the generations."

"Yeah," he said happily, grabbing her and lifting her in the air for another kiss. "We can tell them we're getting married tomorrow at Christmas dinner. But tonight, tonight is Christmas Eve for you and me, so we can wake up together on our first Christmas."

Christmas morning with Tucker. Christmas dinner with a real family. This was going to take some getting used to. It put a whole new slant on Christmas.

"Merry Christmas," she returned, laughing down at him. But a tiny, tinny noise rang out from the fireplace. Puzzled, she cocked her head in that direction.

"What is it?" he asked, sliding her back to her feet.

"Tucker, I could swear I heard sleigh bells in the fireplace."

"Nick?"

"But that would mean..."

They looked at each other for a long pause. "Naaah," they said in unison.

And then Kristina laughed. Gazing into the true blue of Tucker's eyes, she declared, "Maybe, just maybe... I do believe in Christmas."

HARLEQUIN
AMERICAN ROMANCE
brings you

Season's Greetings

When a magical, red-cheeked, white-bearded postman delivers long-lost letters, the lives of four unsuspecting couples will change forever.

Experience all the magic of Christmas with these special books.

Don't miss: #417 UNDER THE MISTLETOE
by Rebecca Flanders
#419 AN ANGEL IN TIME
by Stella Cameron
#420 FOR AULD LANG SYNE
by Pamela Browning

Christmas—the season when wishes *do* come true....

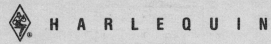